CHANGING PITCHES

STEVE KLUGER

CHANGING PITCHES

Boston • Alyson Publications, Inc.

First clothbound publication 1984 by St. Martin's Press

This trade paperback edition published by
Alyson Publications
40 Plympton Street
Boston, Massachusetts, 02118

First printing: April, 1989

ISBN 1-55583-155-9
LC 88-083330

Dedicated to
NAN and GARRY
who said,
"You've got to be kidding."

CHANGING PITCHES

SPRING

The only thing that bothers me about flying into Washington, D.C., is the Capitol Building at ten thousand feet. It makes me feel exceedingly uncomfortable, as though I were a voyeur—only because at that altitude, it reminds me of an overdeveloped breast. So, for that matter, does the Jefferson Memorial. Not to imply that the city's founding fathers were obsessed with the female form—the Washington Monument cleanly dispels *that* notion—yet, deeply as I admire the nineteenth-century gentlemen who were responsible for putting a new nation onto its feet, I can only assume that Pierre L'Enfant was nothing more than a post-Revolutionary dirty old man.

As we bank sharply to the left for our final approach into Washington National, the stewardess informs us in her breathiest Carole Lombard imitation that traffic is slightly backed up, and we'll probably have to circle the airport for a few minutes. Swell. Considering that I've spent most of the last twelve years in transit to and from every American League city in the United States, I've become pretty adept at reading between the lines. What she's really saying is that, if we're lucky, we may land before Labor Day. Which gives me an opportunity to get down to the business at hand.

I'll be entirely honest—it wasn't my idea to begin keeping this journal. For that I have to credit Benny Fisk, my agent, and the single greatest threat to organized baseball since the invention of the pulled hamstring. Benny's had two forces working against him all his life—his name and his height. In addition to sounding like an amphetamine, he's not much taller than Mr. Machine. Wind him up and he asks for money. He also happens to be pretty much the only reason why, at thirty-six, I'm a two-time Cy Young

Award winner, instead of an aging rookie lost somewhere in the ranks of the Senators' farm system.

"Kiddo," he said to me one July morning thirteen summers ago, "by the time I get through with you, Scotty MacKay's going to be on *everybody's* lips." At the time, I quite naturally assumed he meant the Hall of Fame. Instead, he got me a Chapstick commercial. I didn't really have much reason to complain, however; by the end of the season, my mouth had become standard decor on Rapid Transit buses all across the country.

"Look at it this way," Fisk had said. "It'll get you some nifty introductions."

It was Benny who came up to me last week at the end of spring training and suggested that I start a diary. Considering that I have difficulty keeping my attention span focused long enough to sign a hotel register, I regarded the idea with some doubt—until he pointed out that it might make a great book once my major league career had ended. With that, I clearly sensed that Benny Fisk was beginning to worry about his ten percent, wondering what might happen if I ever lost my fastball.

And judging by my performance in Miami for most of March, that eventuality could conceivably take place as early as the day after tomorrow.

I'll confess right off the bat that I've never been too hot on autobiographies, particularly when they're written by athletes. A full-length treatise on some infielder's neurotic childhood or kinky sexual proclivities has no place on contemporary bookshelves—unless it's filed in the card catalog under "sociological aberration." For that reason, I'll skip the preliminaries and get right down to the important stuff. I bat left and pitch left. My won-lost record over the last twelve years is 271–128, my ERA's an immodest 2.83, and I've thrown thirty-nine shutouts. I also almost pitched a no-hitter once. That was two years ago, up at Fenway Park,

STEVE KLUGER

during a week-long heat wave that had reduced the Boston lineup to one large red and white sweat-stain. I don't remember much of the afternoon, except that I'd spent 8⅔ innings trying to get a sunflower seed out from between my two back molars, when I suddenly realized I'd gone through twenty-six batters without yielding a hit. After a brief moment of introspection, I convinced myself that having come that far, one more strikeout was bound to be a piece of cake. Unfortunately, an especially convincing Red Sock disagreed. Since then, I've made it a point to chase actively after at least a single digit in the column that's headed "No-Hitter," and to dispel once and for all the rumor that second chances only happen in fairy tales. In fact, assuming that one day I find it necessary to die, I can only hope that my epitaph will read "Scotty MacKay—He Lost His Life in Pursuit of the Twenty-Seventh Out."

Favorite movies? *Inside Daisy Clover* and *Star Wars*. Favorite people? Actually there are two. Bucky Harris, my first hero. Bucky was the manager of the Washington Senators during the earliest part of my life, when I spent most of my time growing up and sneaking into the bleachers at Griffith Stadium—not necessarily in that order. The thing that fascinated me most about Harris was his unshakable faith in his club, despite the fact that the Senators were truly the worst team that had ever played baseball. Proof? Their banner year was 1952. That was the season they came in fifth. Still, even as a child, it occurred to me that "Bucky Harris" was probably the most concise definition of the word "dedication" you were ever likely to find. Which is probably why I swore at age eleven that someday I'd be wearing a white *W* on the front of my cap—even if I did turn out to be the only twentieth-century ballplayer who'd ever *wanted* to pitch for the Senators.

My other favorite person in the world also happens to be the one I'm sleeping with. Her name's Joanie Jordan, but you probably know her as the short brunette dancing by the fountain at Lincoln Center singing, "I'm a Pepper, you're a Pepper, wouldn't you like to be a Pepper too." J.J.'s been an actress since she was fifteen, yet despite her above-average talent and unbearably well-defined body, all they ever cast her in are beverage commercials. Lipton Tea paid for her furniture, while Folger's Freeze Dried picked up the tab for her Firebird. Coca-Cola, in the meantime, has taken care of her rent through 1993. "Do I look thirsty or something?" she asks regularly.

Although J.J.'s residual checks are enough to enable her to live the life of Riley, you'd never know it by the way she dresses. As a rule, she generally wears jeans and over-sized men's sweatshirts turned inside out. Period. Understand, I'm not trying to be a snob or anything—as a matter of fact, that's why I fell in love with her. Up until Joanie Jordan, my greatest fixation in life had been Natalie Wood as Daisy Clover. Wood, coincidentally, spent the better part of that film clad in nothing but jeans and an oversized man's sweatshirt—turned inside out. As a result, the first time I set eyes on J.J., I immediately started to believe in kismet. At the time, she was beginning a week's stint as a stand-in for the weather girl at Channel 5 on the same day that I was appearing on the sports segment. Though I tried to conduct myself as a responsible athlete for the duration of the interview, I spent most of my time staring off-camera at a low-pressure area over Nevada. Finally, after the broadcast, I approached her, and in a terrific opening gambit, asked, "Anybody ever tell you you look like Natalie Wood?" Now J.J.'s been around for most of her life and has probably heard every come-on line in the book. Though I'd thought I was being pretty creative, she later informed me that on a scale of one to ten, my originality would have earned me a zero.

"Careful, Lefty," she said casually.

"What's the matter?" I asked, trying to look hurt.

Joanie frowned. "There's a warm front moving in," she replied. "Fast."

Judging by the fact that the Potomac River is now less than three feet below the right engine pod, I'm assuming that traffic has cleared and we're about to land. Either that, or we're in big trouble. One parting thought—Benny Fisk suggested that I come up with a title for these pages, and though I've tried to think of something humorous and teeming with hidden meaning, the only thing that comes to mind is *The Decline and Fall of an American League Pitcher*. I'm not trying to be pessimistic, but with a rapidly tiring thirty-six-year-old arm, you don't have to be a botanist to know that the rose is only a slider away from losing its bloom. Briefly I wish that some Cuban renegade would storm the cockpit and order the pilot to take us to Havana—then just as quickly I tell myself to forget it. If nothing else, we probably don't have enough fuel left to get us to the Carolinas.

I wonder if anybody ever hijacked a jet to Newport News.

* * *

April 4—

According to a survey that appeared in *Time* magazine this week, left-handed people live an average of 2.3 years longer than right-handed people, have a lower divorce rate, and are not as prone to venereal disease. On the other hand, we make an average of $5,000 less than righthanders and drive fewer Stingrays.

I think we're getting short-shafted.

* * *

DO NOT REMOVE

TO ALL STARTERS, FROM DOUG HOYT:
Until further notice, the following will comprise the starting lineup for Opening Day.

Skip Hatten, 1B
Mickey Fowler, 2B
Joey Tobin, 3B
Opie Wright, SS
Don Weinberg, LF
Rick Jackson, CF
Gary Petry, RF
Warren Budlong, C
Bob Delanoy, DH
Scotty MacKay, P

Fellas, I hate to sound like a wet blanket, but we've got 162 games to play between April 9 and October 2. I'd be most appreciative if we could manage to win at least 50 of them. In other words, I want to start seeing some hustle—pronto. If you don't know how, fake it.
Any questions, see me.

DH

●

If anybody finds a silver coke spoon, please return it to my locker. Thanks.

Skip Hatten

●

Sporting News *says that the Dodgers hit over three mil-*

STEVE KLUGER

lion in attendance last year. Anyone know what our figures were?

Buddy

●

Three old ladies and a cocker spaniel.

Rookie Ricky

●

VEGAS SPORTS LINE

Pre-Season High and Low World Series Picks

	Team	Odds
N.L.	DODGERS	FAVORITES
	ASTROS	550–1
A.L.	ORIOLES	FAVORITES
	SENATORS	1000–1

—*Congratulations on breaking 1500.*

The New York Yankees

●

You gotta have heart,
Miles and miles and miles of heart.
When the odds are saying you'll never win,
That's when the grin should start.

Scotty

●

Blow it out your ass, MacKay.

Joey T.

To Management:
     Can we get some uniforms that don't look like feet pa-
jamas?

                              The Outfield

                                 •

     Yeah—when you stop playing like you're sound asleep.

                              The Infield

                                 •

     In an effort to prove that we've got just as much of a
chance of making the playoffs as the Orioles, we're scheduling voluntary practice drills once the season has started. All
those interested, please sign up below:

_____

_____

_____

_____

_____

_____

_____

_____

STEVE KLUGER

•

"Apathy"—lack of interest or concern.

Noah Webster

•

Anybody hear the latest Senators joke?
Q. What's a typical Washington double play?
A. Wright to Fowler to Georgetown.

Buddy

•

Hey, catcher—you looking for a lined foul right in the
nuts?

Fowler

•

Despite the recent spate of rumors, there is no truth to the
rumble that Washington is considering a major trade with
Cincinnati.
Will everyone please stop volunteering?

Doug Hoyt

•

Whoever swiped the strings off my banjo better have his
life insurance paid up.

Opie

•

Don't look at us, Ope. Andy Griffith took 'em and gave
them to Aunt Bee.

Gary P.

•

*Bet you didn't know that the sacrifice fly rule was imple-
mented the same year World War II started.*

Don Weinberg

●

Bet we didn't give a shit.

Joey

●

*If anybody finds a hash pipe, be careful of the finish—it's
made of walnut.*

Skip Hatten

* * *

April 8—

The Washington Bulletin

To the Editor:
   Well, it's obviously spring again—that time of year
when Washington's baseball fans grit their teeth and arm
themselves for yet another season of unrelenting despair.
And once again, we must ask ourselves, "Why?" It is common knowledge that, last summer, the Senators' infield
committed more errors than the Chevy Chase Little
League. It is also an accepted fact that a documentary film
entitled *Season's Highlights* lasted only 2½ minutes. Given
the handwriting on the wall, one wonders why our city is as
determined as it is to invest so much time in a team whose
ultimate goal, with luck, can only be mediocrity. Surely we

STEVE KLUGER

could find other uses for our time and money—urban renewal, perhaps. I, for one, can offer no ready suggestion—only because I have just spent half my savings on season tickets.

COLLEEN WILSON
Silver Spring, MD

To the Editor:
Last year the Senators came in last in batting, fielding, games won, and stolen bases. On the other hand, they led the league in walks, balks, wild pitches, passed balls, infield errors, outfield errors, rainouts, strikeouts, pitchouts, and popouts. Now ask me why I love them. Beats me. But I wouldn't trade them for anything in the world.

GENE ROHRER
Arlington, VA

To the Editor:
The reason I love the Senators is because I'm only nine and I pitch better than they do.

STEVIE SOLOMON
Georgetown, Washington, DC

To the Editor:
The only good part about rooting for Washington is that you don't have to hold off until October to say, "Wait 'til next year." The way *they* play, you might as well do it in March and get it over with.

HILDA AND SAM SHAPIRO
Baltimore, MD

To the Editor:

Yeah, they're losers, all right. But you know what? They're all ours.

Vito Antenotti
Bethesda, MD

* * *

April 9—

Just before I left to go to the ballpark for the season opener, Joanie told me I was a callipygian. I knew I shouldn't let it bother me, but I couldn't keep myself from becoming slightly worried. It's like having a doctor diagnose acute efflorescence without telling you it just means heat rash. The only reason I didn't press the point further was that I hate admitting she knows more words than I do.

"Try not to let it bother you," she advised as I was walking out the door. "Michelangelo's David was a callipygian too. You're in good company." In all due fairness, she knows better than to do something like that just before a ball game. For an entire inning, I misread every one of Budlong's signs trying to figure out what J.J. had been trying to tell me. Finally it occurred to me to ask Don Weinberg. He doesn't know much about playing left field, but he knows just about everything else.

"Callipygian," he said. "That's with a *y*, not an *i*. Webster's Third Unabridged. 'Having shapely buttocks.'"

"Having what?" I asked, a little embarrassed.

"Shapely buttocks," he repeated. "She thinks you've got a cute ass."

I guess I ought to be relieved. At least now I know what she meant by Michelangelo's David. For a while, I thought she was hinting that I pitched like my arm was made of marble.

Actually, if she had been, she might have had a point.

* * *

STEVE KLUGER

The Washington Bulletin

Yankees Shut Out Senators 10–0

BY MARK LITVIN
Washington Bulletin Staff Writer

No matter how you slice it, there's something to be said for reliability. With all of the ever-present, self-perpetuating tremors that shake society's foundations daily, it's nice to know that the Washington Senators will doubtless remain the one constant in an otherwise uncertain world. If the Rockies should tumble and Gibraltar crumble, it won't matter. The Senators will lose. If the price of gasoline soars while the value of the dollar plummets, it will make no difference. The Senators will lose. Should we one day find ourselves engaged in a thermonuclear holocaust that puts an end to life as we know it, rest assured that when the last radioactive ground ball has been bobbled, the Senators will lose.

Keeping pace with tradition, the line scores from yesterday's home opener bore a striking resemblance to a casualty list from Guam. It is true that Senators fans have come to expect no miracles—such as an occasional double play or even a fly ball that gets as far as the outfield—but it is generally believed that they deserve a bit more than a six-run first inning.

MacKay Aced Early

Scotty MacKay (0–1) was the first to fall victim to the visiting New York Yankees. The two-time Cy Young Award winner took the mound with the sort of jaunty confidence that was his trademark ten years ago, when he was regularly knocking the American League on its ear. Unfortunately, that poise lasted only until he threw his first pitch—an anemic fastball to Graig Nettles, which purportedly wound up on the South Lawn of the White House. From there it was all downhill. MacKay's fastball, formerly clocked at 102 miles per hour, is obviously suffering from

See Senators Page Three

CHANGING PITCHES

iron-poor blood. An occasional lapse would be understandable, but three home runs in the first inning alone leads one to believe that if MacKay doesn't come up with a change of pitches fairly soon, that fastball is going to send him down as quickly as it brought him up.

Yankees Not Up to Par

Ironically, the New York Yankees were in much less than optimum form. Coming out of spring training with half of their lineup suffering from a variety of ills, they had yet to rediscover their batting power—and for all practical purposes, should not have been able to come out on top.

But the Senators insisted.

Once Washington manager Doug Hoyt had relieved MacKay of his duties, he sought immediate assistance from his bullpen staff, which regrettably had not had sufficient time to warm up, as they had just sent out for pizza. In fact, although home plate umpire Rene Kern has not officially admitted as much, the real reason Washington reliever Terry Dutton was ejected in the third was not for scuffing the ball, but for getting an anchovy on a slider. Nevertheless, garnished or otherwise, it was hardly the Senators' finest moment. By the time the last pitch was thrown, some five hours and twelve minutes after the singing of the National Anthem, New York had scored 10 runs on 18 hits and no errors, while Washington was left to lick its wounds with no runs, two hits, and six errors. Though the Yankees, behind the powerful arm of lefthander Ron Guidry (1–0), benefitted from home runs by Nettles, Cerone, and Piniella, Washington was able to reach base just twice— once on a bloop single by catcher Warren Budlong, after which he was promptly picked off first—and once by former Yankee Mickey Fowler, who smacked a sinker to left and nearly knocked Guidry's head off when he accidentally let go of his bat.

"They didn't do too badly," offered Yankee manager Billy Martin solicitously. "They just haven't hit their stride yet."

The Senators, like Blanche DuBois, are relying heavily on the kindness of strangers.

Senators Fever Remains

Still, one must assume that there is *something* about a last-place team that compels the

See Senators Page Five

16   STEVE KLUGER

faithful to pack Senators Stadium on Opening Day to cheer for what could only be defeat. It isn't merely a rite of spring—it has become an annual re-adopting of twenty-five somewhat clumsy, often awkward, overage adolescents. When pressed for a reason, your average psychiatrist would have to admit that—next to Senators fever—Oedipus was a snap. And yet, the answer isn't really all that difficult. As you watch Opie Wright drop three consecutive pop-ups, or as you observe Skip Hatten trip over second base, and even as you stare in disbelief as Joey Tobin slides into third—and misses—you can't help but realize that these kids would rather be playing the game than doing anything else on earth. Dedication? Partly. Spirit? That too. Perhaps the sort of enthusiasm that compels an average sportswriter to grope for superlatives when he ought to be composing an obituary. And when all is said and done, it doesn't take much to get to the bottom line.

Love? You bet it's love.

It sure as hell isn't baseball.

* * *

April 11—

One thing I've noticed about being thirty-six is that you tend to have a lot more nightmares than you did when you were thirty-five. Last night was a good example. Maybe it was my first loss of the season that did it, but I kept dreaming that everything I ate tasted like dried figs. I woke up at two in the morning in a cold sweat.

"Are you okay?" asked Joanie sleepily.

"Yeah," I mumbled, trying to be nonchalant in the face of some pretty desperate shaking. "Why?"

"I wasn't sure," she replied. "You kept rolling around, moaning, 'Figs. Figs.'" After a pause, she added, "If you're hungry, I've got some apricots."

I think I forgot to mention it before, but J.J. has a warped sense of humor.

April 13—

So what do you do when you get up one morning two days after the season opener and realize somewhere between your yogurt and your wheat germ that your fastball has, indeed, become yesterday's news? What do you do when you finally face the unpleasant fact that a steady stream of earned runs, cordially invited homers, and an apparent inability to locate the strike zone—even with a divining rod—is no longer due to rotten luck or bad karma? Well, you kick a little, you scream a little, maybe try some TM, and then go back to bed. But when all is said and done, and the tantrum's over, you take a long look at yourself in the mirror and realize that it's time to make a few decisions.

"Want to know what *I* think?" asked Warren Budlong as we were walking through Lafayette Park an hour after workouts.

"Do I have a choice?" I replied.

Buddy squinted at me through his Foster Grants. "Nope."

As a rule, I possess an inbred loathing for anyone who tries to talk down to me, which is a trait that usually brands me "least favorite" amongst managers and pitching coaches. Nevertheless, to borrow a phrase, there's an exception to every rule. Meet Warren Budlong—best friend, past master of the long ball, and American League Exception. Buddy's been catching me for so long now, I've begun to think we're the same person in two different bodies. There's not a single thing I can say or do that he hasn't thought of first. I'm reminded of a game we played last year in New York that found the Yankees trailing us by two runs going into the bottom of the ninth—when, thanks to a variety of thoroughly worthless excuses, I inadvertently loaded the bases with two out, just in time to face Dave

STEVE KLUGER

Winfield and the heart of the lineup. Buddy called time out and approached the mound as Doug Hoyt, with "get the hook" clearly printed across his face, left the dugout to make the same journey. Though Hoyt had intended to feel me out himself before going to the bullpen, he decided, instead, to let his catcher do all the talking.

"The thing of it is—" began Buddy, kicking at the dirt.

"Not necessarily," I interrupted. "If you think—"

"You know we could always—"

"Or something."

After a pause, we looked at each other and nodded, then Buddy readjusted his mask and went back to the plate. Doug scratched his head and returned to the dugout, mumbling, "What the hell was *that* all about?" It wasn't really as confusing as it seemed. Budlong had merely suggested that I jam Winfield at the wrists with the first pitch to rattle him, go high and outside with the second to throw him off, then smoke one over the outside corner. While people had a tendency to laugh at our verbal shorthand, they didn't laugh long. Winfield swung blindly on the third pitch and promptly popped it up to Buddy, who was already waiting patiently for it two feet in front of the backstop. Which is pretty much why Warren Budlong is the only person in the world who can tell me what to do without having me slink off somewhere to sulk.

"You know what you really need?" he asked, ducking a pigeon that was heading directly for his face.

"Yeah," I replied. "An arm that's about ten years younger."

Buddy frowned. "Don't be a jerk. What you need is a couple of new pitches."

"What are you, crazy? I'm thirty-six."

"Big deal," he snapped. "I'm Irish Catholic. What difference does it make?"

It's at moments such as these that I often think the polarized lenses in Buddy's shades are really made of rose-colored glass. Like the Little Engine That Could, he's one of the few people I know whose national anthem is "I Think I Can." Unfortunately, I'm a little bit more cynical.

The fundamental problem, you see, is that I'm a fast-baller. Period. Although at first, one might be inclined to reply, "So what," the simple truth is that I've been throwing that selfsame pitch—or variations of it—since I was nine years old—a development, I might add, that was perpetrated entirely by accident. As I remember, I'd been attempting to teach myself how to skim rocks across a neighbor's pond, growing more annoyed as every last one I tossed kind of hesitated briefly, sighed, then sank like an anchor. Finally, in a fit of pre-adolescent impatience, I snatched up a smoky chunk of slate, muttered a nine year old's equivalent to "screw you," and let it rip. Instead of skimming across the surface of the water, I watched in dismay as it soared up and away, heading in a northeasterly direction, and finally shattering $110 worth of plate glass ninety-eight feet away from where I stood. From that moment on, my fate was inexorably linked to a resin bag and a pitching rubber.

The thing the rule books never tell you is that from the time you take that first faltering step toward the nearest mound until the day you throw your last slider, the entire focus of your life shifts to the peculiar relationship between you and a few pieces of horsehide, which are collectively referred to as a baseball. There's not a single waking instant where your fingers aren't unconsciously scrabbling for a set of seams—either real or imagined—in an effort to perfect that pitch that's uniquely yours.

"Okay," you tell yourself in the middle of algebra class. "Full count, bases loaded. He's looking for something off-speed. So what are you going to do? Smoke him out of there, that's what. Come on, Scotty, fingers spread out along the stitching—cross-seams, kiddo, don't be a coward.

STEVE KLUGER

There's the windup—off the fingertips, MacKay—the stretch—*Struck him out!*"

"MacKay, what's the value of x squared?"

"Huh?"

More often than not, the incessant conditioning of the throwing arm over a period of so many years has a tendency to put people off, particularly when you've trained yourself to regard anything that's round as a potential missile. This holds especially true in bed. I've discovered time and again that pitching style can easily be misconstrued for advanced sexual technique—and usually with no effort whatsoever.

"Boy, that was nice," sighed Joanie, putting her head on my chest and beginning to doze. "What was it, Kama Sutra?"

"No," I confessed, a little embarrassed. "Change-up."

So there you are, four years away from the big four-oh. You've built your career—no, cancel that—you've built your entire life around your fastball, the one pitch you truly believe you can deliver better than anyone else in the world.

And then it's gone.

Gone?

Try telling Robert Frost, after fifty years and thousands of poems, that there's really no such thing as a true rhyme. Or try telling Albert Einstein that he made a mistake and that, in fact, relativity is merely a fantasy. Kind of kicks the bottom out, doesn't it? Makes you wonder what you've been spending all of your time doing. Now go ahead and tell Scotty MacKay that he's going to have to pick up a couple of new pitches.

A couple of what?

"Why not?" said Buddy as we began walking down Pennsylvania Avenue. "You're not the Tin Man. Your arm hasn't rusted. Yet."

CHANGING PITCHES

"Thanks for the 'yet,'" I snapped. He started across the street in an effort to avoid the White House, a practice he's indulged since 1968.

"Besides," he offered, "I'd kind of like to see what you could do with a curve."

"Why?"

Buddy grinned self-consciously. "I never told you this, but I'm getting pretty tired of catching your smoke. One of these days you're going to break my fucking hand." He must have sensed my apprehension at switching horses so late in mid-stream, because he immediately changed his tactics. "Or maybe you ought to call it quits after all," he advised. "Hang up your cleats, Scotty, and try something else. Real estate's big this year." We stopped at the corner in front of the Hot Shoppe for a long moment.

"A curve?" I finally said.

"For starters," he replied. He stepped out from the curb and hailed a cab.

"Where are we going?" I asked mildly.

"Back to the stadium."

"But we just came from there," I protested.

Buddy shrugged and pulled open the back door. "The street goes both ways." He hopped over the jump seats and glanced back at me sharply.

"Come on, MacKay," he snapped. "We got work to do."

* * *

April 22—

Mound Conference

(At Boston. Second inning, Red Sox leading 3–0, with Jim Rice at bat, one man out, and one man on.)

BUDDY*(raising his mask)*:   You okay, Scotty?

SCOTTY: Yeah, but I think it's going to rain.

BUDDY *(surprised)*:   There's not a cloud in the sky and it's eighty-five degrees.

SCOTTY *(squirming)*:   I can't help that. Whenever my toes start itching, it always rains. You think that means something?

BUDDY: Yeah. Athlete's foot. *(Pause.)* You feel like telling me what we're going to do with Rice?

SCOTTY: I was going to walk him.

BUDDY *(incredulous)*:   *Walk* him? With one out, Armas coming up, and the fastball on vacation?

SCOTTY *(defensive)*:   Well maybe he'll ground out. Maybe he'll hit into a double play.

BUDDY: Maybe he'll belt it to St. Louis.

(Scotty stares at the ground.)

SCOTTY: Yeah. St. Louis. *(Looking up.)* What a horrible thought.

BUDDY *(consoling)*:   Don't worry about it. You'll pick up the curveball in no time. Besides, the change-up's got a pretty good spin on it.

SCOTTY: That's not what I was talking about. *(Pausing reflectively.)* Wouldn't it be the pits if I woke up tomorrow and suddenly found out I'd turned right-handed?

BUDDY *(miffed)*:   If you're waiting for me to say yes, forget it.

SCOTTY *(hastily)*:   Oh, no offense, Buddy. I'm not prejudiced against you guys or anything. *(Hesitating and indicating his right hand.)* It's just that I've never been able to make this thing work at all.

CHANGING PITCHES   23

BUDDY *(helpfully)*: You're probably not trying very hard.

SCOTTY: The hell I'm not. Whenever I use it to eat, my sprouts always wind up on the floor. *(Pause.)* And another thing. You ever try your right hand on a push-button telephone?

BUDDY: Constantly.

SCOTTY: Well whenever *I* do it, I always get Information in Cincinnati. You think I have a problem?

BUDDY: Several.

SCOTTY: They say it's because half my brain is slow—

BUDDY *(cutting in)*: Well, you're not going to get an argument there. Your whole head is slow. *(Looking back at the plate.)* Listen, I'd love to stand here and talk, but we'd better do *something* about Rice. You got any thoughts?

(Before Scotty can answer, there is a low rumble of thunder in the distance. Buddy glances up at a suddenly overcast sky.)

SCOTTY: I'm going to try a change-up, Buddy. What do you think?

(Budlong wipes a raindrop off his glasses, stares up at the sky, then down at Scotty's feet.)

BUDDY *(after a beat)*: I think you ought to try Desenex.

(He returns to the plate. MacKay lets loose with a change-up to Rice, who immediately sends it into right field for a stand-up double.)

* * *

April 24—

I could be wrong, but thanks to "Sports Final" on Channel 5, I may have just lost Joanie to Vince Ferragamo.

STEVE KLUGER

We were watching a clip from an old Rams–Cowboys game, and she fell in love with him from behind. Though she professes undying devotion, to the best of my knowledge she still doesn't know what he looks like. I keep trying to tell her that if you can't judge a man by the clothes he wears, the same ought to apply to first impressions of a more anatomical nature.

"Not necessarily," she keeps pointing out. "You don't have to be a Christian Dior to figure out that the cuffs and collars are bound to match."

I hate being hung by my own metaphors.

*   *   *

April 25—

Some people have occasionally observed that whenever I talk to the press, I have a way of sounding like my mouth isn't entirely hooked up to my brain. Normally I become pretty defensive about this kind of accusation—except that this afternoon, I lost the last leg on which I'd been standing.

There was a press conference in the clubhouse just after today's game, during the course of which I found myself involved in an animated interview with Mechelle Plotkin, *The New York Times*' most valuable asset and one of the most competitive tennis players in the country. To Mechelle, "two–love" isn't a set score, it's a social issue. Unfortunately, she also happens to be a feminist—and I say "unfortunately" only because, despite a common interest in the initials ERA, whenever I wind up in a conversation with a feminist, I invariably say something offensive. Part of the reason for this is simply that I'm a professional athlete in a sport that, at least until now, has been restricted to men only, which makes me chauvinistic by association. The other reason: though I try to be excessively careful about neutralizing my nouns, it usually gets out of hand and leaves me sounding like I'm being sarcastic. This afternoon, however, I conducted myself admirably, from my references to the various chairpeople on the Senators' front office staff, to my willing observations on Chris Evert's supremacy over Bjorn Borg. I even managed to avoid noticing the half of my infield that had surrounded us like vultures, gleefully waiting for me to make a slip.

"One last thing," said Mechelle, wiping some Cruex off of her shoe. "With all of the great players you've faced, who do you think is the best hitter in the major leagues?"

"Dave Kingperson," I told her automatically.

I hope I didn't screw up her backhand.

* * *

April 26—

I knew instantly that it was going to be hard to remain tactful the minute Romeo and Juliet appeared on the television screen fighting over a can of diet soda.

"Romeo, O Romeo," mourned the younger Capulet, looking suspiciously like Joanie Jordan, "wherefore art thou Romeo?"

The object of her love appeared momentarily at the foot of the trellis, carrying a rose and a six-pack. "My Juliet," he declared amorously. "I have denied my father and forsaken my name. But you know what else I've done?"

"What?"

"I've discovered Bubble Free. The new, non-carbonated lemon-lime drink that tastes like it just came off a tree."

I closed my eyes briefly and prayed that I was in the middle of a pepperoni nightmare. As farfetched as some of J.J.'s commercials had been, at least she was usually able to rise admirably to the challenge. I recall the time she played

STEVE KLUGER

a coffee bean for Maxwell House. Twenty-four hours later, General Foods had gone up sixteen points on the American Stock Exchange. This, however, was another matter entirely. Fortunately, Joanie seemed to feel the same way, saving me from having to indulge in a series of outright lies.

"Well, I'm dashed," she groaned, standing in front of the Zenith console, whose plug she had just yanked from the wall.

"Ah, forget it," I replied cavalierly, trying to change the subject. "You feel like an ice-cream cone?"

J.J. glared at me. "No," she snapped, "I feel like an idiot." She shook her head slowly and returned to bed.

"I've got news for you," I said as she crossed her legs and stared down at the gameboard between us. "It could have been a lot worse. He could have jilted you for the soda."

"I've got news for *you*," she retorted. "He did." She frowned at the configuration of letters in front of her, then checked her own supply. When she didn't find what she was looking for, she reached across the bed and swiped one of my *B*s.

"'Dumb,'" she finally sighed.

"What," I asked, "the commercial?"

"No," she replied, pointing to the board. "The word. Six points."

Joanie has her own peculiar way of playing by the rules—*anybody's* rules. She could drain me of every letter in the alphabet if she wanted to, and it would be fair play. If I, on the other hand, did the same, I'd be cheating.

I stared down thoughtfully at the board and tried to pay attention to the fractured verbiage spread out over the squares, wondering if I could make something out of W__ K__. It was a hopeless effort. Joanie was wearing my old University of Maryland jersey, which created a rather substantial distraction. In it, I had captured three collegiate pitching titles and the lowest ERA on the East Coast; but quite candidly, it looked a lot better on her than it had on me. Abstractly, I arranged the available letters to spell out LETS MAKE LOVE. This is something with which I've never been entirely comfortable. I have yet to come up with a viable way of asking somebody to sleep with me that doesn't make me sound (a) like a rapist, or (b) ridiculous.

"What's the matter?" asked J.J., glancing up at me. "Something's been bugging you for three days."

I sighed. "It's the curveball," I told her finally, toying with an *L*. "Buddy said that in another couple of weeks we ought to have it dancing."

"So what?" she replied, reaching over and liberating my *S* and my *A*.

"Joanie," I complained, "this afternoon it looked like it was doing a slow waltz."

"'Skywalker,'" she said quietly. "Twelve points. Scotty, you haven't been working at it for very long. You're not Valenzuela, you know."

I frowned noticeably.

"Did I say something wrong?" she asked.

"No," I told her, squinting at the squares, "but how do you spell 'Yoda'?"

"Forget it," replied J.J. "The other *Y* is in 'hyperspace,' and both *D*s are in 'Darth Vader.'"

I carefully scrutinized my remaining vowels and a few unwieldy consonants, fully aware that if I didn't come up with something soon, I'd probably have to switch to "Star Trek." As it was, LETS MAKE LOVE had already been reduced to LEMKELO. Either a Russian dancer or a James Bond villain, I reflected.

"Can I make a suggestion?" asked Joanie, looking up at me.

"What is it?"

"You're worrying too much. When it feels right, throw it."

"That's easy for *you* to say," I snapped. "You know what it's like to make an ass out of yourself in front of fifty-

STEVE KLUGER

six thousand people?" Joanie's eyes flashed, informing me in advance that I was skating on very thin ice.

"Tell me about it," she retorted. "I just got dumped for a case of Seven-Up on national televsion." I backed down hesitantly. Like it or not, I had to admit that she had a valid point.

"No kidding, Scotty," she continued softly. "You've never been afraid to take a couple of risks before. Why start now?"

"J.J.," I said, reaching for her hand, "do you know what the odds are—" Before the question was out of my mouth, she'd successfully painted me into a corner with one of my own brushes.

"1976," she said automatically. "Senators and Oakland. Ninth inning, two men on, Gene Tenace at bat. What did Hoyt tell you to do?"

"He told me to walk him," I replied, bewildered. "Why?"

"What did two coaches tell you to do?" she continued, ignoring me.

"They said to walk him too."

"What did Buddy tell you to do?"

"Walk him."

"And what *did* you do?"

"I threw him a fastball," I admitted.

"Right," she nodded. "And what happened?"

"He flied out to right and we knocked them out of first place."

Joanie smiled indulgently. "See?"

"See what?" I demanded.

"Don't you get it?" she insisted. "If either of us was interested in playing the odds, I'd be sleeping with an accountant, and you'd be stuck with the bases loaded for the rest of your life."

Although I sensed that there was, indeed, a moral in there someplace, I was reasonably certain Aesop would have phrased it a little differently.

"Well?" she asked, brushing the hair out of my eyes. "What do you say?"

I looked up at her and shrugged. "'Wookie.' Eight points. I win."

Joanie stared down at the board in utter disbelief before she finally spoke. "I'm tired of this game." She sighed. "Why don't we make love, Scotty?"

Funny, how everything does work out if you really want it to. Just so long as The Force is with you.

* * *

April 28—

DO NOT REMOVE

From Doug Hoyt:

The Washington Bulletin

THE STANDINGS

American League East

	W	L	Pct.	GB
Baltimore	15	5	.750	—
New York	12	8	.600	3
Milwaukee	11	10	.524	4½
Detroit	10	10	.500	5
Boston	9	10	.474	5½
Cleveland	9	10	.474	5½
Toronto	8	11	.421	6½
Washington	2	19	.095	13½

STEVE KLUGER

At Washington

Baltimore	ab	r	h	bi		Washington	ab	r	h	bi
Singleton, rf	5	0	2	1		Tobin, 3b	4	0	0	0
Sakata, ss	5	2	2	1		Weinberg, lf	4	0	0	0
Dwyer, lf	5	1	2	1		Wright, ss	3	0	1	0
Murray, 1b	3	0	0	0		Jackson, cf	4	0	0	0
Ayala, dh	4	0	1	0		Delanoy, dh	3	0	0	0
Dempsey, c	4	0	0	0		Budlong, c	4	0	0	0
Bumbry, cf	4	1	2	0		Petry, rf	3	0	1	0
Ripken, 3b	3	1	0	0		Fowler, 2b	3	0	0	0
Dauer, 2b	4	0	2	0		Hatten, 1b	3	0	0	0
Totals	37	5	11	3			31	0	2	0

BALTIMORE	010	110	002	5
WASHINGTON	000	000	000	0

BALTIMORE

	IP	H	R	ER	BB	SO
Flanagan (W, 3-0)	9	2	0	0	3	9

WASHINGTON

MacKay (L, 1-2)	6	7	3	2	4	1
Collins	3	4	2	1	3	3

E—Tobin, Wright, Fowler DP—Baltimore, 1 LOB—Baltimore, 16, Washington, 4 HR—Singleton (4) SB—Murray, Ripken, Dempsey WP—Flanagan Time—2:54 Attendance—53,427

Don't let it get you down. We must be doing something right.

DH

* * *

Topps Baseball Series   No. 223

Douglas Franklin Hoyt
(Manager—Washington   Senators)
Born: November 15, 1936
Home: Waynesboro, Pa.
Height: 6'1"   **Weight:** 185

CAREER HIGHLIGHTS

1957—Ranked among AL leaders in seven offensive departments and led the Yankees to another pennant.

1960—One of the league pacesetters in stolen bases, paving the way to another championship season for New York.

1963—Hit three home runs in a game against the Red Sox, again taking the Yankees to the World Series.

1964—In his last full season in the majors, and his seventh on the American League All-Star Squad, Doug batted in the game-winning RBI in eleven consecutive games, and figured as one of the key factors in putting New York back into first place during the pennant stretch.

Douglas Franklin Hoyt. The baseball cards don't do him justice. In fact, I feel safe in saying that I would rather play ball for Doug Hoyt than anyone else in the world. Doug can shout louder than Tommy Lasorda, out-strategize Sparky Anderson, bait umpires with greater aplomb than Earl Weaver, and—when called upon to do so—tap into a deeper well of patience than Walter Alston. What's more, if he ever got into an argument with a marshmallow

STEVE KLUGER

salesman in some bar, he wouldn't belt him in the mouth; instead, he'd probably invite the guy over for drinks, then try to stick him with the tab. Billy Martin has been permanently outclassed.

At the same time, considering his major league playing career, one would assume that Doug deserved a whole lot more out of life than being stuck as manager of the worst team in baseball. Some call it bad luck; others claim that, because he's black, he couldn't possibly expect much more than winding up at the bottom of the totem pole.

"Personally," concludes Doug, "I think that's a crock of shit. Somebody's gotta keep you guys in line. Why *not* me?"

Although he firmly attests that his number-one goal in life is to bring a World Series crown to Washington, I honestly don't believe that's as important to him as is the day-to-day wearing of his numeral. Doug is one of that rare breed of ballplayer that includes Mike Schmidt, Pete Rose, and George Brett—a group whose very religion is steeped in the crack of a bat, the smell of rawhide, and a lifelong membership in Our Church of the Line Drive. According to the precepts of his makeshift Bible, "If it can't be settled between two foul poles, it ain't worth worrying about." I recall the first day of the 1981 baseball strike, which found the Senators in the midst of a two-game winning streak. We had just returned from the West Coast, eager to tempt Fate by trying for three, when the strike was officially called. All of us rather gloomily split up and headed for our respective homes, doomed to spend an undisclosed amount of time in front of our television screens, waiting for the news flash that told us we could go back to work. All except Doug. He showed up at an empty stadium the next afternoon, strolled out onto the diamond in full uniform, and blankly asked, "Where is everybody?"

Doug's only hang-up as a major league manager is a problem he encounters daily—in that, according to him, everybody is under the impression that all black people know each other.

"For God's sake," he snapped, storming into the dugout after autographing a scorecard for an elderly fan.

"What's the matter?" asked Joey Tobin, spitting a sunflower seed into Rick Jackson's batting helmet. Doug jerked his head at the old woman in the stands and growled in disgust.

"She says she can't wait to tell her gardener she met me. Of all the goddamned—" Fortunately, the National Anthem cut him off at that moment, putting an abrupt end to a demonstration of the bluer side of his vocabulary.

The worst offender in this regard is Stu Bishop, a sportscaster for one of the Virginia radio stations. Stu is a fairly competent judge of baseball, but he's so backward, he still refers to Afro-Americans as "colored" (once prompting Doug to show up at a post-game press conference with his face painted green). Apparently, nobody ever told Stu about the Emancipation Proclamation, because whenever he interviews Doug on the radio, he makes sure that none of his words is over two syllables long—a situation that Hoyt finds particularly revolting, since he graduated from the University of Michigan with a B.A. in English.

"Uh, Doug, to what do you attribute—uh, I mean, what do you think is the reason the Senators have gone on such a downslide—er, why they've been losing?" asked Stu, after we'd just dropped six straight.

Doug stared at him in awe. "Well," he began, through gritted teeth. "I suspect it's due to a marked increase in their nocturnal peregrinations, coupled with a growing tendency to put undue pressure on their gluteal muscles."

"Huh?" said Stu.

"They've been staying out till four in the morning and sitting on their asses," Hoyt snapped.

At first, Doug assumed that Bishop's unthinking bias

would wear off over a period of time, but quickly discovered—to his unbridled dismay—that, if anything, it only got worse. Finally, at wit's end, he decided it was time to fight fire with fire, and, if nothing else, yield to the axiom that holds, "If you can't beat 'em, join 'em." We had just completed the thirteenth inning of a five-hour ball game in Baltimore that showed no signs of ending before the following week. To make matters worse, we were due in Boston the next morning, which meant that the longer we played, the less sleep we were likely to get. Understandably, nerves were slightly shredded. That may be why when Terry Dutton inadvertently beaned Rick Dempsey with a 3–2 fastball it didn't take more than twelve seconds for both benches to empty into the kind of encounter you usually only see between Roberto Duran and Sugar Ray Leonard. Doug was standing by the batter's box, shaking his head and praying none of us was going to get killed, when he felt a tap on his shoulder. Stu Bishop.

"Doug," he began, sticking a microphone into Hoyt's face, "do you approve of on-the-field fisticuffs to settle personal differences?" As soon as he realized what he'd said, he immediately began blushing, fully aware that his choice of words might confuse a twelve-year-old; so he rephrased the question. "Some fight, huh?"

Doug nodded once, rolled his eyes heavenward, then smiled broadly, making sure he showed all of his teeth. "Mah, mah, mah!" he declared, indicating the diamond. "Dis sho' is a crazy bunch of folks."

Taking into account Doug's sense of propriety and fair play, I've been more than grateful to have him in my corner. I'm aware that, with the current state of my pitching arm, I need all the help I can get, yet realize I'll always be able to trust him to take up for me when it counts.

"You stink, MacKay," he spat out during this morning's workout. "You call that a fastball? I've seen ice melt quicker." I picked up the resin bag at my feet, debating whether or not to club him to death with it. "Besides," he continued, as I thought better of it and juggled the bag with my left hand, "you and Budlong were supposed to be working on a curve. Let's see it."

I was incredulous. "Are you crazy?" I demanded. "Doug, for God's sake, it's only been three weeks. Who do you think I am, Valenzuela?"

"Spare me the comparisons," he snapped. "Throw the curve."

I shrugged matter-of-factly and turned to face Opie Wright at the plate. Before I unwound with what I was certain would be a laughable result, I went through a mental checklist that I'd recently developed to help myself convert from fastball to curve. It's sort of like switching from fahrenheit to centigrade, except that I keep getting burned.

"Okay," I told myself, "you're throwing from the side, not off the top. And remember, you're releasing with the 'fuck you' finger, not the other one. That's it. Now, aim to the left of the plate so it breaks on the outside corner. Are you ready? Let it go."

In all modesty, I have to admit it was the best curveball I'd thrown yet. My timing was right, my coordination was perfect, and my release couldn't have been more on target. The fact that Opie sent it over the center field fence was something I would have preferred to ignore, but Doug didn't seem bothered by that a bit.

"You know, Scotty," he mused, staring at the plate, "that goddamned thing broke just where it was supposed to."

"Yeah," I reminded him, "but it's on its way to Capitol Hill now."

"Right on the outside corner," he mumbled. "Perfect."

"Capitol Hill," I repeated. "That's on Pennsylvania Avenue."

"You're not going to have any problems with this pitch at all, MacKay." He grinned slowly. "You been holding out on me or something?"

"Capitol Hill, Doug," I said once again, only loudly this time. "Three and a half miles from here."

Hoyt frowned. "Big deal," he retorted. "So you've got control problems. You've only been working on it for three weeks. Who do you think you are, Valenzuela?" He paused to scratch his head, before abruptly adding, "And I want you to try a knuckleball, Scotty."

"A *knuckleball*?!"

"Yeah." He nodded. "You get a grip on the curve, and you're halfway there anyway."

I tried a little logic. "Doug, that last pitch is about four seconds away from beaning the senator from West Virginia. You got something against the United States government?" With that, I snapped his patience entirely.

"Look, MacKay," he growled, "I'm the manager, you're the hired help. You want to hold onto that ticket to the Hall of Fame, you'll do what I say."

"Okay, okay," I replied meekly, recognizing defeat when I saw it. "But I'll tell you something, Doug."

"What's that?"

"My gardener isn't going to like this at all."

P.S. I'm writing this standing up. I've never been booted so hard in my life.

* * *

May 2—

Inside Sports may have just saved my relationship with J.J. I showed her a picture of Pat Haden and told her it was Vince Ferragamo. I suppose I ought to be ashamed of myself, but as long as it keeps her away from L.A.'s other quarterback, she doesn't have to know she's barking up the wrong jersey. The only thing that bothers me is that some day she might meet Pat Haden. I can't imagine what would happen, except that I get this sneaking feeling *somebody* would get burned. Come to think of it, you don't exactly need an I Ching to figure out who that somebody might be.

*   *   *

May 10—

Mound Conference

(*At Cleveland, seventh inning. Jason Cornell at the plate with a 3–0 count.*)

BUDDY (*raising his mask*): What are you doing, Scotty? You were supposed to throw Cornell a fastball.

SCOTTY (*defensively*): No, I wasn't. Didn't you signal for a curve?

BUDDY: No—I was just adjusting my cup. One of my nuts fell out.

SCOTTY: Oh.

BUDDY: I think you'd better relax, Scotty. You're concentrating too hard.

SCOTTY: No, I'm not. (*Indicating the plate.*) I thought Cornell played for the Indians. What's he doing in Detroit?

BUDDY: We're in Cleveland.

SCOTTY (*surprised*): We are? (*Looking at Buddy to see if he's joking.*) When did *that* happen?

BUDDY: I think you'd better relax, Scotty. You're concentrating too hard.

SCOTTY (*staring at the plate*): You know, I really hate Cornell.

BUDDY: I know what you mean. You seen his stats?

SCOTTY: I'm not talking about his average. (*Looking back at the plate.*) How come he gets to have so many teeth? I bet he never even had to wear braces.

BUDDY (*agreeing*): Yeah. (*Peering at the batter's box.*) And look at all that hair. Who's he think he is, Bucky Dent?

SCOTTY (*after a pause*): Let's kill him, Buddy.

BUDDY (*reflecting*): How about if we swipe his Close-Up instead?

SCOTTY (*animated*): Or put a VO-5 label on a can of spray paint.

BUDDY: I've got an even better idea. Why don't you strike him out? That'd show him. (*Beginning to leave.*) Remember, MacKay, when I signal *two* fingers, it's a curve.

SCOTTY: Okay, but do me a favor.

BUDDY: What's that?

SCOTTY: If anything else falls out, just send me a note, huh?

BUDDY: Right.

(*He begins to walk back to the plate.*)

SCOTTY: Hey, Buddy?

(*Budlong turns around.*)

BUDDY: What?

SCOTTY (*scratching his head*): Are you *sure* we're not in Detroit?

* * *

I suspect that maybe I've been playing this game too long. On my way home from the stadium, a red light found me stopped by the Jefferson Memorial. I stared carelessly at the dome for a long moment, wondering what it was that felt so familiar, until I noticed that my left hand was beginning to respond automatically. That was when I realized that if you were to round out the bottom of the Memorial and put a little red stitching on the top, you'd probably be able to pitch it. I mentioned it to Joanie at dinner.

"Don't you think the Jefferson Memorial looks like a baseball?" I asked.

"You want some more sushi?" she replied.

I think it's food for thought. Joanie thinks I ought to be committed.

* * *

Dear Mr. MacKay,
    Could you please send me five autographed pictures for my brother Barry? It's for his birthday and I've made him think he's getting a ten-speed bike.

                            Your friend,
                            Christopher Bridges

Dear Mr. MacKay,
    I'm an Orioles fan and I need your help. The first time you were used in relief, I bet $10 that you wouldn't last the inning. I lost. In 1971, I bet $50 that you'd never win 20 games by September. I lost. Two years later, $100 said that income tax would be abolished before you ever made it to an

STEVE KLUGER

*All-Star Game. I lost. And the following summer, I raised
the stakes to $250 against your beating out the competition
for the Cy Young. Once again, I lost.*

*Now that you're having trouble with the fastball, I see a
clear opportunity to recoup twelve years' worth of unlucky
investments. Yesterday, I wagered $500 that you've come to
the end of the line. My question: when should I make out the
check?*

David Kieserman

Dear Scotty,

*I don't know if you remember me, but I was the one in
the yellow blouse and the Jordache jeans who waved to you
in the third inning of the Red Sox game and you waved
back. Anyway, me and some friends have started our own
Scotty MacKay Fan Club, and we think it would be terrific if
you spoke at one of our assemblies at school. You get to
have lunch in the faculty dining room and I think they pay
you but I'm not sure. Anyway, I hope you say yes, because
all we ever get is city council representatives or somebody's
father who just came back from Egypt or something.*

Love,
Shirley Shor

Dear Mr. MacKay,

*I'm 83, and my husband and I have been watching you
pitch for twelve years, so I hope you'll understand when I
say that I feel like I've raised you. I know you're busy, but I
wonder if you might try to fit a World Series into your schedule some time soon. I don't mean to sound pushy, but quite
frankly, I don't have all the time in the world.*

Fondly,
Judith Stone

CHANGING PITCHES

Dear Mr. MacKay,

Enclosed, please find twelve years' worth of Scotty MacKay baseball cards. When I first started pitching in junior.high, I once traded my glove for six of them. Now, as a starter for Georgetown, I find they're about as valuable as counterfeit currency. And just as phony.

I've been a Senators fan my whole life. It hasn't been easy. Okay, so maybe they aren't the luckiest team in the world. Maybe all of their draft choices have been the ones everybody else has rejected. And maybe they were in last place for my entire adolescence. It didn't matter. When they dropped seventeen straight in 1974, I spent eight dollars on rabbits' feet. When the team plane got lost in '75 and landed in Philadelphia, I didn't even ask for a refund for the canceled doubleheader. But when their most redeeming social value appears to be throwing in the towel just because he's got to toughen up a little, it's time to start looking toward the New York Yankees.

Rich Bruder

*   *   *

May 15—

Rich Bruder is a right-handed pitcher for Georgetown University. This season, he's compiled a 6–0 record, leads his division with a 1.74 ERA, and has a fastball that is virtually unhittable. I saw him pitch against Loyola this afternoon and was thoroughly unprepared for his performance. Maybe perfection is stressed a lot more these days than it was during my stint at Maryland; or maybe it's just that Bruder is one of that rare few who can lay claim to the title of "natural." Whatever the reason, he displayed the sort of unflappable "I-know-exactly-what-I'm-doing" facility that I didn't discover until my second season in the major leagues. One thing is dead certain. By the year 2040, Americans will have put men on Mars, automobiles will be powered by solar energy, and this kid's going to be in the Hall of Fame.

After the game, I hung around the clubhouse entrance, something I haven't done in over eighteen years, waiting to speak to the man of the hour; and when Bruder finally put in his appearance, I saw instantly why he was laying waste to every college team in the Southeast. As he somewhat self-consciously signed autographs for a fairly large detachment of teenage girls, he appeared to be doing it with the same sort of intensity with which he'd pitched nine shutout innings. With his eyebrows furrowed and his pen hovering over yet another scorecard, you almost got the feeling that he was deciding where over the plate he wanted the R to break before he committed it to paper.

"Rich Bruder?" I said, when the crowd had dispersed. He glanced over in my direction curiously until he recognized me. For a brief moment, a shadow of doubt appeared to cross his face.

"Do you have a minute?" I asked. "I'd like to talk to you."

He took a tentative step backward. "You're pissed off about the letter," he guessed. "You came over here to slug me, right?"

"Well, no," I told him mildly. "Actually, I was going to buy you lunch."

He was far from convinced. "You sure you're not mad?" he said warily.

"Yeah, Bruder, I'm furious," I replied, putting an arm around his shoulder. "I'm also hungry. Come on."

"Okay," he warned, "but I've got to pitch again in five days. You break my arms and you're in big trouble."

I took him over to Mr. Natural's in Georgetown, where, for my money, the cuisine can't be touched by any of the city's more elegant establishments. Bruder's willingness to experiment with food of an organic variety was both poignant and touching.

"I thought you said you weren't mad," he frowned, looking up from a plate of alfalfa. "What are you trying to do, poison me?"

"It's good for muscle tone," I suggested.

"I don't *want* muscle tone."

After some strategic prodding, I finally got him to try the sprouts, and only then did I get down to business.

"What did you mean by 'throwing in the towel'?" I asked, carefully lining up the corners of four wheat thins so they resembled an infield.

"Look, I didn't mean to sound off," he grumbled, "but starting when I was twelve, I grew up with two pictures on my bedroom wall." There was an uncertain pause. "Yours and Babe Ruth's." He stared down at his plate for an embarrassed moment, abstractly toying with a sprout.

"Ruth played for twenty-two years," he said, suddenly looking up. "I figured you had at least ten to go. Then all of a sudden, every time I picked up a newspaper, you were mouthing off about being old and losing speed and maybe having to quit, and all the rest of that shitkicking crap."

One thing about college, I reflected—they certainly do teach you how to give a direct answer.

"I couldn't figure it out," he continued. "But you began sounding like your feet weren't made of clay, they were made of concrete." I started to defend myself, but he cut me off.

"I know," he said, eyes blazing. "You're thinking, 'This guy's just a kid, and he's got too much to say, and who the hell does he think he is when I'm picking up the tab.' But I'll tell you something, Scotty. Maybe *you* want to hang it up, but if I ever get my own uniform, they're going to have to *kill* me before I give it back."

In the silence that followed, I carefully picked up a scrap of grated cheddar and placed it smack in the center of

STEVE KLUGER

the mound. Somehow, for the moment, it seemed appropriate that the pitcher was made of cheese; and as I squinted down at my makeshift diamond, it was a long time before I could come up with a reply.

In truth, during the earliest part of my life, nobody had ever believed me when I'd said I was going to be a baseball player. Not that I really blamed them for their lack of support—my parents had been living under the misapprehension that I was supposed to die some time around my eighth birthday. Apparently, I'd been born with a defective membrane somewhere—it was one of those diseases that begins with a *D*, has about twelve syllables, and means, "We don't know what he's got, but don't get too attached to him."

Oh, I didn't really mind the idea of dying. What bothered me was having to do it before I turned nine. It always embarrassed me—as if I were copping out or something. I'd lie in bed each night, staring up at the ceiling and fantasizing about everything I wanted to be and everything I wanted to do—then I'd have to figure out how I was going to cram it all into the next two years. Fortunately, I got a reprieve before I had to take any decisive action.

"I don't know what to tell you," said a puzzled physician, "but the results were negative."

He looked so disappointed that I wasn't going to kick off, I nearly apologized to him. Later that afternoon, I fell out of a tree and broke my leg. I couldn't really complain. It was almost as if God were saying, "You're on your own now, kid. Good luck."

Which brings me to Bucky Harris and the Washington Senators—the team that everybody predicted was going to die. The reasons for such a pessimistic prognosis escaped me entirely. Of course, I never followed the daily standings—that was a practice you left to kids who were going to get to be teenagers. What I did know was that if giving 110 percent had any medicinal value at all, the Senators were dealing with the most potent antibiotic in the major leagues. I remember hearing an interview with Johnny Plitt, a recent Washington acquisition, who said, "When I take the mound, I never worry about winning. As long as you do your best, there's no way you can really lose." When he made that remark, Plitt happened to be 0 and 5. At the time, I had no idea if I could throw a baseball from here to the fence post, but after assessing the available information, I decided that, not only did he and I share the same philosophy, but *I* could be 0 and 5 too. Besides, what difference did it make? It was only the playing that counted.

Years later, when I had, indeed, made it to the minor leagues, it came as a surprise to everybody but me. What no one seemed to understand, however, was that my fastball was not really a pitch; it was the sum total of all of my parts—an extension of everything I'd ever believed in. It was hearing a "no" and perceiving it as a "yes"; it was piloting a leaky sailboat through the Straits of Magellan; it was playing like you were in first place and finding the truth in the lie. And that's why Bruder's observations, like his pitches, had found their mark. Maybe I *had* been too ready to give it up too soon. Maybe I *was* becoming a left-handed contradiction. Or maybe it was just that when you've spent your entire life with your eyes fixed firmly on the stars, you tend not to notice that you've just made a right turn at Orion. Even worse, you sometimes forget why you wanted to make the journey to begin with.

I think Yogi Berra phrased it best when he said, "Pitching is ninety-eight percent of the game."

He wasn't just talking about baseball.

"You know, this isn't half bad," said Rich, plowing through a plate of salad. "What is it?"

"Arrowroot," I told him.

His fork went clattering to the table. "Haven't you guys ever heard of lettuce?" he complained. "Scotty, do me a favor."

"What's that?"

"If we ever wind up pitching together, don't tell anybody I actually ate this stuff."

I examined a wheat germ brownie before I replied, "Maybe, but you're going to have to do *me* a favor."

"What?"

"If you're thinking about relieving me," I warned him, "you'd better work on that slider."

His brow furrowed. "How come?" he asked, puzzled.

"Because," I told him, "in another eight years, I'm going to need all the help I can get."

Rich stared down at the table a little self-consciously before he spoke. After a prolonged moment, he pushed his arrowroot aside and extended his right hand.

"Deal," he said.

I watched him disappear down N Street and wondered at the ramifications of opening a random fan letter. Bruder doesn't know it yet, but in panning for gold, he's about to discover platinum. I hope for his sake that it doesn't happen too soon, because he's got a lot to learn. Then again, so, apparently, have I. According to Ecclesiastes, "To everything there is a season." In his own outspoken way, Rich had reminded me of much the same thing. Winter may be a lot closer for me than it is for him, but, as he pointed out, if I've got to put on my snowshoes and my muffler, I'm not going to do it until the equinox.

I turned up my collar and headed back toward town. *Star Wars* was playing at the Capitol, and for the time being, seemed to be the only remedy for a rather painful moment of truth. On one hand, I chastised Rich for so thoroughly upsetting my equilibrium; on the other, I realized that, sooner or later, *everybody* needs a kick in the ass.

Even callipygians.

*   *   *

May 16—

Joanie saw Pat Haden interviewed on "The Tonight Show" last night. As soon as he stood up, she knew he wasn't Vince Ferragamo.

"Why did you lie to me?" she asked, wounded.

I stared down at the floor, embarrassed that the jig was up. "Because I'm easily threatened," I told her glumly. Instead of finding myself out on O Street, I noticed that her entire expression had softened like a melted marshmallow.

"But, Scotty," she protested, thoroughly confused, "I fell in love with *you* from the front."

Sometimes I really love it when she doesn't make sense.

*   *   *

May 17—

DO NOT REMOVE

To: All Starters
From: Doug Hoyt

1. *Public Relations has asked me to remind you that when you are on the road, you are guests. Not only that, you are representing Washington, D.C. Whoever told the reporter from the* Plain Dealer *that the food in the Cleveland*

STEVE KLUGER

clubhouse smelled like a pet cemetery may expect some disciplinary action.

2. *Also from Public Relations. Next Sunday is Autograph Day. Please remember that the fans are the ones who pay the salaries, so a little respect is in order. If one of the kids gets out of hand, asking him to step aside is acceptable. Telling him to fuck off is not.*

3. *I admit that we will probably not be in the pennant race. I further agree that some of the other teams are playing very competitive baseball. However, during our next road trip to Boston, I would appreciate it if you would* not *root for the Red Sox.*

4. *In case you haven't noticed, we're still in last place. Furthermore, we don't seem to be doing anything about it. As a result, I am presently considering the following:*

> a) *shuffling the lineup.*
> b) *relying more on the bench.*
> c) *rotating the outfield.*

Any questions, see me.

DH

●

Why don't you bury *the outfield?*

Joey

●

Look who's talking. Five errors in six games. Nice hands, Joe.

Rick J.

●

Here's an interesting thought. If MacKay's ERA was Fowler's batting average, and Fowler's batting average was MacKay's ERA, we might wind up in first place.

Skip Hatten

•

Here's another interesting thought: Eat shit, Hatten.

Fowler

•

Why not? It couldn't be any worse than the food in Cleveland.

Buddy

•

In an effort to prove that we've got just as much of a chance of making the playoffs as the Orioles, we're scheduling voluntary practice drills once the season has started. All those interested, please sign up below:

_____

_____

_____

_____

_____

_____

_____

_____

_____

"Malaise"—an indefinite feeling of debility.

Roget

•

For the record, I was born in Shreveport, Louisiana, and grew up in Tallahassee, Florida. I wish you guys would stop telling the press I come from Mayberry. I'm really getting pissed off.

Opie

•

Watch it, guys. Ope's getting pissed off.

Joey T.

•

What do you mean, watch it, Tobin? You're *the one who told them his father was a sheriff.*

Skipper

•

Okay, here's this week's quiz from Baseball News. *The batter foul-tips a third strike, but he thinks the catcher caught it, so he goes back to the dugout. Only the catcher* didn't *catch it, it was a wild pitch, so the batter turns around and runs to first. The catcher tries to throw him out but overshoots, and the ball winds up in right field, so the batter tries for second. The second baseman catches the ball in time for the out, but his foot's not on the bag, so it doesn't count. Okay: where is the batter?*

Gary

•

Washington.

Ricky

•

I need help with the Post *crossword. "8 across—Over the hill." It has six letters and I think it begins with an M.*

Don Weinberg

•

M-A-C-K-A-Y

Bob

•

You want to put your money where your mouth is, Delanoy? Ten bucks to anybody who can reach base against me in a six-inning exhibition.

Scotty

•

You're on, MacKay—

Bob D.

•

You're also nuts, Scotty.

Joey   Opie
Gary   Rick
Mickey   Skip   Jeff
Steve
Bruce   Andy
Phil   Wayne

•

STEVE KLUGER

Actually, I think the word was "mature."

Don W.

*   *   *

May 18—

Skip Hatten	$10
Mickey Fowler	$10
Joey Tobin	0
Opie Wright	$10
Buddy Budlong	0
Don Weinberg	$10
Gary Petry	0
Bob Delanoy	0
Rick Jackson	0
Jeff Stewart	$10
Steve Blye	$10
Bruce Cormicle	0
Andy Stern	0
Phil Brown	0
Wayne Miller	0
TOTAL OWED	$60

This works out to $10 an inning—or what I used to make pitching 1⅔ games in the Winter League. With less gear.

There's a lot of grumbling around the clubhouse. I think everybody expected to take me to the cleaners before the end of the first inning. One thing they didn't anticipate, apparently, was a six-hitter. Or a shutout.

"I smell a mutiny," warned Buddy.

Just so nobody's feathers stayed ruffled, I let them con me into giving them another chance. Act Two of MacKay vs. The Senators takes place Friday afternoon. I just hope my nerve stays up and my curveball stays down. If not, I may become the first major league pitcher ever to wind up in a brawl with his own team.

Joanie and I went to see *The Empire Strikes Back* for the fifth time. In commemoration, she bought me a tailor-made baseball jersey that says WHO'S SCRUFFY LOOK-ING? across the front. Actually, the only reason we've gone back so many times is for one of Princess Leia's lines a third of the way through the film. She's sitting in front of a radar screen, trying to puzzle out the identity of an enemy intruder, when she suddenly shakes her head and grimaces as though she's known all along.

"An Imperial probe droid," she sighs.

I hope she had the good sense to shoot whoever made her say that.

* * *

May 20—

According to this morning's edition of the *Post*, the sportswriters have just named Gary Carter the Player of the Week; and while Gary has my sincerest congratulations, it makes we wonder about the collective power of the press. Somewhere along the line, I sense some operational inequities in a system that subjects over six hundred baseball players to four Judgment Days a month. It's not as if we don't have *enough* to worry about. As such, in putting the cleats on the other foot, I've conducted my own poll, and am pleased to announce Scotty MacKay's three picks for Sportswriter of the Week. The winner will receive a baseball from my next shutout, or a free trip on the next moon shuttle—whichever comes first.

MECHELLE PLOTKIN
The New York Times, Washington Bureau

Mechelle is the most complete anachronism of any sportswriter around. Despite the fact that she works for the world's most important newspaper, her spectrum of knowledge is limited to the confines of every playing field in the world. She recently attended a state dinner for Shultz and came away disappointed. She thought they meant Charles. When she's not out beating the pants off of Jimmy Connors, she's usually crusading against the upper class, of which she is grudgingly a member. She attends the opera with a pea shooter. I also understand that, much to her dismay, the *Times* rented her a Mercedes on a recent trip to the Super Bowl. Before she returned the car, she'd stripped it clean and donated the parts to the Shop department at the Holy Conception Academy in Ossining, New York.

The other thing I like about Mechelle is that she's the only person in the world who calls me "Scott." While I used to find this disconcerting, it's noticeably more appealing than some of the other names thrown my way during press conferences. One writer in particular has a grating way of referring to me as "Scotty-Boy." Every time I talk to him, I begin feeling like an Irish folk song.

NOELLE BIANCHI
Time magazine

For using a pen the way da Vinci used a brush. Noelle not only has the most perceptive insight into sports journalism of anyone in the business, but she's also the only woman who's demanded—and received—an opportunity to try out for the Ft. Lauderdale Yankees. When she didn't make the cut, she did the next best thing and married Yankee shortstop Michael Buckner. Noelle also happens to be a perfect "ten," but I won't let that influence my judgment. Not much.

MARK LITVIN
Washington Bulletin

Mark isn't really one of the *best* writers around, but he's the only local who's stuck with the Senators from Day One without even flinching. If loyalty were measured in thoroughbreds, Mark would have a string of stables from here to Denver. Some samples of Litvin's prose:

"Scotty MacKay's fastballs were largely in fine form, despite the fact that four of them cleared the outfield wall."

"Pitcher MacKay has committed three errors over his last two starts, although he is purportedly suffering from food poisoning."

"MacKay was hit up for six runs before he was pulled—but, much to his credit, he gave up no walks."

Now *that's* a sportswriter.

* * *

May 22—

Wright	$10
Fowler	$10
Budlong	$10
Tobin	<u>$10</u>
	$40

This raises my total indebtedness to the Washington Senators to $215. Not that it isn't paying off. The curveball's been getting such an unplanned workout, I only threw 106 pitches in tonight's game. Of course, if you do a little calculating, you figure it's cost me $2 a pitch. It really set me thinking. I've earned a number of wins in the past, but this is the first time I ever *bought* one.

Buddy told me he's been feeling a little guilty about getting that hit off of me in yesterday's exhibition. I pointed out he'd have to be crazy not to take advantage of an easy ten bucks. On the other hand, I also mentioned that if he *wanted* to feel guilty, he didn't have to stop on my account. He did anyway.

* * *

May 23—

A doubleheader with the Cleveland Indians happened to coincide with Autograph Day at Senators Stadium. This is an annual ritual that is enormously soothing to the ego—provided you're twenty-eight years old. I was signing my name for my fourteenth Little Leaguer, when I happened to glance across the field toward the Indians' dugout. Jason Cornell was making time with the entire contingent of Dallas Cowboy cheerleaders; all I had waiting in *my* line were the Silver Spring Shriners.

I *hate* Jason Cornell.

* * *

May 24—

I just read another in a continuing series of articles in *The Sporting News* condemning Philadelphia's Steve Carlton for refusing to speak to the press. While I respect the media's irritation, I wonder if they realize that in devoting so much time to Steve's vow of silence, they're giving him more copy than if he ever opened his mouth.

* * *

Weinberg	$10
Hatten	$10
	$20

Doug came out onto the field this afternoon to watch me two-hit the Washington Senators. He didn't say a lot, but then again, he didn't have to. His face told the whole story. It wasn't so much my nine strikeouts that did it; it started when Joey Tobin corkscrewed himself three feet in the air to keep a line drive out of the ionosphere. Before he'd come back down to earth, he'd shot it to Opie, who dove into second, rolled over, and flipped it to Hatten at first for perhaps the only triple play that has ever taken place beneath the bleacher lights at Senators Stadium. Of course, one might have wished that we'd been playing a team other than ourselves, but if beggars can't be choosers, Doug was making do with his coppers.

"I don't get it," he said to me later on in the dugout. "If you didn't know any better, you'd think they were ballplayers, wouldn't you, boy?" I hate it when Doug calls me "boy."

"What about the curveball?" I asked offhandedly.

"Did you see the way Tobin made that catch?" he mumbled. "I haven't seen him move so fast since you guys put the Ben Gay in his jock."

"What about the curveball, Doug?" Sometimes when I talk to him, I get the feeling my needle's stuck.

"The what?" he asked, turning to me.

"The curveball," I repeated patiently.

Hoyt frowned. "Were you throwing the curve?"

He stared back toward the field in muted disbelief, then slowly got up to leave; but just before he reached the dugout steps, he turned back to me.

"I know what you're doing, Scotty," he said quietly, indicating the rest of the team out on the diamond.

"Who, me?" I asked, feigning confusion.

"Yeah, you," he nodded. "I've been playing this game for thirty-two years, and I know every pitch in the book."

That's why Doug Hoyt is the manager, and I've never been very good at poker.

*　*　*

May 26—

Once in a while I find myself suspecting that Joanie only fell in love with me for my fastball. Because that now happens to be a past-tense pitch, I've begun wondering how long it's going to take her to become bored—so I chose tonight to have her tell me I have an overactive imagination.

I had it timed perfectly. We were watching a rerun of *Inside Daisy Clover* on the "The Late Show," and I'd waited until Natalie Wood eloped with Robert Redford, knowing that J.J. is a sucker for that scene.

"Can I ask you something?" I whispered, as she nuzzled her chin into my neck.

"What?"

I nodded toward the television screen. "Would you sleep with Robert Redford if I lost my pitching arm?"

J.J. put her hand on my chest and sighed. "I'd sleep with Robert Redford if you *didn't* lose your pitching arm."

I have to learn to stop asking questions like that.

*　*　*

I stopped by Mr. Natural's on my way to the stadium for some ginseng and sprouts, and encountered an unfortunately repetitive sociological phenomenon. I was sitting at the counter at the time, minding my own business and poring through an *Inside Sports* article on Mickey Hatcher, when a complete stranger turned to me as I was about to swallow a mouthful of food.

"Southpaw, huh?" he said.

There used to be a time when this sort of comment would invariably make me feel guilty, as though I were a second-class citizen. Kind of like the time I traded in my 1972 Vega for a Porsche. For three months, I was so concerned that my friends were going to think I'd gone high-hat, I'd only drive it at night. The thing that irks me to no end is that people are constantly excusing my shortcomings when they find out I'm left-handed, as if that were the reason. In truth, I don't especially *mind* being a fallible human being with my own lineup of faults—particularly when I've spent most of my life cultivating them.

"Lefty Scotty MacKay was knocked off the mound in the second." The "Lefty" is supposed to explain why I failed. Notice how they never say, "Righty Nolan Ryan couldn't get past the first out." Of course, when I win, that's a different story entirely.

"The six-foot-two fastballer went the distance." No mention of which hand I did it with. Is that fair?

For the time being, I think I've figured out a solution to the problem. The next time somebody accosts me with, "Left-handed, huh," I'll come right back with, "Yep. And what about you? Bald, huh?" The possibilities are endless. "Wear glasses, do you?" "A little overweight, right?"

The only thing that stops me is that, sooner or later, I'd probably wind up in a fistfight in the middle of Constitution Avenue. Oh, it isn't the broken nose I'd mind so much, it's

STEVE KLUGER

the headlines in the evening edition of the *Washington Bulletin:* SOUTHPAW SCOTTY MACKAY JAILED IN BRAWL.

It's enough to drive you right up a wall—and to the left.

*   *   *

May 28—

Jackson $10

It's funny what a well-timed double play can do for a team morale that's either sagging or nonexistent. After yesterday's game with Detroit, there was a new jingle floating around the clubhouse. Well actually, it was an old jingle with a facelift.

> *These are the saddest of possible words,*
> > *Opie to Mickey to Skip,*
> *Faster than lightning and fleeter than birds,*
> > *Opie to Mickey to Skip.*
> *Ruthlessly pricking an Indian's bubble,*
> *Making a Tiger hit into a double,*
> *Words that are heavy with nothing but trouble,*
> > *Opie to Mickey to Skip.*

Wherever they are, you figure that Joey Tinker, Johnny Evers, and Frank Chance are smiling. A lot.

The team finally let me off the hook after our last workout, when they informed me I wouldn't have to pitch against them again.

"I think you've learned your lesson, MacKay," said Bob Delanoy. This was almost funny coming from him. It was Delanoy who'd challenged me to begin with, yet he's the only one who hasn't been able to make it to first base.

I suppose I'm just as happy that the whole thing is over.

The guys tell me that my curveball's in good shape, so I really don't need the extra practice anymore. In truth, I suspect *they* don't need the extra practice anymore. It's served its purpose. Besides, at ten bucks a throw, and with my pitching arm, I've been losing my shirt.

But we've been winning ball games.

* * *

May 29—

The Washington Bulletin

Senators Trounce White Sox 2–1

BY MARK LITVIN
Washington Bulletin Staff Writer

Yes, Virginia, there is a Santa Claus. And sure as Hell has frozen over, he's arrived just in time for Mother's Day. Perhaps the tricycle he promised you is a little dented, and maybe Raggedy Ann is missing an arm; but rest assured that those funny noises you heard on your roof last night were unmistakably reindeer. And when you open your stocking this morning and find that silver box with the red ribbon, don't be surprised when you pull out a six-game winning streak.

Christmas first came to Wash-

ington, D.C., last Monday afternoon, when the Senators defeated the visiting Chicago White Sox 3–2. In the ensuing week, graces have been showered upon the pure of heart in the form of five stand-up doubles, four two-run homers, three stolen bases, two double plays, and a partridge in a pear tree. Not only has mistletoe been strung out all along Connecticut Avenue, but with last night's victory over those same White Sox

See Senators Page Three

STEVE KLUGER

at Comiskey Park, the Senators have achieved their longest unbroken string of wins since 1972. This is not to imply that they've climbed out of the cellar—yet—but until the last carol has been sung, every hall in the metropolitan area will continue to be decked with boughs of holly.

Sox Can't Cut It

Yesterday's hero was undoubtedly Yesterday's Hero, Scotty MacKay, the former Cy Young recipient and future Hall of Famer, who, earlier this season, seemed to be heading for an involuntary retirement. MacKay has been developing a curveball, which, though it doesn't exactly curve, manages to pull off a few cleverly disguised imitations.

"Don't ask me what he was throwing," said Sox catcher Carlton Fisk, who went 0 for 4. "The first two looked like they were sinking, the third one broke around my knees, and that last one just sort of hung there." After a pause, he added, "That damned ball did everything but sit up and beg."

"Junk," snapped Greg Luzinski. "Nothing but junk." Indeed, the perplexing nature of MacKay's pitches led a number of media members to inquire what, exactly, he was doing differently.

Unfortunately, the six foot two lefthander didn't seem to have much more of an answer than they had.

"I'm not quite sure," he was quoted as saying. "When I tried to make it break, it would drop, when I tried to get it to drop, it broke. It's sort of like fried wonton. Until you cut it open, you don't know *what's* inside." The only slip he made was a 3–2 pitch to shortstop Harry Chappas. MacKay had set up Chappas with a series of breakers, trying to catch him unawares with a fastball for a called strike three.

"As soon as I let go of that pitch," admitted MacKay, "I knew that the next people to see it were going to be Canadian."

MacKay Shines

Yet, it takes a lot more than a series of lucky pitches to effect the kind of panache that MacKay displayed last night. Despite a near-brilliant run-saving dive by shortstop Opie Wright, a double steal by Fowler and Tobin, and a two-run homer by catcher Buddy Budlong, it was still the pitcher's night to shine. Scotty MacKay has often been accused of getting by on a pass of sorts. His

See Senators Page Five

legendary fastball, which first put him on the map, had become so routine, one often got the impression that he could have phoned in his turn on the mound. And when that fastball began losing its velocity, there were those who predicted that, like so many who had never learned how to work, MacKay was only a fungo's drive from unemployment. After last night, those self-same wags now find themselves dining on crow sandwiches. Granted, MacKay still has a long way to go toward mastering control—seven walks in as many innings speak for themselves—but it was the total concentration and sweat-stained decisiveness he devoted to every pitch that stripped away thirteen seasons of active duty and—in the case of this observer—instilled one with the same sort of excitement you experienced the first time you saw Valenzuela pitch. Scotty MacKay may yet become the only 36-year-old lefthander ever to earn the title "Rookie of the Year."

Which is not to overlook the other key participants in last night's victory. A fan once said of the Senators, "The reason I love them is because whenever they take the field, they actually look like they believe they've got a chance." By the top of the eighth inning, they looked like they believed a lot more than that. Although Chicago reached base eleven times, only Harry Chappas managed to make the 360-foot journey from home plate to home plate. It wasn't so much the throwing accuracy of catcher Budlong, as he thwarted three consecutive White Sox steals, nor was it necessarily the outfield acrobatics that consistently eliminated the threat of extra bases. What it was—pure and simple—was the consummate intermeshing of some formerly disparate cogs, who, after season upon season of perpetual disappointment, are beginning to earn the right to call themselves a team.

"This is a last-place club?" groaned Chicago manager Tony La Russa. "Give me the Yankees any time."

Yes, Virginia, there is a Santa Claus. Multiply him by twenty-five and call him the Washington Senators.

Oh—and have a Merry Christmas.

*　*　*

　　　　　　　　　　STEVE KLUGER

Mound Conference

(At Minnesota. Third inning, one out. Kent Hrbek at bat with a man on base.)

BUDDY *(raising his mask)*:   What's the matter now?

SCOTTY *(visibly perturbed)*:   I just thought of something. What if you get traded someday?

BUDDY: Then I get traded. So what?

SCOTTY: Well, what if they send you to another American League team and I have to pitch to you?

BUDDY: I still don't get it.

SCOTTY *(exasperated)*:   Don't you *see*? You know me too well. Whenever you come up to bat, you'll be able to figure out what I'm going to throw you.

BUDDY *(comprehending)*:   Oh. *(Pausing, then grinning slowly.)* Hey, you know, you're right.

SCOTTY *(coolly)*:   You think that's fair, Warren?

BUDDY: Warren?

SCOTTY: Yeah. I wouldn't take advantage of *you* like that.

BUDDY: I'll tell you what. If I guess what you're going to pitch, I'll close my eyes before I swing.

SCOTTY *(irritated)*:   No, you won't. You'll look. *(Pause.)* I hope they trade you to Milwaukee.

BUDDY *(surprised)*:   Why?

SCOTTY: Because you hate Milwaukee.

BUDDY: No, I *like* Milwaukee. I hate Detroit.

SCOTTY *(amazed)*: You never told me that.

BUDDY: Yeah, I did. You just never listen. *(Looking back toward the plate.)* What do you want to pitch to Hrbek?

SCOTTY: I'm not going to tell you.

BUDDY *(exasperated)*: Scotty, we're not on different teams *yet*.

SCOTTY *(capitulating)*: Make me a promise, okay?

BUDDY: What's that?

SCOTTY: When they trade you, ask them to send you to the National League.

BUDDY: I'll write it down. *(Putting on his mask.)* Besides, what if they trade *you*?

SCOTTY *(putting on his glove)*: That's *your* problem. Go on back to the plate, Budlong. I want to hit Hrbek with a curve.

(Buddy turns around and walks back to the plate. When he gets halfway there, he stops and returns to the mound.)

BUDDY *(plaintively)*: Scotty?

SCOTTY: What?

BUDDY: Don't ever call me Warren again.

* * *

The Washington Bulletin

Budlong Out for Season

June 2—Minneapolis, Minn.— Washington Senators catcher Warren Budlong has been placed on the disabled list for the remainder of the season, a spokesman for the Senators said tonight. Budlong, a former American League batting champion, was injured in the third inning of this evening's game with Minnesota when he chased a pop foul by Twins' first baseman Kent Hrbek into the stands. According to an eyewitness, who was later treated for injuries after the catcher had fallen on her, Budlong had miscalculated his proximity to the wall and flipped over the box seat railing as he was making the catch. An unconfirmed report indicates that his left arm was broken in four places.

In a related story, the Senators completed a deal with the Cleveland Indians to send four of their minor league players to Ohio in exchange for Jason Cornell, considered by some to be the best defensive catcher in the American League. Cornell is expected to arrive in the Twin Cities some time tomorrow to complete the series with the Twins and to take over Budlong's spot in the lineup for the rest of the season.

* * *

What they didn't say was that Buddy never let go of the ball. He would have broken both his legs, too, before he'd done that.

On one hand, I'm happy it wasn't his throwing arm; on the other, that's not going to mean a whole lot to a dedicated dirt-eater like Budlong. Then again, there were a few equally immediate problems, not the least of which is the fact that during twelve years in the major leagues I've only pitched one game that Buddy hasn't caught. That was half of a doubleheader with the White Sox in 1973. I gave up seven runs on three homers, and committed two errors—as well as the first balk of my career. Although nobody really takes me seriously when I say as much, the only reason I won those Cy Youngs was because there were two of us on the mound.

"How's your other half?" asked a friend of Joanie's who'd once come to see me pitch.

"He's fine," I replied automatically, indicating Buddy behind the plate.

Which is why I can't accept Jason Cornell as the best defensive catcher in the American League. The best defensive catcher in the American League is lying in a bed at Twin Cities Presbyterian Hospital. And with only one arm, he can still outdistance anybody else with two. Even so, Cornell's stats can't be overlooked. He has led the division in nearly every category for four out of his six seasons in the majors. He has been named to the All-Star team three times. He has won a pair of batting titles.

He also does those commercials for Jockey shorts and for Johnson's Baby Shampoo. He spends more time with a blow dryer than he does with a batting helmet. On a scale of 10, Cosmopolitan rated him 11. And he knows it. He's also only twenty-eight. I *hate* Jason Cornell.

I've got a bad feeling about this.

SUMMER

Suggestions for Pissing Off Jason Cornell

1. When he gives you the signal for a change-up, brush him off, then throw it anyway.

2. Remind him constantly that you'd rather be pitching to Yogi Berra.

3. When he's warming you up in the bullpen and asks you to take it easy on his hand, throw fastballs.

4. Volunteer to help out with the gear on the road trip to Oakland, then make sure his equipment winds up in Seattle.

5. When he's quoting baseball stats and claiming he has total recall, tell him so does a Betamax, only they don't cost $750,000 a year.

6. When he calls a mound conference and implies that your fastball is rising away on him, tell him it's because he's too short.

7. Ask him if his slow reflexes are an acquired trait or hereditary.

8. Tell him you accidentally broke all of the teeth in his comb, then watch him panic.

9. Remind him constantly that you'd rather be pitching to Johnny Bench.

10. If he ever goes into a batting slump, imply that you know what he's doing wrong, but don't tell him.

11. The next time he tells you he's having trouble seeing your change-up, suggest he cut his hair.

12. Wait until he puts on all of his gear, then tell him he's wearing your undershirt, and make him give it back.

13. Imply to the press that his jockstrap is a boy's medium.

14. Wait until the next time they're taking pictures of him for *Sports Illustrated*, then ask him why all of his teeth are capped.

15. When the bases are loaded with no outs and he asks you what you're going to pitch to Robin Yount, make him guess.

* * *

June 10—

Mound Conference

(At Detroit. Kirk Gibson at the plate with a 1–1 count.)

JASON *(taking off his mask)*: Look, Scotty—I know you're getting a little tired, so maybe you'd better walk this guy, huh?

SCOTTY:

JASON: Okay, bad idea. *(Pause.)* You want to try the curve?

SCOTTY:

JASON *(putting on his mask)*: Right.

(He goes back to the plate and signals for a curve. Scotty throws a fastball, which Gibson sends to Pontiac.)

* * *

June 11—

This is obviously not going to work at all. And that includes everything. The curveball, the knuckleball—even the seventh-inning stretch doesn't play the way it used to. Of course, it's all Cornell's fault. He says fastball when everybody knows it ought to be a breaker; slider when it ought to be an intentional walk. That's why I take everything he says into consideration and then do the opposite. Yesterday I was walking through Georgetown and ran into him outside of Mr. Natural's. He said he was going my way and volunteered to walk with me—so I turned around and headed in the other direction. I wound up in Virginia.

* * *

June 12—

Topps Baseball Series   No. 521

WILLIAM SCOTT MACKAY
(Pitcher—Washington Senators)
Born: October 4, 1945
Home: Washington, D.C.
Height: 6′2″   **Weight:** 190

Every time I pick up one of my baseball cards, an event that has been occurring less and less frequently, I inadvertently find myself wincing. It isn't so much the stats (although they are not exactly cause for trumpets themselves) as it is the name that appears at the top: WILLIAM SCOTT MACKAY

This is not to imply that I have anything against my name. On the contrary, I find that over the years I've grown quite accustomed to it. Fond, almost. I also find,

CHANGING PITCHES

however, that it lacks any music of its own. Understand, I don't expect a moniker to inspire a symphony, but I do believe a player's name should spark at least a couple of verses of "Take Me Out to the Ball Game." Case in point: Tony Conigliaro. Obviously spelled with two *i*'s and a fastball. Or Rocky Colavito. You can already smell the horsehide.

It's all in the name.

Deep down, I think this is the reason baseball has gone soft. It's not that we're any less competitive than we used to be, but nobody takes us seriously anymore. Do you blame them? Time was when you could face a lineup with names like Boomer, Ripper, Moose, Duke, and Tank. Today your starting nine is liable to feature Bobby, Ritchie, Ross, Scotty, and Geoff, with an occasional "Scooter" thrown in just to remind us that we haven't wandered into an underclass meeting at Groton.

For this reason, I accept the criticism that I would normally pin on the designated hitter rule. We *have* gone soft. There are those who blame it on artificial grass, and others who claim that we've forgotten how to tough it out. Personally, I think this is a crock. I remember my first season in Winter League ball. The dinners consisting of Fritos and Yoo-Hoo's, and the all-night journeys from Pensacola to Ocala in a World War I school bus. Or the times they'd forget about a little thing called accommodations and three of us would wind up having to share the same bed—all for a doubleheader played in front of six people and a stray cat. I hated it then and I'd hate it now. But I'll tell you something. I wouldn't trade a single one of those lumps— and believe me, there were plenty—for anything in the world. So how did *I* get soft? I think it was our manager. I had a great deal of difficulty believing I was a minor league baseball player for a man who insisted that we call him "Winky."

So, when Mechelle Plotkin asked me whom I would include in my own all-time All-Star lineup, I found myself putting aside Ruth's average and Mantle's slugging percentage and heading straight for the thirteen men who, by virtue of nothing more than a surname, were most certain to inspire abject fear in the hearts of anyone who ever picked up a bat.

Roy Campanella, C
Candy LaChance, 1B
Rabbit Maranville, 2B
Pee Wee Reese, SS
Pie Traynor, 3B
Tris Speaker, OF
Zack Wheat, OF
Dummy Hoy, OF
Christy Mathewson, RHP
Lefty Grove, LHP
Dutch Leonard, P
Dazzy Vance, P
Mickey Lolich, P

There is a footnote. Although my choices are representative of the names that most clearly spell "baseball," there is nevertheless one conspicuous omission, and one that deserves special mention. It is a unique combination of letters that cannot and will not be duplicated. Because no matter how you try—and you can barter, trade, borrow, or rob— for the sheer feel of the game, no one will ever be able to top the fellow who decided to call himself Tom Tresh.

And maybe that's where we can find a solution. If *everybody* were called Tom Tresh, or Rabbit Maranville, or Pee Wee Reese, we wouldn't have to worry about whether or not we could still tough it out. As a matter of fact, we could probably dump the DH without a second look. Hell, we wouldn't even need Astroturf anymore.

It's all in the name.

June 13—

I visit Joanie on the set, and she tells me I'm being juvenile because I won't talk to Jason. I have a great deal of difficulty taking her seriously, considering that when she makes this remark, she is dressed as a pitcher of Kool-Aid.

* * *

June 14—

Somebody at *Playgirl* saw Buddy doing the color commentary on Saturday's Game of the Week and asked him if he would consider a five-page spread in next month's issue. They didn't even mind that he'd be wearing a cast—provided that was *all* he was wearing.

"What do you think?" he asked skeptically. What did I think? I thought it was undignified, in poor taste, and counterproductive to the essence of competitive sport.

"You're jealous as hell, aren't you?" He smirked.

It's difficult to defend yourself when the nail has been hit squarely on the head.

* * *

SPORT Interview

SCOTTY MacKAY

**the lefty that batters have loved to hate
for thirteen years**

When he was 25, he was unhittable. When he was 30, he had guaranteed himself a plaque in the Hall of Fame. And when he was 35, it had all turned sour. The fastball had lost its pop, the earned runs were multiplying like guppies, and retirement was never more than 90 feet away. Yet, at 36, Scotty MacKay is not tending his organic garden or watching the World Series from an armchair. He has discovered the fountain of youth in a curveball, and has already earned himself the title, "The Comeback Kid."

SPORT: *Last year, you probably racked up the worst season ever for a Cy Young winner. Four and eleven, I believe?*

MacKay: Four and fourteen. You forgot September.

SPORT: *Any reason you were so underwhelming?*

MacKay: Uh-huh. I stunk. It was one of those years when nothing went right. I know that's a pretty lame excuse, but when you need a pair of binoculars just to find the plate, you've got to figure there's *some*thing wrong.

SPORT: *There was obviously a reason why nothing went right. Any ideas?*

MacKay: I used to have a lot of them, but they all turned out to be bum

CHANGING PITCHES

steers. *You* know—the usual party line. Bad lighting, artificial grass, too many left-handed hitters, too many right-handed hitters. . . .

SPORT: *It doesn't sound like you believed any of it.*

MacKay: That was my problem. I did. And maybe if I'd faced the truth a little bit sooner, I'd have had a better year.

SPORT: *What was the truth?*

MacKay: The truth was, I was scared to death. I never *used* to be, but all of a sudden somebody would mention my name, and people would say, "MacKay? Is *he* still around?" And then when I'd go out and win a game, everybody made such a big deal over it because I was 35, you'd have thought it was the Second Coming.

SPORT: *How did that ultimately affect your performance on the mound?*

MacKay: In a couple of words? It destroyed me. Made me start wondering if I was for real, and if I wasn't, when I was going to turn back into a pumpkin. And once I started worrying about that, I lost my nerve along with my next seven starts.

SPORT: *Were you able to make the connection at the time?*

MacKay: I couldn't help it—but it didn't make it any better. See, baseball's no different from anything else. All you've got to sell is yourself, and when you start doubting that, you might as well hang it up. I remember how I used to feel at the beginning, when I'd be facing—oh, I don't know—Robinson or Yastrzemski—and I'd have them down to a 3–2 count, and I wouldn't be afraid to challenge them because I had 50,000 people standing up and screaming, telling me I could do it. Well, last year, it hit me for the first time that even with all that, *I* was still the one who had to push the ball across the plate. It's this terrible feeling of aloneness, and when it gets ahold of you, it can really louse up your karma.

SPORT: *Is that why—*

STEVE KLUGER

MacKay: That's why.

SPORT: *Was there ever a time last year when you decided you were going to call it quits?*

MacKay: About a dozen. But I wasn't going to give it up without a fight—so I promised myself one more year to pull it together.

SPORT: *What made you decide on a curveball?*

MacKay: I didn't. Buddy did.

SPORT: *Warren Budlong?*

MacKay: Uh-huh. He nearly had to break my arm to get me to try it, but I figured, "What have I got to lose?"

SPORT: *Do you always do what your catcher tells you?*

MacKay: Except for one time back in '74, when he told me to throw Bobby Grich a fastball and I threw a slider instead.

SPORT: *What happened?*

MacKay: Last I heard, the ball had penetrated the ozone layer and was gaining speed.

SPORT: *Just how important is the pitcher/catcher relationship?*

MacKay: Are you kidding? It's *everything.* They say it's like a business partnership, but actually it's more like a marriage.

SPORT: *What's the formula for judging a successful battery?*

MacKay: If the pitcher and catcher were to switch brains and nobody knew the difference.

SPORT: *So it's all chemistry?*

CHANGING PITCHES

MacKay: Chemistry and compassion, I think.

SPORT: *If a Little Leaguer were to come up to you and ask you for advice, what would you tell him?*

MacKay: Not to listen to anything I had to say. I'm not a role model.

SPORT: *You don't think so?*

MacKay: No. Things came a little to easy for me and I got spoiled fast. Also, I'm not the world's most patient human being, I tend to sulk when I don't get my own way, and—face it—I'm not that great a pitcher.

SPORT: *Who do you think is?*

MacKay: Tom Seaver. There's your role model.

SPORT: *Why do you say that?*

MacKay: Because he stayed pure. He never lost sight of who he was and what he wanted, which is why he stayed on top and I'm learning a new pitch.

SPORT: *Now that you've added the curveball to your roster of specialties, do you think it's made you a better pitcher?*

MacKay: No, it hasn't made me better. Just more determined.

SPORT: *About what?*

MacKay: About sticking around until I'm too old to walk to the ballpark. Up until now, I've only been afraid of age in terms of what it might do to my fastball. And since those days are gone and I'm still here . . . I'm working on a knuckleball now.

SPORT: *Any speculations on when you'll be able to use it?*

MacKay: Not until Kirk Gibson retires from baseball.

STEVE KLUGER

SPORT: *Why?*

MacKay: Because facing him is like pitching to a condominium.

SPORT: *Do many mind games go on between pitchers and batters?*

MacKay: Some—but mostly that's an overrated concept. Sure, we try to outguess each other—I'm thinking fastball, he's looking curve—and maybe once in awhile I'll step off the rubber just to rattle him or he'll take a walk to shake *me* up. But the rest of it is a lot of media hype. They'll cut to my face and I'm all creased brows and frowns, then they'll cut to Carlton Fisk, who's ditto, and they'll say we're outpsyching each other. Well actually, he's wondering whether or not he's going to have spaghetti after the game, and I'm trying to remember where I left my Vitamin B.

SPORT: *How long have you been a health food nut?*

MacKay: As long as I've been left-handed.

SPORT: *I don't see the connection.*

MacKay: How sad.

SPORT: *Do you find that being a lefty has its advantages?*

MacKay: Always . . . except at dinner parties. See, it gives us a psychological advantage that very few of us have learned to tap.

SPORT: *How so?*

MacKay: People tend to regard lefties as surreal. We are the human abstract. Ask a southpaw a question and you'll get an answer you think you understand—then three hours later, you'll realize you don't have the slightest idea what he meant. You follow?

SPORT: *I'm not sure.*

CHANGING PITCHES

MacKay: See?

SPORT: *So the key to being left-handed is a degree of confusion?*

MacKay: Speak for yourself. It makes perfect sense to me.

SPORT: *Do you have any predictions for yourself this season?*

MacKay: I'd rather not say.

SPORT: *Superstitious?*

MacKay: A little. I just don't like tampering with a good thing.

SPORT: *How about just one?*

MacKay: I won't be traded to the National League, okay?

SPORT: *Why?*

MacKay: Because if I ever had to face Mike Schmidt or Ron Cey, I'd cash in my chips and move to another table.

SPORT: *Are you a gambler?*

MacKay: I'm still playing, aren't I?

*   *   *

June 16—

Even my subconscious is rebelling. Last night I had a dream that made the dried figs look like a Roman holiday. It went something like this:

I am standing on the mound at Senators Stadium, warming up for the first batter. Jason is crouched behind the plate, ringed by a circle of MVP and batting trophies.

STEVE KLUGER

As he catches a perfectly executed fastball, the announcer speaks into the mike. "Catching for the Senators, number Eight, Jason Cornell. Cornell is currently batting three fifty-six and has done seven ads for Jockey shorts. His teeth are all real."

The crowd stands and gives him a standing ovation that lasts for eight minutes. Like a schmuck, Cornell rises and takes off his cap, bowing first to the box seats, then to the loge, and finally, in a sweeping gesture, to the bleachers. While I fight off an overwhelming desire to throw up, I contemplate beaning him with a curveball, aimed to break right over his mouth. I wind up scotching the idea, however, as by now he has appropriated a microphone and is singing "Strangers in the Night" to the current Miss America, who is sitting over the dugout. I wait through his encore, noting with satisfaction that Frank Sinatra has left the stadium in disgust, and get back down to business when Cornell reluctantly replaces the mike in its stand and returns to his crouch.

"And pitching for the Senators," begins the announcement; I brace myself for my own moment to shine, "number Thirty-Seven, Scotty MacKay." There is a deprecating pause. "He's thirty-six, and once did a commercial for Uniroyal Tires." I remind myself that I've got to do something about my public relations right around the time that the crowd begins booing and throwing things. Jason shrugs sheepishly from his crouch and looks over at me.

"Sorry." He smiles.

I pretend to ignore my environment, remembering that courage in the face of adversity is the stuff that made Rudyard Kipling famous. I am so intent on striking out the first batter, I do not even raise an eyebrow when that turns out to be Honus Wagner, who, considering he's been dead for twenty-seven years, is in remarkably good shape.

Jason trots out to the mound, a look of impatience on his face. "Throw him a curve," he snaps.

I am thoroughly nonplussed. "I was going to pitch a fastball."

Jason turns away. "Suit yourself," he growls. "I don't have time to argue."

"You don't?"

"No. I'm hosting 'The Tonight Show' in two hours. Step on it, MacKay."

He returns to the plate and resumes his crouch. I ignore his suggestions and throw the fastball anyway, achieving the impossible by striking out Wagner on one pitch. The announcer is quick to hand out the kudos.

"Struck him out on a fastball!" chortles the disembodied voice. "What a *brilliant* call by catcher Cornell!" Jason, of course, is up taking his bows again, though, to be entirely honest, he does have enough shame to turn to me, obviously embarrassed, as I dodge some overripe vegetables.

"Sorry," is once more his contribution to injustice.

I am ready to throw in the glove and let Cy Young relieve me when my attention is suddenly drawn to the bullpen gate. My eyes narrow suspiciously, just before I suddenly see a large coach, in the shape of a baseball and driven by four white horses, making its way across the outfield toward home plate. Doug Hoyt is the coachman, and he is swearing at the steeds. "One more inning," he groans. "One more inning."

While I don't know for sure what is happening, I do know that I don't like it—and in short order, I am proven right.

"Ladies and gentlemen," says the announcer, "Mr. and Mrs. Jason Cornell." And down the aisle behind home plate rushes Joanie. She is wearing a white bridal gown with a large number 8 on the back. As the organist begins playing the wedding march from *Lohengrin*, Jason lifts her over the railing and into the coach. The crowd roars. I, for one, am finally shocked.

STEVE KLUGER

"I hate this," I mumble.

The coach moves toward center field, and passes me slowly. Joanie cannot help but notice me and at least has the good taste to look uncomfortable. She leans across the sill and shouts apologetically, "I fell in love with *him* from the front, too."

Jason, of course, turns and smiles. "Sorry." He shrugs. And they disappear beneath the scoreboard.

Son of a bitch.

*   *   *

June 17—

Further Suggestions for Pissing Off Jason Cornell

1. Remind him constantly that you'd rather be pitching to Ted Simmons.

2. The next time you brush off his sign and then give up a homer, blame *him*.

3. Take him aside and tell him management would be stupid to trade him for Bobby Grich. When he asks you what you're talking about, act embarrassed.

4. Ask him if he wouldn't be happier in the National League.

5. The next time you work a full count with the bases loaded, act confused and call time-out. When he asks you what's the matter, tell him you have amnesia.

6. When he shows you his latest baseball card, ask him which figure is his batting average and which one's his weight.

7. Wait until he throws somebody out at second, then, instead of congratulating him, ask him if he's feeling all right.

8. Remind him constantly that you'd rather be pitching to Johnny Gooch. When he points out that Gooch is dead, tell him you'd *still* rather be pitching to Johnny Gooch.

9. Ask him if he's heard the latest statistics that link excessive crouching to impotence. If he hasn't, make some up.

10. If he asks you for ideas on what he ought to do during the All-Star break, suggest he become a free agent.

* * *

June 18—

Apparently, Joanie isn't the only one who's been making a living courtesy of Benton and Bowles lately. Last night I turned on the television during "Sports Final" in time to catch Buddy Budlong holding a box of Wheaties.

> *"With sugar or with honey,*
> *It's a breakfast-time home-runnie."*

I behaved like the responsible adult that I am. I locked myself in the bathroom and howled for three hours. Somebody finally called the police, who showed up at the front door wanting to know if anyone was hurt.

"You know, thanks to you I almost wound up in jail," I told him this afternoon.

"Serves you right for being a smart-ass," he retorted, sidestepping me and taking aim on a foul shot. Buddy's apartment looks like a miniature sporting goods store. Scattered about the living room are a couple of footballs, three

STEVE KLUGER

hockey sticks, half a dozen assorted pucks, and a year's supply of used sweatshirts. "Good vibes," he insists. At that moment, he was keeping his muscles limber with one of several basketballs—dribbling in front of the fireplace, pivoting at the kitchen door, and shooting from behind his VHS. Understand, this is a man who has three pins in his left arm, which also happens to be encased in a cast up to his shoulder. Buddy hasn't heard of the phrase "never say die"—he invented it.

"Time-out," he panted, sinking an improvised lay-up. "You want a Gatorade, Scotty?" Every time I go to his home, it always feels like I'm sitting in a dugout. Come to think of it, it smells like it too.

"Sure," I replied, anticipating just such an opening. "It's an afternoon home-runnie." Buddy froze and turned to me calmly.

"See the cast?" he inquired, pointing to his arm. I nodded. "You want a couple to take home with you? Say it once more." Despite a usually staid poker face, I lost it all over again.

"For Christ's sake, Buddy," I gasped between wails, "couldn't they have let you say something *else*?" Fortunately, my temporarily ex-catcher has a well-developed sense of humor. Things like that don't bother him. When he returned from the kitchen with the quart of Gatorade, he inverted it over my head.

Considering that Buddy lives on raw energy twenty-four hours a day and now finds himself with no ready outlet, I didn't really blame him for being touchy. Baseball is evidently out of the question until next spring, as are all of the rest of your contact sports. For awhile, he briefly considered soccer, seeing as you don't need any arms at all for that—then changed his mind when he realized you do need two hands to get into the jock. This is why he's gravitated toward the media. There is nothing more attractive to the public's eye than an athlete who has injured himself in the line of duty—nor is there ever a dearth of opportunity in that direction. Wheaties had grabbed him just after NBC gave him the color commentator spot for the summer on the Saturday network games. Buddy seemed to be eating it up with a shovel. Seemed to be.

"Know what it's like, Scotty?" he said, handing me a towel. "When you've been a starter for twelve years, and then boom!—you're pulled, it's like tearing down Suitland Parkway at seventy-five, shifting into reverse, and watching the drive shaft shoot straight up through the hood." I wiped the residue of lime out of my ears before I replied.

"Can you live with it until March?" I asked. "That's only eight months, Buddy."

He shrugged. "Are you kidding? This is the first summer vacation I've had since college." He sat down in a canvas director's chair opposite me and leaned in, his eyes flashing brightly.

"I'll tell you something, Scotty. There's a whole 'nother world out there. You don't have to worry about pulled hamstrings or whether you've gotten enough sleep to be able to call nine innings. . . . I always thought it'd all be over when it was over, but . . ." There was a thoughtful pause. "Know what it's like to *breathe* for the first time?"

I didn't say anything at all; I merely stared at him. Partly because it was a tough monologue to top, and partly because we both knew he was lying through his teeth.

"You're thinking I'm full of shit, aren't you?" he guessed finally.

"Uh-huh."

Buddy reached out in front of him and began toying lightly with a lacrosse stick. "You don't know everything, Scotty."

But I do.

Buddy and I had first met about two hours after I'd been called up from Pensacola. He was the rookie everybody was talking about; I was the lefty who had posted a 22–1 record in his first season of minor league ball. We hated each other instantly.

"Listen, phenom," he snapped. ("Phenom" is a compliment when you're talking about someone—an insult when you say it to his face.) "This isn't the 'Glades, it's for real—and nobody's going to hold your hand up here. When I call a fastball, you throw a fastball. And when I say breaker, you do that too. Understand?"

"What if I tell you to go fuck yourself?" I asked.

This lasted for about twenty minutes—which was roughly how long it took for us to realize that, between us, the American League didn't have a prayer. I remember that first game as though we played it this morning. White Sox at Washington. We were fighting for last place, as usual; they were telling anybody with ears that they'd have the pennant sewn up by the first. Three hours later, Buddy and I had clearly proven why Chicago is famous for wind. But it wasn't the shutout that impressed me. It was how I knew in advance every call that Buddy was going to make. There is a technical term for this—sympatico, I think they call it. It explains why two complete strangers will meet and wonder why they feel they've known each other their whole lives. There are no bridges to cross, no obstacles to overcome. That afternoon, Buddy stopped using signs in the third inning. He'd merely look up at me, a question mark on his face, and I would nod. The exchange meant something different each time we used it, yet there never was, and never has been since, a crossed signal.

After the game, we each took our time dressing. Neither of us wanted to be the one to make the first move, so we figured if we were the last to leave, circumstantial aloneness and a lack of prying ears might render it easier. Only it didn't work out that way. We were left sitting side by side in self-conscious silence, not a word spoken, until he finally turned to me and shrugged.

"Surf 'n Turf?"

I nodded. "Giorgio's?"

So did he. He didn't have to ask if I liked lobster, any more than I had to wonder whether or not he liked sangría. It was understood. As a matter of fact, we polished off three carafes between us, and wound up passing out in the front seat of my car. I have since learned that when two people get drunk together the first time they meet, fraternity is considered sworn in blood.

This is why I would go to the mat for Buddy, without hesitating and without questioning whom I was fighting or why, until I had won. When I see him trying to pretend that his unplanned summer off is a welcome holiday, all I want to do is give him *my* right arm. He needs it a lot more than I do anyway.

I don't hate Jason Cornell. I resent everything he's taken away from me—and, even worse, everything he's taken away from Buddy. I know it's not his fault, but somebody's got to take the rap, and at least for the moment, he's won the part. Buddy was born to *hit* home-runnies, not sing about them; and crouching behind the plate, wearing a numeral as foreign to me as a middle-Eastern hieroglyph, Cornell is concrete evidence that—modern technology notwithstanding—one item we have never learned to make foolproof is justice.

"Come on, let's get out of here," said Buddy, catching the towel I tossed to him.

"Where are we going?"

"Tuesday—early workout. I thought maybe I'd go over with you and catch a couple of—I'm trying this right-handed thing that—" He broke off and tried to stifle the self-conscious flush that had begun to surface as a result of my penetrating stare.

"Okay, okay," he shrugged, hands raised. "Maybe I miss it a *little* bit."

STEVE KLUGER

Buddy Budlong is a pretty good liar, but then sometimes he forgets who he's talking to.

* * *

Jason is really beginning to get on my nerves. It isn't so much his smugness, which is considerable, nor is it his reputation, which, as far as I am concerned, is entirely lacking in credibility. What bothers me more than anything else is his unwillingness to fight back. In all honesty, I don't especially mind pitching to him. I've even managed to convince myself that his lack of worth as a human being is something he can't help. But baiting him is like trying to play badminton by yourself. A few examples:

ME: You look like you're playing with two broken arms.

SUGGESTED RESPONSE: You should know.

JASON'S RESPONSE: I'll work on it.

•

ME: You call that a throw-down?

SUGGESTED RESPONSE: You call that a pickoff move?

JASON'S RESPONSE: Maybe I was a little late.

•

ME: Did you ever consider contact lenses?

SUGGESTED RESPONSE: Fuck you.

JASON'S RESPONSE: No.

I'm beginning to suspect that if I hauled off and socked him in the face, he'd apologize for bruising my knuckles. Maybe my disposition is irresistible.

* * *

June 21—

FAMOUS RIGHT-HANDED PEOPLE

John F. Kennedy	Jesus Christ
Albert Einstein	Lucille Ball
Ty Cobb	William Shakespeare
Eleanor Roosevelt	Elizabeth Taylor
John Glenn	Orson Welles
Ethel Merman	François Truffaut
Charles Dickens	George Washington
Jackson Browne	Barbra Streisand
Anne Bancroft	Richard Burton
Lou Gehrig	Henry Fonda
Winston Churchill	Louis Pasteur
Bruce Springsteen	Ludwig van Beethoven

FAMOUS LEFT-HANDED PEOPLE

Jack the Ripper
Gerald Ford
Marie Dionne (one of the
Canadian quintuplets)

* * *

June 22—

I stopped by the clubhouse this afternoon to pick up my jacket, and on my way up to the parking lot level, the elevator stopped at the second floor. Know who got on? That guy with the blue eyes and the mask. Apparently, he'd just had an interview with *Cosmopolitan*.

"With or without pants?" I inquired. He didn't answer—and before I had a chance to level any more curare-laced darts in his direction, the car stopped between floors. With no hesitation, I will freely admit that I panicked. Not about dying, but about having to do it with Jason Cornell. Of course, considering the depth of our relationship, we had plenty to discuss while we were waiting to be rescued.

"Nice elevator." I nodded. Jason merely glared. End of conversation.

We must have stood in dead silence for close to twenty minutes until we felt the welcome jerk that informed us in advance that we were about to rejoin the human race as free men. Still, as the doors slid open, I found it impossible to keep my mouth shut any longer.

"Where's your blow dryer?" I asked.

Jason froze as he was stepping out, then turned to me very slowly.

"Up your ass," he snapped.

Now he's catching on.

* * *

June 23—

Joanie says my disposition is *not* irresistible.

* * *

June 24—

Dear Mr. MacKay,

The only reason my husband and I were Senators fans was because he had been transferred to Chevy Chase, and there was nobody else to root for. Well, we have just relo-

cated to Boston, where we presently support the Red Sox. You can start losing now.

A former fan,
Harriet Pure

Dear Mr. MacKay,
    A couple of years ago, you autographed a baseball for me, but when you started losing all those games, I got mad and threw it at you during a doubleheader with Texas. Can I have it back?

Sincerely,
Ritchie Blair

Dear Scotty,
    Every time I see you starting to sweat, I am filled with an uncontrollable urge to rip the clothes off of your body and let you have a taste of savage femininity. All you have to do is say the word, and I will be there in the flesh. All of it. You turn me on, Scotty—and I won't stop until I've made you mine.

Really had you going there, huh?

The Bullpen

Dear Mr. MacKay,
    I have a new invention I've been working on. It's a pitching machine for kids that adults can use too, which can be reset to four different types of pitches. Of course, it still needs a little work. The sliders come out as grounders and the fastballs go straight up, but that's why pencils have erasers.
    It should be ready to market in another year, and I

would like you to endorse this product. *If you are interested, please send me a check for $20,000. I'm sure you could write it off to taxes, couldn't you?*

> *Best wishes,*
> *Chuck Tinker*

Dear Mr. MacKay,
   I am seven years old and I met you at a game and you said if I wanted to be a pitcher just work at it. So at school when they told us to write about the greatest American that ever lived I wrote mine about you. Except Mrs. Thompson my teacher said that didn't count because of Lincoln and all and besides I was too young to know what I wanted to be yet. Would you come to my school in the fall and hit her?

> *Love,*
> *Brucie Ercole*

Dear Mr. MacKay,
   By golly, I'm getting sick of reading all this baloney about free agents and money. Fooey! When I saw Babe Ruth pitch at Oriole Park in 1913, he considered himself lucky to have a place to stay.
   Why don't you boys get jobs?

> *Samuel Glasser*

*   *   *

June 25—

   I think we're breaking the ice a lot faster than we were. Tonight we were facing the Brewers, and I actually paid attention to three of Jason's signs. Oh, I made him sweat just the same, but it's the first game we've won together, and I began to suspect there's something here worth looking into. So I called time out in the middle of a 3-2 count with the bases loaded, and signaled him to come out to the mound. He looked scared to death, figuring I was probably running out of steam.

"You'd better calm down," he snapped, reaching me. "I almost lost that last pitch."

"Maybe if you grew a couple of more inches," I suggested.

Jason squared off and removed his mask. "Can I ask you something?"

"What?"

"I may be wrong," he said solicitously, "but you don't like me very much, do you?"

I placed a fraternal hand on his shoulder. "You're not wrong."

"Gee, that's too bad," he sighed. "Because I've always looked up to you. I remember how happy I was when you won Rookie of the Year."

Well, this rocked the hell out of me. There's nothing worse than having somebody turn sincere on you in the middle of a put-down.

"Oh, yeah?" I asked, a little uncertainly.

"Yeah." He smiled. "I was twelve. Throw him the curve, MacKay." With that, he turned around and went back to the plate.

Yeah. This is *fun*.

* * *

June 26—

It's about this time of year that athletes across the country begin collecting lucky charms and avoiding cracks in the sidewalk. It's a ridiculous practice, but it's also insurance,

STEVE KLUGER

because just around now, the first votes are being counted for the "Sportsman of the Year"—an annual choice made by the Sportswriters of America. According to the published procedures, performance counts for only a small percentage of the vote. Sportsmanship, citizenship, community involvement, and fan appreciation make up the rest. This is why, as far as I am concerned, the elements clearly point to Wayne Gretzky or Joe Montana. Nobody else comes close.

"I don't know," says Joanie skeptically. "I think there's going to be an upset."

"By whom?" I inquire, suspecting what she's getting at.

"By a left-handed pitcher who did what everybody said was impossible."

"I love you," I tell her.

"Not you," she replies. "Tommy John."

I go for a long walk.

* * *

June 27—

Okay, so maybe I was wrong—maybe there's more to the guy than just underwear ads. I'm not too proud to admit that I made a mistake. That takes character. That takes nerve. That takes reading a piece on him in *Sports Illustrated* where he tells the whole world that you're one of the five best pitchers that ever toed a rubber.

"Did you see this?" said Joanie, looking up from a lotus position.

"Sshhh!" I told her, similarly occupied. "You're not supposed to talk." She handed me the copy of *SI*.

"I think you'll find this a lot more enlightening than your mantis."

"Mantra."

I took the magazine and stared down at the page. The first thing I saw was Jason's teeth.

"Are you trying to be funny?" I demanded.

"Read on, Lefty," she said, standing up. "I've got to teach myself how to walk again."

She left the room while I focused on the newsprint. At first I wondered whether or not J.J. was merely trying to torment me. The interviewer had spent a good six paragraphs telling Cornell what a gifted catcher he was. Jason, in turn, had spent another six agreeing with him. I was all ready to trash the whole thing entirely, when my eye was drawn to my own name at the bottom of a page.

"Are you sorry you were traded to a last-place team?" he was asked.

"Standings are only temporary," was Jason's reply. (Tactful little pecker, I thought. Translated, that means "yes.") "Besides," he added, "I never caught a legend before." I could feel myself beginning to shrink.

A what?

"See, the thing is," he went on, "a catcher's only as good as the guy who's making the pitches. Okay, maybe Scotty MacKay ran into some bad luck, but he's one of the only guys around who isn't afraid to take chances. He's sort of a Crusader Rabbit with a curveball."

Joanie entered the room, holding a half-eaten bag of apricots, and I didn't have the nerve to look her in the eye.

"Did you get to the rabbit part yet?" she asked. I mumbled something noncommittal. "That's what I thought." She nodded. "Yeah, Scotty, he's a real creep all right." Joanie extended the bag in my general direction. "Crow, anyone?"

I tried not to let it affect my game that afternoon, but every time I stared down the pipe at Jason, I had to turn away. It was as though his eyes were twin blue mirrors— and all I saw in them was my own conceit, my own ego, and my own bruised pride. What I also saw was the friendship and the respect I had rejected out of hand without even first acknowledging. Yet, in his expression, there appeared to be no rebuke; only a reluctant acceptance. It was at that moment I realized that in my quest for a second chance, in my bid for a revitalized future, there was one award I had just won hands down. Without a doubt, I was unquestionably the American League's Shit-Heel of the Week.

Moments after we had fanned Brian Downing, and Fred Lynn had moved to the plate, I called time. Jason raised his mask and trotted out to the mound, an impassive look on his face.

"Tired?" he asked brusquely.

"No."

"Then what's the problem?"

I paused and took my first adult breath since Buddy had disappeared behind the box seat railing in Minnesota. "Look, Jase," I began. Another first. It had always been "Cornell" or "asshole." "I wouldn't blame you if you said no, but do you think we could start over? I mean you and me."

All things being equal, Jason would have been thoroughly entitled to (a) break my arms, or (b) tell me exactly where and in what direction I could stick my truce. Instead, all he did was toss it around for a minute. "Yeah," he finally replied. "I think it's about time." I did notice, however, that when he said it, he was doing his best not to show me a relieved smile.

It was that simple.

"Okay, do we have that settled?" he asked.

I nodded.

"Great. Then we got work to do. Throw him the fastball, Scotty."

I pointed to the plate. "Look, Cornell," I snapped, ready to tear up the surrender, "that's Fred Lynn."

"So?" he demanded.

"Don't you get it? Fastballs. He eats them."

Jason extended his mask, irritated. "*You* want to catch?"

Under the circumstances, I deferred. Having settled our first argument since we had become friends a minute and a half earlier, my catcher started back toward home plate. A few feet away from the mound, he stopped, turned, and leveled me with a thoughtful stare.

"Later," he finally said, nodding.

We fanned Lynn on the fastball.

"Later" was after the game at Mr. Natural's. That Jason was the only other person I knew who patronized that particular establishment of his own free will and not under my customary duress, was one of the many factors I had been deliberately overlooking in an effort to render him entirely useless. Even Buddy, as close as we were, had steadfastly refused to accompany me on my organic forays, insisting emphatically that God hadn't meant for human beings to eat grass.

"How come you changed your mind?" asked Jase, looking up from a plate of seaweed.

"About what?"

"About me."

"What do you think?" I frowned. "I can read, you know."

Jason grinned a little self-consciously. "Yeah, I thought that'd get to you. Anyway, I hoped it would."

"You mean you did it on purpose?"

"Well, I had to get through to you *some* way," he insisted. "And it was a lot cheaper than Western Union, see?"

While the afternoon began to shrink around us, we talked about—what didn't we talk about? Where we'd been, where we thought we were going, why the American League was decaying, how we'd both contributed to the No Nukes demonstration at Diablo Canyon, and why Billy Joel was the only musician to come along in a decade who was likely to make people forget Paul Simon. In almost no time, it seemed as if we had lived parallel pasts, if indeed we hadn't shared the same one. Our voices took on a staccato-like tattoo as we compared notes, two people who were no longer shackled to the verbose conversation of strangers.

"Sex," he said. "First time."

"Seventeen," I replied.

Jason smiled. "I've got you there. Sixteen. Back seat of a Mustang."

"Volkswagen."

"*Volkswagen?*"

Or:

"First real game."

"Little League. I was nine."

"So was I. Score?"

"Seven-up. We got called in the eighth."

"Rain?"

"Dinner."

"Ours was four–three, us."

"Any homers?"

"Porky Tannenbaum. But I went two for four."

This might have gone on indefinitely, but for the intervention of restaurant management. Normally, they were pretty easygoing about letting me stick around as long as I wanted, but in this instance, they had legitimate cause for concern. Jason and I had become so wrapped up in whatever earth-shattering issue we were momentarily discussing—our first beer, I think (mine was a Natty Bo, his was a Black Label)—that we were oblivious to everything except ourselves and a bowl of sprouts on the table. At least that's what we assumed they were. It turned out we were eating the centerpiece.

"I thought it was dessert," he mumbled, after we had been shown the sidewalk.

We headed east toward the Tidal Basin, every step a

continuing lesson in self-discovery. We both, for instance, disdained a Mercedes parked by the curb, confessing simultaneously that we each owned a Porsche.

"Mine's a Nine Twenty-Four," I said.

"Mine's a Nine Twenty-Eight."

"Mine's got velour interiors."

"Mine has rawhide," he replied.

"I've got two speakers."

"I have four."

I stared at him ominously. "You ever been beaned by your own pitcher?"

We also found that we both shared identical passions for football and *Star Wars*, although to be entirely honest, he had seen the latter a mere eight times, while I had long ago stopped counting at an even dozen. Having finally attained the upper hand, I should have known when to quit—while I was ahead; instead, I added, "Know what else? I once had fifty-yard line for the Super Bowl."

Jason shrugged. "Friend of mine's a quarterback for the New York Giants." So much for staying on top. Jason chuckled. "How about if we call it a draw, okay?"

I thought about it for a minute, then realized I had already used up my entire arsenal of impressive achievements—for nil, I might add—so I had no choice but to accept the armistice. After a moment, I nodded.

"Draw."

By the time we reached the Tidal Basin, dusk had already bathed the city in an orange-pink glow. The lights of metropolitan Washington were twinkling beyond the stark white marble of the Jefferson Memorial, making me wonder for the thousandth time why anybody would want to live anywhere else. Civic pride, I think, is what they call it.

We sat on the grass by the water, where, from our vantage point, we might as well have been staring at a Michelin

STEVE KLUGER

guide. The Capitol Building rose up majestically to the east, falling under the shadows of a winking Washington Monument, while Abraham Lincoln guarded the western boundary, a silent watchman protecting the banks of the Potomac River—and us. Though our eyes met several times, neither Jason nor I spoke for many minutes, each of us wrapped in a cocoon of thought—perhaps a little weary, certainly a little wary. Vulnerability does that. For myself, I've always had an irritating habit of doubting new-found gold; when I first discovered my fastball, I immediately began wondering if it might disappear the same way it had surfaced. When I first realized I was in love with Joanie, I promptly started worrying that she might not be similarly inclined. Sitting next to Jason, listening to his silence, I realized with foreboding that friendship carries the same hazards. Yet, as quickly as the fears arose is as quickly as they were doused.

"If I tell you something, will you promise not to laugh?" he asked quietly.

"I won't laugh."

He pointed to the Jefferson Memorial. "See the dome?"

"What about it?"

"If you squashed it down to make it rounder, and then painted red stitching on the top . . ."

Home free.

* * *

June 28—

Jason says he lied. He was really fourteen.

* * *

Joanie thinks I ought to cultivate a new image.

"You're too clean," she insists.

We discuss it at length, as we do every eight weeks, and try to come up with an optimum way of making me a little raunchier. It is J.J. who ultimately suggests chewing tobacco.

"It tastes terrible," I advise her mildly.

"Yeah, but it looks hot."

I give in, as I always do, knowing in advance that I'm wasting my time. These things never work. When I return with a package of Red Thunder, we spend three hours positioning my jaws so that my face is crammed and my expression fierce.

"You need a little more," she says, dipping into the pouch. By now my mouth is too full to speak—not that I really have anything to say. When Joanie finally gets the look she wants, she steps back, satisfied, to admire her handiwork.

"That's it, Lefty," she nods. "*Now* you look like a pitcher." There is one problem. My cheeks are now so puffed out, I can no longer see the batter. J.J., of course, is appropriately disappointed. I am both relieved and ashamed.

"You want to try something else?" I ask, hoping she says no.

"Yeah," she mumbles, flipping through a newspaper. "Why don't we go see *Blade Runner*?"

Sometimes I'm very grateful for the length of her attention span.

* * *

Mound Conference

(At California, bottom of the fifth. Bases are loaded, Brian Downing is at the plate.)

JASON *(lifting up his mask)*:   If I tell you something, will you promise not to get paranoid?

SCOTTY: What is it?

JASON: We're in a shitload of trouble, Scotty.

SCOTTY *(offhand)*:   It's just your imagination, Jase. The curveball is breaking just where I want it to.

JASON *(doubtfully)*:   In Long Beach?

SCOTTY *(after a pause)*:   Okay, so maybe there's a little control problem.

JASON: A *little*? *(Pausing as he kicks the ground.)* You know, that's why I never wanted to pitch. My form was okay, but somehow the ball never went where it was supposed to. *(Hesitating.)* Except when I was pitching fruit.

SCOTTY *(taken aback)*:   Pitching what?

JASON: Fruit. You know—like limes.

SCOTTY *(incredulous)*:   You pitched *limes*?

JASON *(hastily)*:   No, no. That was just a for instance.

SCOTTY *(relieved)*:   That's better. For a minute you had me worried.

JASON: I pitched apples.

SCOTTY *(patiently)*:   Why, Jase?

JASON: Well hell, Scotty. They always did what I wanted

them to. *(Pause.)* You should have seen my slider. *(Remembering.)* Pow, y'know?

SCOTTY: Applesauce?

JASON: For real. You know, Scotty, if they only made baseballs with stems, you wouldn't be facing Downing now. *I* would.

SCOTTY *(solicitously)*: Speaking of Downing—

JASON *(cutting in)*: Change-up.

SCOTTY: Forget it. I was going to toss him a curve.

JASON: But Scotty—

SCOTTY: I said forget it, Jase. Stick to fruit, okay? I know what I'm doing.

JASON *(shrugging)*: You're the boss.

(Jason returns to the plate. MacKay sends Downing a curve ball that promptly clears the center field wall for a grand slam. As the scoreboard changes to reflect the four additional Angel runs, Jason trots back to the mound.)

SCOTTY *(amazed)*: What did I do wrong?

JASON *(politely)*: Maybe you ought to try pitching pears.

* * *

July 1—

Jason and I have been getting into some serious disagreements lately over literature. He says he wants to sound more intelligent when he's being interviewed, and asked me if he could borrow some of my books, seeing as most of the material *he* reads comes in plain brown wrappers. I lent him a couple of classics, and that was where the problem started.

"I don't get it," he said, pointing to page one. " 'Call me Ishmael.' Is that like 'asshole,' Scotty?"

"Ishmael was his name," I sighed.

Jason frowned. "Why?"

This led to a discussion of Herman Melville, the likes of which I have never encountered before. We took the story apart, piece by piece, then put it back together Jason-style. By the time we were through, the novel began, "Call me Arthur," and promptly went downhill from there. The *Pequod* was a nuclear submarine, Moby Dick was now a great white shark, and Captain Ahab was portrayed by Robert Shaw.

"See?" He smiled. "If you look under the surface, Scotty, you'll find a lot you never thought was there before."

I'd be fascinated to see what he could do with John Steinbeck.

* * *

July 2—

I just read in *The Sporting News* that Winky Gillis, my old minor league manager, was brought up from Florida and named assistant pitching coach with the Philadelphia Phillies. While I wish him the best of luck, I find myself taking great exception to his comments on the promotion.

"I feel like I've just been released from prison," he said. Uh-huh, that's what they all say.

Whenever a ballplayer tells you that playing in the minors was the worst experience of his life, don't believe him. And if, in these pages, I have made similar statements, don't believe me either. Sure, we say we hated it, and maybe we even mean it—but that's only because, as every busher knows, it's the place where each kid who wears a glove must ultimately face that sink-or-swim decision. Robert Frost called it "The Road Not Taken." In baser terms, it's more like, "Am I for real or am I full of shit?" Those who opt for the latter usually become chemical engineers. As for the rest, they have reached the point of no return. Gone is the sanctity of the Little League trophy; dimmed is the glory of staking title to the Pony League's Most Valuable Player. Up ahead and around that bend lies the real thing—and after tiptoeing through college, afraid of upsetting your equilibrium, you have been claimed by the First Round Draft—formerly an ally, now a threat.

There are no promises. You stand alone, armed only with a supply of Neat's Foot Oil and a piece of rawhide that has been appended to your hand since you were sixteen, and you realize there is a good chance you have come to Golgotha. Your worst enemy, indifference, might permanently bury your adolescence in a crypt of "might have beens." On the other hand, acceptance is sure to unlock every door. To what? Frustration, anguish, fear, doubt, envy, grief, and pain.

Welcome to the minor leagues.

To some of us, the minors were a beginning. To others, they were an end. It didn't matter at first what our stats were. There were those who were brilliant, those who were adequate, and those who really should have studied law. Yet, until success taught us how to be smug, there were no class distinctions. We were all in this thing together, and unless you were a past master at the art of lone self-survival, you learned pretty quickly what teamwork was all about, because all you had was each other.

"You know something? I'll tell you something." This was Tommy Higgins, my roommate. "If we hadn't of wound up here—and here is definitely the asshole of the world—we could of wound up in Duluth. And if you've ever been to Duluth, you'll know I'm right. Am I right?"

Tommy was, at various times, my mentor, my teacher, and my best friend. He was also a minor league veteran, having arrived in Pensacola six months before I did. In baseball, that's a lifetime. I don't know why we gravitated toward one another—maybe because we were polar opposites. I'd gone to college, Tommy had spent four years in the sandlots. If absolutely necessary, I could discuss Proust and make it sound like I knew what I was talking about. Tommy, on the other hand, eschewed intelligence, regarding it as a definite threat to organized sport.

"Know what *I* say, Dobie?" he'd insist. "Brains are for people who know what to do with them. Not us." "Dobie" was what he called me—my first and last nickname—due mostly to the fact that, with my crewcut, I bore a certain resemblance to a certain television character.

"And you know what else?" he added. "All the diplomas in the world aren't going to buy you street smarts. You know why? Because when you're up at the plate with a three–two count, you're on your own. And that's when you use this." He tapped his heart. "Because if you use this"— his head—"you know what you're going to get? Bad wood."

So now you've made it to the minor leagues. You can forget about that closet full of varsity letters that was once your only concrete assurance that you were going to have a future. You can forget about the college plaudits you once employed to belie adult skepticism. You can even smirk at the yearbook that listed you as "least likely to succeed" just above the jock who used to sit across the aisle from you in Physiology who swore he was going to pitch for the Yankees but who's now working for his father. *You're* making your bones in Florida, fulfilling an adolescent's fantasy by spending so much time in a baseball uniform it's begun to attach itself to your skin—the same skin under which the sport itself crept years ago. You discover a peculiar kind of energy in fatigue every time that fastball burns a hole over the outside corner. And when you wake up to find you've won your first three starts, you also find that yesterday's pain has become today's panacea. So you've braved the nor'wester and it's clear sailing ahead, right? Wrong.

"Dobie, I hate to bug your ointment," said Tommy, "but there is a distinct chance your bushness is showing." "Bushness" was Tommy's word for inexperience, and though we often disagreed on issues of a horsehide variety, it didn't take him long to prove his point here. In fact, it became evident immediately that making it on the Class-A level had very little to do with baseball.

Tommy and I lived with the rest of the team in a run-down motel that had been pledged to the wrecking ball shortly before the Senators first purchased the Pensacola franchise. It had been the opinion of the Board of Health that the accommodations weren't fit for farm animals, let alone human beings, but they had capitulated when they learned the facilities would be housing a minor league roster.

"I'm tellin' ya, Dobe," groaned Tommy, surveying the interior of our room, "we're an engendered species." Well, if we hadn't been, we sure as hell were by the end of the season.

Having just come from the University of Maryland, I was used to a certain kind of inconvenience that is supposed to come part and parcel with dormitory-style living. What I didn't know—yet—was that, compared to Florida, Prince Georges Hall might well have been Versailles. We had two cots, regulation Army variety, whose functions—allegedly—were to allow for sleeping, poker, letter-writing, and some of the more earthy repasts for which one might require a mattress and springs. Normally, each of us would have appropriated one of the cots at the outset, except that our room possessed a personality of its own that precluded sole proprietorships. It seemed that the left side of our ceiling—or what remained of it—housed the plumbing, and if one of the other guys on our corridor noticed that they had run out of hot water, that was usually because it was on our floor. As a consequence, it became necessary to play musical beds on a daily basis, so that one of us wouldn't prematurely end his career with double pneumonia. "Whose turn is it to sleep wet?" quickly became a routine question.

Finances were always a problem. The days of the megabuck contracts and inflatable signing bonuses were still fifteen years off, and unless you were Tony Conigliaro, you were lucky to get transportation. My parents weren't rich, but they weren't poor either, so I'd never had to worry about money before. In Florida, I was definitely out of my element. Tommy wasn't. He'd never owned a thing in his life that he hadn't fought for. When he was twelve, he'd sold newspapers to pay for his first glove. In junior high, he'd worked nights in a bicycle repair shop to cover his first pair of regulation cleats. When he graduated to automobiles, he learned how to rebuild transmissions so he could bankroll a six-week training program at Lake Placid. And all this was done while he put in eight hours a day on the diamond—running, fielding, drilling, and telling himself through four layers of grease that he was the best shortstop that had ever squeezed a runner home from third.

So it wasn't surprising that I let Tommy do the rationing for both of us, seeing as he was an old pro at economy. Quite frankly, I doubted that he would be able to make much with what they gave us for meal money, but Tommy wasn't fazed.

"The thing is, Dobe," he'd say, "we're looking at this all wrong. Hunger is something without which we might starve. Understand?" I understood. We ate a lot of potato chips that year.

We split our responsibilities down the middle, but we lived by the same set of rules. Clean uniforms were obviously a necessity; a decent blanket was not. If we were thirsty, it was a Yoo-Hoo or a Bud. Ripple was out of our league. We even had rules for the potato chips. When Tommy bought them, they were usually the barbecued variety. Whenever I did the shopping, they were invariably organic. I was already learning how to be a pain in the ass.

Reading material? Expendable—except for *Sports Illustrated* and *The Sporting News*. And with those, you made sure the rest of the team had seen them before you threw them away. This was how we survived. None of us owned much, but what we had, we pooled. As a matter of fact, by season's end, we were all so used to sharing, nobody could remember what belonged to whom anymore. I remember a game in Tampa when we were playing a Cincinnati club, and Pete Mahoney was at the plate with one of Tommy's bats. It was an old Louisville model that he'd had since he was seventeen, and one of the only possessions he cared about. He used to talk to it in the on-deck circle, asking if it had a couple of hits in it. Anyway, that afternoon, Pete swung on an 0–1 fastball and turned the old wooden slugger into thirty-three ounces of splinters. Tommy sat bolt upright on the bench, his face a mask of pain.

"My bat!" he cried. "He broke my bat!" Then, as if he thought he'd abrogated our all-for-one-motto, he added hastily, "Well, it was *his* bat"—pause—"but it was *mine*."

In the minor leagues, there's really no such thing as recreation. It isn't that there's no inclination, there's just no time. What's more, considering where most of the teams were located, there wasn't anything to do even if we'd *had* the time. In Pensacola, for instance, there were no movies and no women—anything female was either a wife or a daughter. So all we had left was poker. None of us was particularly good at it, but it didn't make much difference; we didn't play by Vegas rules anyway.

"I'll raise you," said Pete Mahoney, throwing in a chip.

"Oh, yeah?" demanded Eddie Young. "With what?"

"The Red Sox." Pete was always trying to unload the Red Sox. "Tell you what," he added. "I'll even throw in the Wellsville franchise."

Tommy frowned. "You already bet that," he said.

By the end of a game, Tommy usually owned most of the American League, Pete had laid claim to the National, and Eddie had sewn up the minors. As I said earlier, I've never been very good at poker. My only chance came with a full house, and Mahoney implying that he had a royal flush. I thought he was bluffing, so I called him. That's how I lost the Cleveland Indians.

One thing we never had to learn was when to call it a night. Curfew is one of those things you can afford to break after you've played in your first World Series. Not only that, Winky Gillis was a strict disciplinarian. He had received his training in the Instructional League after he'd apprenticed with the gestapo. Looking back, I've often felt that Winky was the only person in my life I've ever hated. He knew nothing about baseball and even less about human nature. If we made mistakes, we were torn apart in front of the rest of the club. If someone belted a three-run homer, he was greeted with silence. Winky cared only about prestige, about money, and about the day when he could dump us and "work with *real* players." Yet, the older I get and the more I see of the new crop coming in, the more I wonder whether I didn't underestimate Winky Gillis. At the time, we were young, we were inexperienced, and we didn't know what we were doing. And perhaps the fastest way to get a group of people to work together is to give them a common enemy. Did he do it on purpose? Beats me. But we were in first place for the entire season.

Lights out was probably the best part of a given day. To

understand why, you have to take a close look at the peculiar makeup of what sociologists broadly refer to as athletes. Although it was never discussed, it was unspoken knowledge that every one of us saw his name on a first-class ticket to Cooperstown. This was not confidence—it was fear and it was self-defense. Maybe deep down a lot of us knew we'd never make it to Washington, let alone the Hall of Fame, but we had to believe we would. This obsession is not as perplexing as it might seem, because if you've ever felt the electricity that accompanies slipping on a jersey, if you've ever paid special attention to the collection of smells that make up a clubhouse, and if you've ever seen your own name in a box score, you'll know why we would have killed before we'd have given up any of it. Still, we never talked about the future, because we didn't want the other guys to know we weren't cool. When Eddie Young hit the season's first grand slam, you knew instantly by the look on his face as he was circling the bases that he was calculating how many copies of the next day's papers he was going to buy, and how much he was going to have to spend on postage in mailing them back home. But when he returned to the dugout, all he said was, "Check it out."

There is only one person you have to level with, and that only because there is just no way you can hide anything from a roommate. So, after lights out, Tommy and I would drop the daytime facades and map out our plans.

"Dobie," he'd say, "here's what we'll do. We'll make a pact [that's P-A-C-T, it means 'deal']. If *you* make it first, you'll put in a word for me, and if *I* make it first, I'll make them bring you up too."

"What if we both make it?" I'd ask, staring at a darkened ceiling. I could hear his face splitting into a wide smile.

"Then there's no problem. All we'll have to worry about is how to spend the money."

This would continue until one of us would start nodding off. Tommy decided on a two-toned Rolls, even after I pointed out that they got lousy mileage. Those being my pre-Porsche days, I settled on an MG (despite the fact that, when I finally could afford a car, I rather meekly went for a Chevy). One thing we were both in agreement about was the matter of personal records. We decided that we'd win as many titles as we wanted, but we'd stop short of dethroning the legends.

"I mean, it's not fair," said Tommy. "Whoever heard of *us?*"

So he made up his mind that he would hit as many home runs as he wanted, but he'd never best Ruth; I vowed that I'd pitch exactly three no-hitters, stopping short of encroaching on Koufax territory.

"One more thing," he said, beginning to doze. "I think we ought to do something for the kids."

"Whose?" I asked.

"Everybody's." There was a pause. "You remember when you were nine and Maris would come to the plate and you'd scream 'hit it out' and he would and you thought you had done it *for* him?"

I nodded in the darkness.

"Well, the thing is," he said slowly, "maybe we did." He sat up and turned to me. "So how about if we buy a bunch of seats and give them to the kids and—" He cut himself off, obviously embarrassed, as the moonlight filtered in through the window. After a moment, he spoke quietly.

"Don't tell anybody I said that, Dobe. Okay?"

I loved Tommy Higgins.

* * *

Jason says he read in the *Bulletin* that Gary Carter is the frontrunner for "Sportsman of the Year." I disagree, only because Jase is never entirely happy unless I do.

"No way," I advise him. "If it's going to be a catcher, there are a lot of other choices."

"Such as?" he counters hopefully.

"Carlton Fisk, Bruce Benedict, Jody Davis, Rick Dempsey, Brian Downing . . ."

He leaves without a word and returns to the plate.

". . . Rick Cerone, Darrell Porter, Ted Simmons, Steve Yeager, Bo Diaz. . ."

Within three minutes he has signaled for two curveballs, both of which he knows are going out of the park—and they do.

Jason hates to be provoked.

* * *

July 6—

❦he Washington Bulletin

At Washington

Boston	ab	r	h	bi	Washington	ab	r	h	bi
Remy, 2b	4	1	3	0	Tobin, 3b	3	0	1	0
Boggs, 3b	4	0	2	1	Weinberg, lf	4	1	2	0
Rice, dh	3	0	0	0	Wright, ss	4	0	2	0
Armas, cf	3	0	1	0	Cornell, c	4	1	1	2
Evans, rf	1	0	0	0	Delanoy, dh	3	1	1	1
Gedman, c	4	0	0	0	Jackson, cf	1	0	0	0
Hoffman, ss	4	0	1	0	Fowler, 2b	3	0	0	0
Stapleton, 1b	4	0	0	0	Petry, rf	3	0	1	0
Miller, lf	3	0	0	0	Hatten, 1b	3	0	0	0
Nichols, lf	3	0	1	0					

Totals	33 1 8 1			28 3 8 3

BOSTON	100	000	000	1
WASHINGTON	012	000	00x	3

BOSTON

	IP	H	R	ER	BB	SO
D. Mitchell (L, 9-6)	8	8	3	3	3	3

WASHINGTON

	IP	H	R	ER	BB	SO
MacKay (W, 11-3)	7⅓	8	1	0	1	2
Collins (S, 8)	1⅔	0	0	0	0	3

E—Jackson DP—Boston, 2, Washington, 4 LOB—Boston, 4, Washington, 7 HR—Delanoy (12), Cornell (18) SB—Tobin, Weinberg Balk—D. Mitchell Time—2:33 Attendance—52,662

* * *

July 7—

DO NOT REMOVE

From Doug Hoyt:

𝕿𝖍𝖊 𝖂𝖆𝖘𝖍𝖎𝖓𝖌𝖙𝖔𝖓 𝕭𝖚𝖑𝖑𝖊𝖙𝖎𝖓

THE STANDINGS

American League East

	W	L	Pct.	GB
Baltimore	49	35	.583	—
New York	47	35	.573	1

CHANGING PITCHES

Detroit	43	38	.531	4½
Washington	41	41	.500	7
Milwaukee	40	41	.494	7½
Boston	39	41	.488	8
Cleveland	37	46	.446	11½
Toronto	36	47	.434	12½

●

AMERICAN LEAGUE ALL-STAR TEAM

July 5—New York, N.Y.—The American League offices today announced the roster for next week's All-Star Game at Veteran's Stadium in Philadelphia.

Murray, Balt.—1B
Grich, Cal.—2B
Yount, Mil.—SS
Brett, K.C.—3B
Cornell, Wash.—C
Henderson, Oak.—OF
Bonnell, Tor.—OF
Gibson, Det.—OF

Barker, Cle.—P
Davis, Balt.—P
Gossage, N.Y.—P
MacKay, Wash.—P
Burns, Chi.—P
Quisenberry, K.C.—P

Reserves
Carew, Cal.
Hatcher, Minn.
Rice, Bos.
Owen, Sea.

STEVE KLUGER

Bell, Tex.
Fisk, Chi.
Dauer, Balt.
Cooper, Mil.
Armas, Bos.
Harrah, Cle.
Cerone, N.Y.
Dent, Tex.

*   *   *

July 8—

Mound Conference

(Versus Baltimore, fifth inning. Two men on, none out, Kenny Singleton at bat.)

JASON *(removing his mask and scratching his head)*: Scotty, I hate to sound like a wet blanket, but what the fuck do you think you're doing?

SCOTTY *(feigning bland innocence)*:   Just bad luck, Jase. The curveball's got some pretty good stuff on it.

JASON: It sucks.

SCOTTY *(defensively)*:   Oh yeah? It struck out Thompson, didn't it?

JASON: My cat could strike out Thompson. It sucks.

SCOTTY *(irritated)*:   Watch your mouth, Cornell. I've broken every pitching record in the book.

JASON (calmly):   It *still* sucks. *(Scotty stares at the ground thoughtfully.)* What's the matter?

SCOTTY *(after a beat)*: You're right. It sucks rocks.

JASON: No, it doesn't. It sucks dog legs.

SCOTTY: Jason, that's disgusting.

JASON: So is a two-run fifth.

SCOTTY: Are you kidding? Lots of guys throw two-run fifths. Even sixths, sometimes.

JASON: Yeah, but who are they? *You've* broken every pitching record in the book.

(He puts on his mask and starts to leave.)

SCOTTY: So what should I throw him?

JASON *(turning around)*: Pitch him a curve.

SCOTTY *(incredulous)*: Are you crazy? I thought you said it sucked dog legs.

JASON: I don't have a dog. Besides, it's got some pretty good stuff on it.

SCOTTY *(solicitously)*: Jason, don't you ever miss Cleveland?

(Cornell goes back to the plate. MacKay pitches nothing but curves and promptly strikes out Singleton and Ripken.)

* * *

July 9—

An advance copy of Buddy's issue of *Playgirl* came in the mail at ten this morning. They even gave him the cover—broken arm and all—and I've been in a rotten mood since eleven.

"What's so special about a cast?" I grumbled.

"Is he wearing a cast?" asked Joanie, slightly dazed. She turned the page over to expose the centerfold—as if Buddy hadn't already taken care of that particular infinitive. J.J.'s eyes widened automatically.

"Buddy?" she said to herself in a state of mild awe, as a slow smile began creeping over her face. "*Buddy?*"

I snatched the magazine away from her immediately. "That's enough," I snapped.

"Aw, come on, Scotty," she said, retrieving it. "I want to read the article."

"Like hell you do." She returned to the first page and attempted to mollify me by pretending she was absorbing the printed text. Apparently, she has become a very slow reader.

"I don't get it," she complained, going back to the centerfold. "Why did they make him cover himself with his hands?"

"Because if you've ever noticed," I retorted, "Buddy's got very small hands." J.J. looked up at me and smiled cryptically.

"Sure, he does."

I wonder what she meant by that?

* * *

July 10—

Jason came out to the mound while Rick Cerone was at bat, a look of concern on his face.

"I just thought of something," he said, raising his mask. "What if we both get elected to the Hall of Fame at the same time?"

"So?"

He frowned. "You ever been to Cooperstown, Scotty?"

"Once."

"They maybe have two hotels there, and they're always

filled." I picked up the resin bag and balanced it carefully on my left hand.

"What's the problem, Jase?" I asked quietly.

"Don't you think one of us ought to do something about reservations?"

Decisions like that are always tough to make in the middle of the eighth inning.

* * *

July 11—

𝕿𝖍𝖊 𝖂𝖆𝖘𝖍𝖎𝖓𝖌𝖙𝖔𝖓 𝕭𝖚𝖑𝖑𝖊𝖙𝖎𝖓

"Who *Are* Those Guys?"

BY MARK LITVIN
Washington Bulletin Staff Writer

Twenty-five years ago, there was a musical play running on Broadway. The heroine was a red-headed seductress, the villain was the Devil, and the comic relief was provided by an inept band of ballplayers called the Washington Senators. During the course of the first act, a young man from Hannibal, Missouri, named Joe Hardy appeared out of nowhere, knocked the mud off of his cleats, took a few practice swings, and led the team to the World Series. People stopped laughing at the Washington Senators.

More than a decade later, somebody decided to bring the legend of Butch Cassidy and the Sundance Kid to the screen. The heroine was a schoolteacher, the villain was The Law, and the comic relief was provided by an inept band of renegades called the Hole in the Wall Gang. During the course of the first reel, two young men named Butch

See Senators Page Three

STEVE KLUGER

and Sundance appeared out of nowhere, knocked the mud off of their boots, took a few practice shots, and cleaned out the Wild West. People stopped laughing at the Hole in the Wall Gang.

For those who find it inconceivable to comprehend the black-and-white evidence called the A. L. standings, skepticism is inevitable. On the other hand, there is no need for an explanation; Joe Hardy has once again risen from the ashes and picked up a Senators' glove—only this time, he has cloned himself into the Butch and Sundance of the American League.

It's MacKay and Cornell

It has often been held that the cornerstone of a truly great team will invariably be traced to an unbeatable battery. Scotty MacKay and Jason Cornell, obviously, have been sent to us courtesy of Duracell. In fact, so electric is the spark they have provided to their cleated Hole in the Wall Gang, others in the league have been moved to utter repeatedly one of Cassidy's more well-known lines. "Who *are* those guys?"

Take, for example, last night's 7–2 romp over the New York Yankees. Joey Tobin's two stolen bases now rank him third in the league in thefts. Banjo-

strumming shortstop Opie Wright has extended his errorless inning streak to 36, and the Wright–Fowler–Hatten 6–4–3 has turned a formerly penetrable infield Maginot Line into the Berlin Wall. If you *don't* believe, you are either a cynic or Rod Serling.

And yet, it all comes back to MacKay and Cornell.

The Nucleus

Baseball is probably the one sport where teamwork is not an elective, it is required credits. In football, a star quarterback may take a team to the Super Bowl. In hockey, a brilliant goalie may push his club toward Olympic gold. And in baseball, if you rely on a similar individual talent, you will surely wind up in last place.

Scotty MacKay was once the most overpowering pitcher in baseball. His left arm was a Sword of Damocles to anyone who faced him. Yet all he really had was power, and for awhile that was enough. Enough to earn him his awards, enough to put him on magazine covers, and enough to keep the rest of his team from having to exert itself. When the tide began to change, it was catcher Warren Budlong who noticed it first and pushed MacKay into the curve-

See Senators Page Five

CHANGING PITCHES

123

ball. Now it is Cornell who is picking up the legacy.

Between them, MacKay and Cornell have established the most fundamental element necessary in competitive sport. Neither of them could do the job alone. Cornell must rely on MacKay's arm, and Scotty must rely on Jason's instincts. The curveball requires a great deal of finesse—not the same sort of "who cares" delivery one associates with a fastball—and, in mastering it, Scotty MacKay has finally earned his wings as a working pitcher. He sweats.

"Scotty's a pro and he'll be the first to tell you," grins Cornell. "Everything he is he owes to his catcher."

The Catcher's Job

How, exactly, does Cornell make the difference? MacKay need no longer be fearless. In the humanizing process, he had learned how to be afraid, and that is what keeps him on his game. The curveball, by nature, is not a strikeout pitch, and it is up to the catcher to decide who might turn it into a ground out and who would be likely to send it for a ride.

"Jason Cornell says *he's* the reason you're knocking off the American League," MacKay was told.

"Who said that?"
"Cornell."
MacKay shook his head. "Who's he?'"

The Last Word

Which is why the Senators have become the catharsis they now are. With the one-hoppers and fly balls that come part and parcel with the curve, the entire roster has become responsible for every victory MacKay has notched. And they know it. Of course, the facts speak for themselves. The Washington Senators, formerly the clowns, formerly the court jesters, have moved into third place for the first time since—well, for the first time.

There is something almost dreamlike in watching them play, as though one is still dozing before the alarm clock shatters a post-sunrise reverie. And when the harsh realities of the electronic buzz fail to materialize, there is an insane resurgence of hope, as it becomes clear that this is for real, and it is now the *rest* of the world who must find solace in slumber. For those of us who have borne the slings and arrows of outrageous for-

See Senators Page Eight

124   STEVE KLUGER

tune ever since we were old enough to cry, "Go, team," we can now rest assured, in our smugness, that everybody else is suddenly taking notice of the unspoken message we have known all along.

We told you so.

* * *

July 12—

DO NOT REMOVE

To All Starters, From Doug Hoyt:

For those of you who haven't been paying attention, it suddenly seems we have a ball club here. A couple of pointers:

1. Everyone not involved in the All-Star Game is to report to the field during the three-day break each morning at 11:00. Workouts will run until 2:00. There will be a $500 fine for absences, and $20 per 15 minutes for all latenesses. *No excuses will be accepted.*

2. We have an eight-game road trip coming up next week. There is an old saying that you play to tie on the road and win at home. This is now bullshit. I expect a .750 trip and will accept .625 only if absolutely necessary. You drop any more than that, you'd better have a good reason.

3. Whoever wrote the note to me on the men's room wall in Detroit, please be advised that that is a biological impossibility.

4. A number of you have brought it to my attention that our extended workout schedules have been interfering with your personal lives, particularly with vacations planned for the All-Star break. In thinking matters through and taking everything into consideration, I understand the problem and direct your attention to Point 1.

Any questions, see me.

—DH

•

What do we do about the breadfruit, sir?

—Fletcher Christian

•

Anybody see Litvin's column? He says we're a catharsis. Is that good or shouldn't we talk to him the next time he comes back?

Ope

•

What kind of a moron are you? Catharsis means land-mark. Like the Capitol.

Bob D.

•

If anyone's taken the time to measure the basepaths lately, you'll notice that none of them are exactly parallel, and two of them are an inch longer than the rest. This means we're not playing on a diamond, we're playing on a trap-ezoid.

Don W.

•

I thought those were the things you get up your ass. Like Brett.

Joey

•

STEVE KLUGER

Go write on the john, Tobin.

Fowler

●

Take a look at Sports Illustrated. *Who says we're not getting better? Cornell just won Player of the Week.*

Skip

●

Big deal. Pinocchio won an Oscar.

J.T.

●

If I were you, I'd be very careful the next time I went for my Cruex, Joe.

Jase

●

Who wants what from the All-Star Game?

Scotty

●

Bring back a piece of ass from Philly, will you? There's nothing left in D.C. that we haven't already had.

Mick

●

You're crazy, Fowler. They don't have sex in Philadelphia.

Rick

●

Yeah, they do. Carol B. 505–2311. Urinal, Penn Station.

Little Joe

•

Hey, Jase and Scotty—in case we forget to say it, go for it.

Skipper

•

Yeah—us too.

The Team

* * *

July 15—

Philadelphia may not be the garden spot of the world, but it sure won *me* over. It wasn't Independence Hall, and it wasn't Rittenhouse Square. What it was was three innings, no hits, and no walks. And for that, I have to credit the guy who makes my left arm work the way it did when I was a rookie.

Jason must have known that I didn't want to be there, and he probably knew why. I wasn't afraid of making an ass out of myself—I've had a lot of practice at that, and it gets easier each time. I *was* afraid that I didn't belong.

A spot on the All-Star roster was a privilege I had been awarded three times in the past—yet each of those instances had occurred before I'd turned thirty. This is not to imply that veterans have no place in the lineup, as long as you're Pete Rose, Mike Schmidt, or especially Yaz. But other than a select few, the All-Star Game is really a celebration of youth; a spotlight for that rare talent called the phenom, whose every move, every swing, is the daily substance of club car conversation on commuter trains across

STEVE KLUGER

the country. Jason was one of them, I was not—and to include a relic from an earlier time frame was not only unwise, it was unjust.

"This is wrong, Jase," I insisted once again. "They need Righetti. They need Martinez."

"Yeah," retorted Cornell, "but they picked you. Look, Scotty, you may think you've got a long way to go, but they think you're there already. So play clam, huh?" We were in our room at the Warwick Hotel, the All-Star Game now only a matter of hours away, and I was not entirely sure I'd make it as far as the elevator.

"You know what we need, Sundance?" said Jason thoughtfully. "We need a way to get you loose."

"Good luck," I groaned. Instead of replying, he walked over to the window and stared out at the street, craning his neck all the way to the left.

"Scotty, how far are we from Logan Circle?" he asked, turning back to me.

"Mile or two," I shrugged. "Why?" He tossed his head in the general direction of my dresser.

"Put on your sweats, Sundance. We're going out."

Fifteen minutes later, we were jogging up 17th Street, heading north. *Why* we were jogging up 17th Street was another matter entirely. Apparently, Jason was under the impression that exercise under coercion was calculated to take my mind off the game. Equally evident was that he obviously didn't know me as well as I thought he did, if he believed such a strategy had even a ghost of a chance.

"Step it up," he called out over his shoulder. "We don't have much time."

For what? I wondered.

We continued to dodge taxicabs and eight-axle jobs for another few minutes, sidestepping pedestrians who recognized us immediately and who wondered if we hadn't lost our minds on our way to the first inning. Quite frankly, I was wondering the same thing myself.

My skepticism lasted only another moment, as we

reached the intersection at Benjamin Franklin Parkway and turned left. By that time, I was all ready to call it quits, when I looked up and suddenly understood the method to Jason's madness. Looming in front of us, about a mile and a half down the Parkway, was the Philadelphia Museum of Art. And the course that Jason had chosen led straight up to the front steps; the same route that Rocky Balboa had run just before he took the heavyweight title away from Apollo Creed. I quickened my pace and caught up with Cornell.

"You . . . crazy . . . son . . . of . . . a . . . bitch," I panted.

"You still want to call it off?" he asked, catching his own breath.

I swallowed once before I challenged him. "I'll race you."

And in moments, we were tearing down the Parkway, heading for the steps, heading for the title, and heading for anything that lay beyond. The stakes, I was well aware, were far greater than a mere sprinter's victory—I was running for my life, and I knew it.

As the museum grew larger, my mind was filled with a thousand jumbled impressions, some real, some imagined. I saw the Schuylkill River, blending into the background against the railroad tracks, and beyond it, I could clearly make out the University of Pennsylvania. I also saw the next six years of my life, which until that moment I had not been willing to admit I was going to have. Jase was right. The comeback was no longer luck, nor was it impermanent. It was here. It was real. And it could not be undone.

I don't know if Jason started off thinking he was going to let me win—but by the time I had reached the bottom step, he was trailing me by thirty yards, his legs pumping desperately. I took the steps two at a time, three at a time—any way I could have them. Feet were no longer a necessity once I discovered I had wings. And after I had

STEVE KLUGER

reached the top, my lungs gasping for air I did not need, Jason came up behind me and put an arm around my shoulder.

"Okay?" he panted, drenched in sweat. "Okay?"

I closed my eyes briefly and tried to make the moment last as long as I could, knowing I was going to need every bit of it if I didn't want to lose my nerve again. When I reopened them, I took a deep breath and turned to Jason.

"Okay," I said.

Six hours later, I had earned the save, and he was the American League's Most Valuable Player.

"Your attention please. Batting for Valenzuela, number Sixteen, Rick Monday of the Los Angeles Dodgers."

The last out was not particularly significant, insofar as historic value was concerned, but it was one of those rare spots in time that, even as you're living it, you know for sure will never again be tolled—at least not in this lifetime. As Rick Monday stepped into the batter's box, Jason signaled time and jogged out to the mound.

"Problem?" I asked, as he reached me.

"No," he said pensively, raising his mask. "But you know something? Right now, there's probably a couple of million people watching you and me, and wondering what we're talking about."

"What *are* we talking about?" I inquired.

"Well, I was just thinking," he mused. "In a couple of years, they're going to be running highlights of this thing, and when they come to this part, they're going to think we're talking about what to do with Monday."

"Isn't that why you came out here?"

"No," he replied. "I thought maybe we ought to make this something special, so that when *we* see it, we'll be the only people in the world who know what was really going on." He stared down at the ground and kicked at the rubber abstractly. "You feel like making a wish, Scotty?" If it

had been anybody else who had made that particular statement, I might have been inclined to say something not especially flattering; but considering that it was Jason, I knew
he was serious.

"Out loud?" I asked.

"No. To yourself."

So while Howard Cosell and Joe Garagiola expressed
concern in front of a nationwide audience over what was
obviously trouble on the mound, we lowered our eyes and
indulged for a very brief moment in that special practice
generally reserved for birthday candles and wishbones only.
My thoughts spun silently through my cerebrum, propelled
by the knowledge of what was undoubtedly about to trans-
pire between the foul poles of Veteran's Stadium, and I
wondered whether anybody north of the stratosphere was
really listening to what was less a wish and more a prayer.

"Okay," said Jason quietly, suddenly looking up. "Now
let's nail this guy, Sundance."

He returned to the plate for what we both knew in advance was destined to be one of the most anticlimactic moments of our lives. As a matter of fact, Monday had come
to the batter's box first-pitch swinging; and when that pitch
happened to be the breaking ball he didn't expect, it was all
over. I suppose it was only fitting that it was Jason who
caught the final pop-up; Jason, whose two home runs had
clinched it for the Americans by the fourth; Jason, whose
signals had provoked the pitches that had baffled the Nats
all evening; and Jason, who has now become a master at
cleaning up my act. When the out had been officially re-
corded, and the media descended on us like lensed locusts,
we glanced at each other briefly—just before we were en-
gulfed in a tidal wave of humanity—the same thought running through both of our minds.

Somebody *had* been listening after all.

"Can I tell you something I've never told anyone before?" We were sitting on board the American Airlines 727

that had just taken off on its way to National, the afterglow of the evening's accolades and trophies heady enough to propel the three Pratt and Whitney engines without any fuel whatsoever.

"Go ahead," replied Jason. "I won't tell anyone." I paused for a moment, wondering why I was doing this.

"When I was in the minors," I began, "we had this three-game series against Tidewater for the division title, and it came down to the last inning with me on the mound."

"That's a secret?"

"Not that part," I told him. "But there were two out with the bases loaded and a one-run difference for us, and the guy at the plate had a three–two count on him when I let him have it with the fastball."

"What happened?" asked Jase.

"They called it strike three, and we won it."

"So?"

I stared at him guiltily and lowered my eyes. "Jase, it was ball four. That pitch tied the game for Tidewater, and nobody's ever known it but me."

He must have suspected that there was nothing he could say, so he didn't. I, on the other hand, felt a pronounced sense of shame, mitigated only by a wave of relief that I had finally gotten it out of my system.

"I don't guess it means anything in the long run," I added, "but after tonight, I just wanted somebody to know that *I* know."

We sat in silence for a few moments, before I faced to him. "It's your turn," I said.

"For what?"

"Isn't there something *you've* never told anybody before?" He appeared to be thinking about it for a long time, before he replied.

"Yeah, there is," he finally said, weighing his words carefully. "Scotty, say I trusted you more than anybody in the world. Say I knew I could tell you anything." He paused, a look of discomfort on his face. "What would you say if I told you—"

"Would you care for a cocktail?" The stewardess had materialized out of nowhere, as though she had sprung from an armrest. Once we had dispatched her with a polite negative, Jason no longer seemed quite as willing to part with whatever it was he had planned on spilling.

"What if you told me what?" I asked.

He smiled sheepishly. "Later," he replied. "It was just a joke."

I glanced out of the oblong Perspex to my right, just in time to see the City of Brotherly Love fading into a deep blue oblivion. If you looked hard enough, you could almost see the museum in the distance, its facade an invitation to anyone with a dream. Beyond that was the snaking form of the Schuylkill, and on its banks, in the foreground, were the glittering lights of Veteran's Stadium; a beam penetrating the darkness as though it were a living thing, vying for equal time with the moon.

I'll tell you something. Philadelphia may not be the garden spot of the world, but it sure won *me* over.

* * *

July 17—

Good news and bad news. Buddy just found out that he'll be removed from the disabled list and returned to the roster around the last week in September, which means he'll be eligible for post-season play. This is obviously not as imminent as it sounds. If you scan fifty years of Senators history, it's like saying I'll be eligible to run for president.

That's the good news.

The bad news is that, after his success with the Wheaties people, he rounded up a couple of other injured players and formed his own country and western group. Though he had intended on calling the combo "Buddy Budlong and his Wounded Infielders," he backed off at the last moment—a wise idea—figuring that pseudonyms were a lot safer in the event that serious music lovers began looking for someone to blame. That afternoon, he came up with a new name when he inadvertently stumbled across an ad for Western footwear in the *Bulletin*. This is how Washington, D.C., first became blessed with Acme Durango and the Texas Boots.

So far, their popularity has been limited to the Rawhide Saloon ("A Little Bit of the Alamo on O Street"), and I suspect it's not going any further than that. Oh, I've heard worse—but not by much. Firstly, their costumes—which look like somebody blew up a Salvation Army truck—are as mismatched as their accents, which are a cross between Southwest and South Bronx. There is also the matter of teamwork. The drummer, a Phillie, has no sense of rhythm whatsoever, and the backup guitars are manned by a Yankee and a Red Sock, who naturally spend the better part of the evening fighting for the lead. Buddy, on the other hand, accustomed as he has become to the limelight, has managed to pull it all together and actually comes across with a goodly amount of poise. Unfortunately, his singing voice is enough to make a grown man cry.

"Fer our next number—" he drawls.

"Take off your clothes," shouts a woman who has obviously heard about *Playgirl*.

Buddy grins. "That's the *second* set, sweetheart. Stick around. But fer our next number, ah'd like to dedicate a song to mah old pardner, Texas MacKay." I am at the front table at the time, and immediately wish I were in Louisiana. "Hit it group," commands Buddy.

As the introduction staggers weakly through the speakers, Buddy picks up the mike, and adds new dimensions to the term "inner rhyme."

"Last night ah had a dream ah was in Phoenix,
And, ah swear, it sure did seem ah was in Phoenix."

This is what happens to those of us who stay out in the sun too long.

* * *

July 16—

Mound Conference

(At Boston. Tie score of 1–1 in the eighth. Bases are loaded with two outs, Carl Yastrzemski at bat with a 3–2 count.)

JASON: Can I ask you a favor?

SCOTTY *(through a pronounced sweat)*:   Yeah, but would you make it brief? I'm a little busy right now.

JASON *(taking off his mask)*:   Could I borrow your Billy Joel tapes?

SCOTTY *(accessibly)*:   Before or *after* we take care of Yaz?

JASON *(abstractly)*:   Whenever. I'm trying to remember that sax solo in "Marzipan."

SCOTTY: "Zanzibar."

JASON: Yeah. Anyway, it's the instrumental after he stops singing, when it goes "Dum de dum, dum de dum, yadda dada, yadda dada, dada dada dum."

SCOTTY *(interrupting)*:   You did that wrong.

JASON: I know. That's where I always screw up. I think there ought to be another couple of "dums" in there, but I can't figure out where they go. What do *you* think?

SCOTTY: I think you'd better forget it. It's like Louis Armstrong used to say—if you can't feel it, I can't explain it.

STEVE KLUGER

JASON *(starting back toward the plate, then turning around)*: You know that part at the beginning where he sings about Pete Rose's batting?

SCOTTY: So?

JASON: Well, I was just wondering. You think they'll ever write a song about ours?

SCOTTY: They already have. "The Sounds of Silence." *(Jason starts to leave.)* Hey, Jase?

JASON: What?

SCOTTY: What about Yaz?

JASON *(blankly)*: Who? *(Remembering.)* Oh, yeah. *(Pause.)* He thinks you're setting him up for a curve. Give him the fastball.

SCOTTY *(protesting)*: But *anybody* can hit that.

JASON: Yaz won't.

(Cornell returns to his spot; MacKay nails Yastrzemski on a called strike three.)

* * *

July 22—

1 lb. brown rice	*8 oz. raw shrimp*
1 lb. fresh seaweed	*8 oz. raw squid*
8 oz. raw eel	*8 oz. raw octopus*
8 oz. raw bass	*1 bottle oil*
8 oz. raw tuna	*Teriyaki*

This is what the Japanese call dinner. And they wonder why they lost the war.

Actually, this particular genre of alleged food is Joanie's fetish, not mine; but considering that she didn't even flinch the time I presented her with an alfalfa burger, I figure the least I can do is reciprocate.

"Where do I put the eel?" I called out to her.

"In the oil."

"Where's the oil?"

"Next to the wok."

"Which one's the wok?"

"Are you trying to be difficult?"

I really wasn't—it was merely the price I had to pay for volunteering to be helpful. Joanie was in the living room, memorizing the script for a Swiss Miss commercial and teaching herself how to yodel. As a xonsequence, the more mundane aspects of cohabitation devolved to me. I didn't especially mind. We've always made it a point to switch roles whenever possible anyway: one day I'll be adjusting the wiring in one of the appliances while she's doing the laundry; the next, I'll find myself wrestling with a poor excuse for a hospital corner while she's changing the plugs in the Firebird. Unlike similar setups between Lucy and Ricky, ours had never backfired—although this particular evening promised to be a true threat to non-marital bliss.

I stared down at the counter, trying to make sense out of some very perplexing alternatives. The component parts to what I hoped would come out as dinner were strewn about the kitchen in no logical order, making me speculate on whether or not I could get away with tossing the whole thing into the blender and praying it came out all right. My lack of enthusiasm for the chore at hand was, I think, the result of a pre-teenage obsession with a pair of goldfish that I had inadvertently starved to death when a Pony League doubleheader went into extra innings and I didn't get home until close to midnight. Since then, I haven't even been able to look at a piece of smoked salmon without flinching.

"The eel in the oil in the wok," I mumbled to myself, recalling, for no good reason, Cole Porter. I know I fol-

STEVE KLUGER

lowed instructions to the letter, but moments later, the fish had turned a fairly unattractive shade of jet black, as had the wall behind the stove. Freud would have had several opinions—"There are no accidents" being one of the first. I emptied the wok into the trash and reached for the octopus.

"Strike one," I mumbled.

Yuet Sun is one of the best Chinese restaurants in Georgetown. Chow mein. Moo-shu pork. No fish.

"I don't get it," frowned Joanie. "Couldn't you save *any*thing?"

"Just the teriyaki," I told her.

"What about the shrimp? You didn't even have to cook them." I shook my head impatiently.

"They swam upstream and spawned," I replied. "Look, can we just forget it?"

We were sitting at a front table, J.J. somewhat mollified over losing thirty dollars' worth of groceries by the fact that I had promised her first choice on the fortune cookies. Generally, I was the one who exercised that prerogative, moving her to complain that she always felt like she was being handed her future by default.

"You want some more tea?" she asked, handing me the pot. I declined on grounds of oversaturation. "You know, you'd better get used to it," she warned. "I just got the job with Lipton." There was a slight pause as she grimaced. "Another beverage. Can't they get me a dog food commercial?"

"Quit while you're ahead," I advised. "With your track record, they'd have you playing a biscuit."

When the fortune cookies had been brought over, my luck—or lack of it—continued to run true to form. I was usually the one who got the put-ons, while Joanie invariably opened the one that contained the cliché. Tonight hers read, "Where there's smoke, there is always fire."

"Swell," she groaned, depositing the fragments in an

ashtray. "I knew that as soon as you started making dinner."

"Look," I reminded her, "you wanted first choice."

"Okay, Lefty," she countered. "Your turn."

I opened mine slowly, knowing how that makes her crazy. I'm a Libra, which means that I do things in a planned-out, balanced, and methodical manner. It takes me fifteen minutes to unwrap a Christmas present. J.J., on the other hand, is a Cancer. She gravitates toward chaos.

"Well, *this* is different." I frowned, looking down at the grainy print.

"What's it say?"

I held it back briefly before finally handing it over to her. "You're not going to like it," I cautioned her. Nor did she.

"'You will find new love,'" she read slowly. There was a moment of dead silence before she looked up. "I dare you." Obviously, the time had come for a change of topic.

"Why don't we get out of here?" I suggested hastily. "We could go somewhere for dessert, okay?"

"I have a better idea," she replied, brightening instantly. "Why don't we go home and make popcorn?"

There was my opening. I leaned in and lowered my voice. "Uh, listen. Why don't we go home and make love?"

J.J. stared at me thoughtfully before she smiled. "I *really* wanted to make popcorn."

She lost that one.

Sexuality and baseball have been mutually inclusive terms since the days of the Polo Grounds, the American Association, and Charlie Ebbets. It's probably the nature of the sport that has perpetuated the relationship between the two—curfews have grown looser while our uniforms have grown tighter. I would be a liar if I said that the below-the-belt attention constantly focused on us is anything but an essential part of a player's ego. There is no such thing as lack of appeal, and performance anxiety is a foreign term. If you wear a numeral, you're hot sex. Period.

Of course, a number of us are able to enjoy the reputation without necessarily having to do anything about it. I am told by a former Senator who presently plays for the Cardinals that there is a woman in St. Louis who insists she still owns the sheets I slept on—or didn't sleep on, according to the innuendo—during the ostensibly athletic weekend I spent on her Sealy Posturpedic. Naturally, I am grateful for the compliment; I would be a lot more grateful if I'd ever *been* to St. Louis.

On the other hand, there are also some of us who not only take advantage of circumstance, but who carry it to the farthest extreme possible. Mickey Fowler, for instance, has a waiting list in eleven American League cities. He has stopped short of the "Take a Number" system, but I suspect that's merely because those things only go up to double digits. For myself, I generally wind up making excuses for what has turned into a voluntary abstinence. I never used to be that way, but then again, after seven years of leaving your scent all across the country, you find you breathe a lot easier when you start coming home to a double bed instead of the usual twin. And when that happens, it's then that you usually discover that sex begins with an *L.*

"Can I ask you something?" said Joanie quietly. She was propped up on her side, playing with the few chest hairs I have managed to cultivate over the years.

"What?"

She turned away and spoke softly, as though she were having a great deal of difficulty finding the words. "You don't have to, Scotty," she began, "and I don't want to make you do anything you don't want to . . ."

In advance of the question, my blood turned to ice.

Since Joanie and I first began going together five years

ago, we have made it a point never to discuss marriage, knowing that if and when the time were right, it wouldn't even have to be decided—it would be automatic. I freely admit that I have often wished we weren't so independent; identical last names have been on my agenda since the first time we said, "I love you." It's just that we can never seem to train our individual needs to coincide. If we could only manage to be weak together, or strong together, or feel in the mood for raspberry ripple at the same time, maybe we wouldn't still be two half notes looking for a chord. As it is, whenever one of us says "left," the other invariably chooses that moment to say "right"—which is why we're constantly traveling concentric circles in different directions.

Tonight, it is obvious that it is my turn to be on the outside looking in. I don't know why the prospect of tying the knot is as especially frightening now as it appears to be. I suppose I could blame it on the curveball, I suppose I could pin it to the All-Star save, labeling both as the reason I require more space now than I ever did. There is also the distinct possibility that I am full of shit. All I know for sure is that there is something that has been nagging at the back of my mind that precludes the word "commitment" from my vocabulary just yet. It has taken several forms in the last few weeks. J.J. will be in the shower, and I'll be ready to jump in with her—surprise!—when I suddenly find myself pulling back, as though there were an unnamed force restraining me. Sometimes it becomes so tangible, I can almost feel it taking hold. It has a size, it has a shape, and it probably has a name. But it is still opaque enough to remain a mystery. The funny thing, though, is that it picks the most unusual times to change its face. When I'm with J.J., it feels like fear. When I'm on the mound, it feels like somebody has just unleashed a moth collection in my stomach. Anticipation, almost. *I* don't know—maybe I'm losing my mind. More likely is that I've been infected with that

STEVE KLUGER

disease that hits everyone when they realize youth is a finite wellspring that is about to go dry. I'm beginning to feel mortal.

In any event, I decided that I was going to tell Joanie with as much love as I could put into the spoken word that it just wasn't time yet, and hope she'd understand. The last thing I wanted to do was crush her.

"What is it?" I whispered.

She looked up at me bravely. "Do you think you could wear your uniform pants a size bigger?"

I paused. "What?"

"You heard me. I don't want anybody getting any ideas, okay?"

You're not going to find *that* in St. Louis.

* * *

July 23—

The question, of course, is why did I lend him the *Iliad* in the first place?

"First of all the title," Jason insists. "I mean you're not going to go out of your way to read something called *Iliad* unless you're stuck in a waiting room somewhere and they don't have the *Bulletin*, right?"

I decline to reply for two reasons. One, I am not up to the intellectual pressures of this conversation; and two, the first time *I* read it, I was stuck in a waiting room somewhere and they didn't have the *Bulletin*.

"You see my point, don't you Scotty?" he says. "They loused it up from the beginning."

Delving back into mythology, Jason contends that the most serious flaw in the legend is the ease with which the Hellenese were able to play on the enemy's gullibility. Nobody, he claims, could possibly be that stupid.

"No kidding, Scotty. If somebody gave *you* a fifty-foot

horse, wouldn't you think something was fishy?" Feeling as though I am required to argue for the defense, I ask him if he has an alternate solution. You'd think I'd know better by now, wouldn't you?

"If I was the Greeks," he says sagely, "I'd've dressed up as gypsies and then told them we got lost on the way to Yugoslavia. You *know* they'd let us spend the night. Then when they were asleep we just open the door and let the other guys in. See? They really could've blown it with the horse." When I mention that Troy is not walking distance from Yugoslavia, Jason does not know what I am talking about.

"What do you mean, Troy? Scotty, don't you remember the part where he kidnaps the girl and takes her to Paris?"

I sigh. "Jase, Paris was the guy's name."

Jason is clearly thrown. "No."

"Yeah." Evidently, this news does not greatly alter his opinion of the Trojans.

"You see? You see? That's the dumbest thing I ever heard in my life. What if *we* did that? I mean, suppose you named your kid 'Detroit.' Don't you think people would talk?"

He may have a point. I know *I've* been doing a lot of mumbling.

* * *

July 24—

Buddy says he knows who's going to get "Sportsman of the Year."

"Are you kidding?" he demands. "How can they argue with three pins and a cast?" He walks over to a bat rack and stands behind it, as though it were a podium. "Hey, Scotty, how's this?" he asks, reciting. "'What I find especially touching is that this award comes from the sportswriters of America. These are the same guys who took one look at my Wheaties commercial and said the only thing more wooden than my acting was my bat. Pretty funny, huh?"

"For you or Carol Burnett?" I ask.

Actually, there is one bright side. If he does wind up making an acceptance speech, at least he's not going to sing it. I hope.

* * *

July 30—

Sports Illustrated

FOR THE RECORD

MILEPOSTS. Awarded, to a group of investors, the Atlanta franchise in the new USFL. **Adrian Allen** will coach the team.

NAMED. As Sportsman of the Year, **Scotty MacKay**, 36, pitcher for the Washington Senators, by the Sportswriters of America.

TRADED. From the New York Jets to the Washington Redskins, quarterback, **Ken Campbell.**

TRADED. From the Montreal Expos to the New York Yankees, first baseman, **Scott Sklar.**

DIED. James H. Wellington, Jr., 68, of a heart attack, in Waterloo, Iowa. Former track star for Harvard, and 1936 Olympic gold medal winner.

DIED. Tommy Higgins, 35, of a drug overdose, in Detroit, Michigan. Former minor league shortstop for the Washington Senators.

* * *

Tommy Higgins is dead in Detroit at age thirty-five. Drug overdose, they called it. It didn't get much space—six lines at the bottom of the column, just above the photo credits. Then again, it's not especially surprising, considering that not many people knew who Tommy Higgins was.

Baseball has often been accused of possessing a heartless transience that makes lasting friendships an impracticality. Though the "here today, gone tomorrow" philosophy is something with which we all live, Tommy and I always managed to rise above that level. As our first season wore on, I found myself relying on him for everything: moral support, psychological counseling, an occasional kick in the ass, and even pointers on how to dress.

"The white socks have got to go."

I also found, as so often happens when two people are thrown together for long periods of time, that he became a barometer by which my own growth could be measured. When I lost a series opener to St. Petersburg by the ignominious score of 11–0, Tommy put an arm around a bereft yours truly and said, "Aah, what are you worried about? Everybody needs a vacation. You're the best thing that ever happened to this club and you know it." And when *The Sporting News* named me Rookie of the Week and I used the wire press photos to turn our room into a shrine to myself, Tommy's only comment was, "So what? You're not that great."

Tommy was the one who kept the rest of us loose at the times when a man's true mettle is tested, if not sorely tried. It wasn't that he was any more easygoing than the rest of us, but that he possessed an unquenchable optimism, fueled by a thirst for baseball that could not and would not be slaked. While we grumbled that we had lost both ends of a doubleheader, Tommy was still gloating over the fact that we'd each had eleven at-bats in a single day. If one of us complained that he was wasting his time in the minors, Tommy would immediately counter with his favorite argument. "It's mathematical," he would say. "The sooner we get out of here, the sooner we go to the majors. The sooner we go to the majors, the sooner we're out of that too. I'm not in *that* much of a hurry." I've often thought that if I had a blueprint of Tommy Higgins' mind, I'd discover that his brain stem was carved from a spoonful of sugar.

My clearest memory of Tommy was something he said on July 23, 1970. The date is important only because it was the day before he took the belly dive that ripped his rotator cuff and put him out of uniform. Permanently. We were in the middle of a road trip that had begun in Ocala, proceeded to Jacksonville, and was presently peristalsing in St. Pete. Nobody was ever in a good frame of mind on the road. We played all day and we drove all night, in a 1919 bus that didn't like any of us. Its only friend was Charlie Graham, our driver, whom we called "Jervis," and whom Tommy referred to as "Jergens." Jervis seemed to understand the feminine changes of mind in the cranks and shafts under the hood and was always capable of coaxing the transmission to get us as far as the next town. Not that night. We wound up pushing the bus to Clearwater, making it to the ballpark five minutes before we would have had to forfeit. Now, obviously, in a situation such as this, a team is automatically excused for not being, shall we say, on its game. Errors are forgiven, wild pitches accepted, and the strikeout becomes a pardonable companion. Even Winky Gillis, who was always quick to hand out $20 fines to those of us who weren't hustling, suspended the rule this once, grumbling, "Just get the goddamned thing over with." The only one who wasn't buying, of course, was Tommy. He belted a double, a triple, and a home run, putting the Senators on top without any help at all from the rest of us. As a matter of fact, as we went into the eighth, some wise-ass radio announcer broadcast the score as "Higgins—two,

Clearwater—zero." But when Tommy next came to bat, the fatigue was beginning to show. He took the first pitch high for a ball, then watched, immobile, as the next one sailed across the plate for a called strike. He reddened slightly, but resumed his crouch and kept his mouth shut. When the third pitch breezed by, also unchallenged, and was called "strike two," Tommy stood up slowly and faced the umpire with a deadly calm.

"What?" There was a moment of silence.

"I said, 'strike two,'" countered the ump.

Tommy removed his cap and tapped his head. "Are you sure you don't want to change this?" he said tightly.

Clearwater's catcher looked up. "Aw, shut up, Higgins," he snapped. "You heard him."

Nobody knew how the fight started. Apparently, when Tommy turned to face the catcher, he said something innocuous like "Go fuck yourself," just before the fists started flying. In moments, the rest of us were on the field, pounding anyone we could lay our hands on. This is a much-maligned practice, yet one not without its own good reason. None of us had anything against Clearwater—but when somebody raises a hand to one of your own guys, they'd better be ready to take on eight older brothers as well. That afternoon, no real damage was done, outside of the usual bruises and cut lips. Tommy was ejected from the game for causing the thing, and as I helped him back to the dugout, blood streaming from his nose, I really let him have it for opening his mouth.

"Are you crazy or something?" I demanded. "It was a *strike*, Tom."

He looked around uncertainly to make sure no one was listening, then lowered his voice.

"*I* know that," he said, looking down. "But I was losing it, Dobe."

"Losing what?"

"If I hadn't made him toss me, I'd've struck out."

Not that it would have made much difference anyway, because with Tommy gone from the game, my 2–0 shutout quickly turned into a 7–2 laugher for Clearwater. Later that night, I paced our room, throwing whatever wasn't nailed to the floor and swearing at any deity who was listening for making me a pitcher. Tommy, for once, was uncharacteristically silent, as he listened to two solid hours of my self-indulgences. When I'd calmed down enough to get into bed and snap off the light in a well-practiced sulk, Tommy finally spoke.

"I don't get it, Dobie," he said quietly. "What more do you want?"

"What more?" I frowned. "We're stuck in a swamp, we've lost four straight, and we're not going anywhere."

There was a pause.

"But isn't this enough?" he asked, bewildered. "We're *here*, aren't we?" He sat up and switched on the light. "I think we'd better have a talk, Scotty." It wasn't just his tone of voice that shut me up, it was the name. Tommy had called me Scotty exactly twice before, and both times it had meant I was in serious trouble.

"I don't know why *you're* here," he said, "but I know why *I* am. Do you remember what it felt like the first time you told somebody you loved her?" I nodded. "And remember how it felt the first time you found a quarter on the street and you were all of a sudden rich?"

"So what?"

"How about when you thought you'd never stop being a kid, and then you woke up that morning and you were finally sixteen?"

"What's the point, Tommy?" I sighed.

"The point is," he replied, "if you take all of these things and put them together, and then tell me you don't feel the same way when you slide into second base, then we don't have anything to talk about. Ever." He leaned across the chasm that separated our beds and glared at me through narrowed eyes. "Now maybe you'd better think about it for awhile," he said slowly, "because if you ever say anything like that to me again, you're going to wish you hadn't." And only then did he turn off the light, roll over, and go to sleep.

For a long while, I stared out of the window at a deep blue Florida night—Tommy's last in professional base-ball—and tried to blot out everything he had said. Of course, I didn't take him seriously. Sometimes you have to learn when to turn a deaf ear and not let things get to you.

Six hours later I dozed off, ashamed of myself.

Tommy Higgins is dead in Detroit at age thirty-five. Drug overdose, they called it. I know better. Tommy started dying in Clearwater the minute he hit the basepath and felt the rip in his shoulder. Somehow though, you knew he'd never let you see the pain—not out of a sense of consideration, but because he refused to acknowledge it himself. When they carried him off the field, all he was concerned about was whether he could make his next at-bat. And when I visited him last year at his meat market in Hamtramck, he kept joking about how he was going to be the minors' oldest Comeback Player of the Year.

Tommy Higgins is why I play baseball—because, through him, I learned the hard way that where we ul-timately wind up is irrelevant. It's how we get there that counts. Tommy never cared about awards or contracts or commercial endorsements; all he asked was to be left alone with his diamond. After he was released, I felt I owed it to him to play for both of us, just the way he would have—by forgetting about tomorrow and concentrating on today. And the funny part of it was that four weeks after that, I was called up to Washington, and until now, I've never had to look back.

These days, whenever I think of Tommy Higgins, I re-member something he once said to me. It was his credo of sorts, a code by which he lived that made adversity itself bearable. He'd stare at the cracked gray walls that comprised our room, toss aside the schedule for a grueling road trip, and chuckle.

"We don't care, Dobe," he'd say. "And you know *why* we don't care? Because a little ways down the road (and it may be a couple of years), we're going to make the All-Star team on the first ballot. And when we do, we're gonna grab a couple of beers, you and me, and we're gonna look back on all this, and we're gonna laugh our asses off."

I wish we could, Tommy.

* * *

August 2—

Last night's doubleheader with the White Sox provoked a serious difference of opinion between Jason and myself. It was his contention that the new Chicago uniforms make their team look like an ad for Ringling Bros. I, on the other hand, insisted they looked more like the Legion of Super Heroes.

"You're crazy," said Jason, while Carlton Fisk waited patiently at the plate. "Those guys had antennas."

"Some of them did," I reminded him.

"Look Scotty." He frowned. "I'm not leaving until you tell me they look like a high-wire act."

I figured it would probably be in everyone's best interests if I humored him—Jason prefers having his own way whenever there's the slightest opportunity, and if I didn't agree with him, we were likely to remain in the third inning until Tuesday.

"Come to think of it," I pretended to muse, "you know, you're right?"

Satisfied, he went back to the plate, and I struck out Lightning Lad.

* * *

The Washington Bulletin

To the Editor:

I have been engaged for six years, mostly because I'm not especially anxious to get married yet. My fiancée is not a baseball fan, and I've managed to hold her off this long by promising her we'd set a wedding date when the Washington Senators won the American League pennant.

I'm obviously in a lot of trouble. To whom do I complain?

JOHN COSTANZO
Baltimore, MD

To the Editor:

The Yankees say that they've got the most powerful lineup in the division. The Orioles say they've got the bullpen with the most depth. The Sox say they've got the market cornered on home run balls, and the Indians say they can't be out-hit by anybody.

They can *all* get stuffed.

KEITH MARSHALL
Gaithersburg, MD

To the Editor:

The real reason the Senators can't lose is because I have a Toronto Blue Jays T-shirt I started wearing eight weeks ago, and every time I've worn it to a Senators game, they've won. The only thing is, I don't know whether or not it would break the spell if I washed it, so I haven't. I hope they win the division soon, because nobody will go to the games with me anymore.

> JoAnn McLaughlin
> Quantico, VA

To the Editor:
Know what? The Senators used to go into a June swoon in April, which means that even if they go into one now, at least they'll be late for once. Doesn't that make you feel secure?

> Stevie Solomon
> Georgetown, Washington, DC

To the Editor:
Ever since my letter appeared in your column several weeks ago, I have received quite a bit of hate mail from your readers. Therefore, please give me this chance to clarify myself. I did not say *all* of your fans were animals. I merely pointed out that here in the shot-and-beer town of Pittsburgh, we do not run onto the field and behave like savages when a game is over. Further, I did not mean to imply that your facilities were a disgrace. What I tried to point out was that, compared to our Three Rivers Stadium, *your* park is a little outdated. I hope this clears things up.

> Mrs. J. J. McNichols
> Scott Township, PA

To the Editor:
You ever see Three Rivers Stadium from the air? It looks like a yellow toilet seat.

> Vito Antenotti
> Bethesda, MD

August 4—

The Sporting News says that Jason and I have the best winning percentage of any battery in baseball. Jase is inclined to chalk it up to hard work; I claim it's because of the combination.

"Libra and Gemini," I point out. "We can't miss." Not only that, since Cornell's birthday is May 21, he's borrowed enough Taurus willpower to force our two sides into an even one.

"What do you mean Taurus?" he frowns. "*I'm* not a Taurus."

"You were born on the cusp," I remind him. Jason merely chuckles.

"Shows what you know, Scotty. I was born in Ohio."

I can take him anywhere but out.

* * *

August 5—

You are looking at a man who is in very serious trouble.

At the outset, it didn't especially appear to be the kind of day that was going to turn my whole life upside down. I mean, when I woke up this morning, the sky was still blue and my wheat germ was still brown. I even managed to do eight extra sit-ups. Hallmarks of normalcy. Yet, if I'd had any clue as to what was about to happen, I'd have locked myself in a closet for the rest of my life. Instead, I went to the ballpark.

I'll be entirely honest. Facing the Kansas City Royals— even on the best of days—is not my idea of a pleasant way to spend a Saturday afternoon. Over the years, they have systematically roasted me alive—time and again—to the point where I can almost hear the chatter in their locker room just before the game.

"Hey, what are we having for lunch?"

"Scotty MacKay."

Consequently, I was a little surprised to notice the line scores at the top of the seventh in this afternoon's game.

| ROYALS | 0 | 0 | 0 | 0 | 0 | 0 |
| SENATORS | 0 | 0 | 1 | 1 | 1 | 1 |

Ours looked like a picket fence. Theirs looked like Orphan Annie's eyeballs.

Oh, I wasn't fooling myself. I knew that half their lineup had the Hong Kong flu and could have been knocked over by a stiff breeze. Even so, I hadn't pitched six consecutive shutout innings all year—and if I had to pin my thanks on an Asian virus and some stomach cramps, that was okay by me. Except that George Brett didn't see it quite the same way.

Brett—and I have no qualms about admitting as much—is the one batter who genuinely scares the hell out of me, if for no reason other than the fact that he's one of the only pure athletes in the game today. If there's a fielding play he hasn't made or a pitch he hasn't hit, it's only because they haven't been invented yet. As a result, given a choice between either facing him at bat, or having all of my teeth pulled, I would promptly head straight for the dentist. Even Jason, who normally prides himself on knowing the opposition's weaknesses, won't get near Brett, because, according to him, he doesn't have any.

"On the other hand," observed Cornell, "they didn't think Achilles did either, did they, Scotty?"

"Or Samson," I added.

Jason nodded. "Yeah," he replied. "Want me to get you a pair of scissors?"

We were standing on the mound at the top of the seventh, with two men on, two out, Brett at the plate, and my shutout vaporizing before my eyes.

"What do you think we ought to do with him?" I asked apprehensively.

"What are your choices?" said Jase.

"Well, we could walk him or take our chances. You got any other options?"

Cornell looked up at me and frowned. "We could always ask him to forfeit the out," he said, "but I wouldn't hold my breath." He kicked at the ground for a minute, then added, "You know, it could be a lot worse. We could be playing the Tokyo Giants."

"That's worse?"

"Yeah," he insisted. "You ever see 'em play? They're only a couple of feet tall. Their strike zone's around their ankles." His brow creased with concern. "The other thing is, can you imagine how tough it would be to pitch to yellow outfielders? If you weren't careful, you might lose them in the sun."

"What about Brett?" I demanded, abruptly bringing him back from the Far East. Jason weighed the alternatives before he spoke.

"Nail him on the knuckleball, Scotty," he said quietly.

I was nothing short of shocked. "Have you been smoking the resin bag?" I cried. "This isn't batting practice. Everybody knows I can't throw the knuckler yet."

"*I* don't," he declared flatly, turning back toward the plate. "Neither do you, Scotty. And outside of you and me, who else counts?"

He returned to his spot behind the batter's box and resumed his crouch. Though I tried to focus on Brett and hold onto my concentration, I couldn't keep from chuckling. Jason. If it wasn't yellow people, it was Billy Joel. If it wasn't Billy Joel, it was dog legs, or pitching fruit. Momentarily I wondered if it was more than just coincidence that I'd begun streaking again around the time he'd started catching me. Don't get me wrong—it didn't have anything to do with lack of ability on Buddy's part. Experience-wise, nobody can touch him. It was just that, while Buddy knew exactly what he was doing, he always left me to make all of our decisions. Jason, on the other hand, was not about to do as much and give me a chance to get weak in the knees.

I instinctively stepped back on the rubber, as Brett finished his last practice swing, and stared intently at the steely blue glint in Jason's eyes. Briefly, I saw the smile there, and as I unwound with my first pitch, I read the message that only I could translate.

"Outside of you and me, Scotty," it said, "who else counts?"

And in one awful instant, the world stopped spinning.

I don't know why it took me so long to make the connection. I don't know what it is about self-deception that compels a lefthander of above-average intelligence to detour so suddenly from the path of simple logic. The strikeouts, the wins, Joanie—of *course* there was a common denominator. I do know, however, that as Brett fouled off my first pitch, raging comprehension plumbed the depths of every last corner of my mind, and forced a virtual *Titanic* of awareness to come shooting straight up to the surface.

I'm in love with Jason Cornell.

Now, I understand fully that this is not the run-of-the-mill type of admission that one might expect from a curveballer. I further realize that a number of people—particularly Little League mothers—would find themselves somewhat perturbed to learn as much. In defense, all I can say is, "How the hell do you think *I* feel?" For nine hours and fifty-three minutes, I've been living with what some would call "the awful truth," and have become convinced that if I force myself to see it on paper in black and white, I might be able to accept it.

I'm in love with Jason Cornell.

I was wrong. I can't accept it.

To be quite blunt, I find myself—at the very least—sufficiently out of my league and have little or no idea of what I'm supposed to do next. I mean, for God's sake, I'm so used to breasts. I've even spent most of the evening with an old copy of *Playboy*, praying that my biological reactions to Miss October remain what they have been ever since I discovered her eleven years ago. On the one hand, I'm pleased to note that everything still works. On the other hand, she also keeps growing a catcher's mask and the number 8. Oh, shit.

I have an idea. Don't they play baseball in Brazil? Sure, they play baseball in Brazil. What's it called? Oh, yeah. The Brazilian League. Maybe I'll tell Doug Hoyt that I need some time to work on my arm, then move to Rio and play there. I'll even teach myself to tolerate coffee. No, I can't do that. I can't leave Jason behind. Okay, so I'll take him with me. What am I, crazy? If I take him with me, why leave in the first place?

No, maybe I'd better stay right here. Maybe I'd better stay right here and face the music. Maybe I'd better stay right here and face the music and stop the rumors before they start. Nobody suspects anything yet anyway. Fine. I'll show up at the stadium tomorrow night and belt Jason in the mouth. Make people think I hate his guts.

Jason.

Funny, how it all comes back to Jason. The worst part of it is, if I felt revolted or pissed off or depressed, I might be able to do something about it. But I don't. As a matter of sorry fact, I kind of like it. No, strike the "kind of." I like it. I think it has something to do with noticing that every time I'm around him, I smile a lot more than I normally do. Maybe because he makes me feel confident, or maybe it's just because there never seem to be any shadows around him. I like the way he thinks, I like the way he acts, I like the way he talks, I like the way he dresses, I like the way he moves, I like the way he catches, and I like the way he looks at me after I've just struck out a side. In short, if I had to be anybody else other than myself, I'd want to be Jason Cornell. Seeing as that's not the case, however, I'll take the next best thing. I'd like to be as much a part of him as one human being can be of another, and have him as much a part of me as I am of him.

Does that sound like the end of the world?

On the other hand, I could always take the easy way out. Ask Doug for a new catcher and tell him that Jason is lousing up my concentration. Nobody would fault me for that. What's more, considering the rather disturbing emotional turn of events of this afternoon, he can't possibly be doing any good for either my pitching arm *or* my frame of mind.

Oh, yeah, that reminds me. I nailed Brett on the knuckleball and pitched my first complete-game shutout in over a year and a half.

You are looking at a man who is in very serious trouble.

FALL

Joel Humphries is a psychoanalyst. That implies that he practices psychoanalysis. Period. The distinction is important, because the one time I unwittingly referred to him as a psychiatrist, he nearly threw me out of his office.

"But it's the same thing," I protested.

"Oh, yeah?" retorted he. "How would you like it if I got *you* confused with the peanut vendor? You both work in the same ballpark, don't you?"

Joel is into what they call "pop psychology." This means that we shout at each other three times a week. I *will* say one thing in favor of his technique, however—during our sessions, I am so busy being irritated with him, I have no time to worry about Jason. Who, of course, is why I'm there in the first place.

I was referred to Joel by Sonny Hackford, a reliever for the Orioles who used to have a heavy drinking problem. If there is any credence in rumor, he was about one shot-glass away from waivers, when his head was put back together by the shrink who hates Freud. (I should also mention that Sonny presently has an ERA of 1.83, with seven wins and eight saves. That speaks louder than any degree.) Naturally, my queries about professional guidance were couched in terms of, "I have this friend . . ." If Sonny suspected anything, he was sensitive enough to pretend he believed me.

I did not know quite what to expect of Joel. My exposure to therapy of a medulla oblongata variety was limited to what I had seen in various movie houses over the last three decades. On the one hand, Joel does not look like Sidney Greenstreet. On the other, he doesn't look like Bob Newhart either. If I had thought his office was going to be a study in cold clinicism, I was disappointed there too.

No spiky chairs or tastefully upholstered ottoman. He has furniture you can sit on. Nor are his walls festooned with the usual crap one normally associates with persons of his ilk; there is one diploma, which hangs, sans frame, over the telephone answering machine, and which is generally employed less as evidence of his intelligence and more as a scratch pad to scribble down numbers in the absence of a ready piece of paper. There *is* an obligatory abstract that looks as if someone threw up on the wall, but it's tucked away in the far corner of the room, by the lavatory, appropriately, permitting the rest of the hanging space to be devoted to a few framed shots of his dog. He has a dog too, whom he permits to sit in on working sessions—a situation that makes me extremely uncomfortable. The animal always seems to understand exactly what I'm saying, and, furthermore, possesses an intellectual air of its own that clearly implies it skipped obedience school altogether and went right on to Princeton. I'm sure that when I leave, they discuss me at length.

Although I had been less than honest with Sonny Hackford about my real reasons for seeking counseling, I realized that it was not a wise idea to be equally as enigmatic with Joel, considering that, after a while, he was bound to wonder what I was doing there. Even so, I spent much of the first session talking about anything and everything—except what really mattered. I doubt that he was fooled; I must have mentioned Joanie at least a dozen times, interrupting myself only to describe—in detail—some of my more lurid sexual forays over the last thirteen years. In the legal profession, this is what's known as leading the witness. And for a while, it looked like it was working.

"Well, you don't seem to have any problems in *that* department," he chuckled. "So what brings you to me?" The inevitable question. Could I really expect to evade it any longer? I tried.

"Do you follow baseball?" I asked, stalling for time. He nodded. "Well, if you want to know the truth, it all started when I began losing my fastball." This was good for a solid twenty minutes on the comeback—the doubts, the insecurities, the fears about hanging it up. I was so convincing, after awhile even *I* believed that's why I was sitting in his office. He didn't.

"Can I say something?" he asked, interrupting me in the middle of a 1–1 pitch.

"What?"

"I'm waiting."

The jig was up.

I suppose I knew from the minute I said, "Dr. Humphries, I'd like to make an appointment," that, sooner or later, I would have to locate the strength to utter the few more words that would undoubtedly brand me—first in his eyes, then in my own. Thinking it had been one thing. Saying it made it true. Had I been given half a chance, I gladly would have remained silent and shrouded myself in a pocket of lies for as long as they protected me from whatever it was I did not want to face. I guess I should have known better.

"Well?" he repeated.

After a moment of silence, I finally replied. "Will you be shocked?"

A negative shake of the head and I realized the time had come. A fast gulp, a quick prayer.

"There's a problem."

"There usually is."

"This is different."

"Want to bet?"

And to my unbridled dismay, I heard the words coming before I could stop them. "I'm in love with—" Uh-huh. Those prepositions are deadly, Scotty. "—my catcher."

The dog yawned. Joel remained impassive.

"Go on," he said evenly. Well, I was finally appalled.

This sort of thing might have been a standard menu to him, but I was the one who was ordering à la carte, and I would have been most appreciative of a gasp or a little astonishment. Even a raised eyebrow would have been welcome.

"Isn't that enough?" I demanded. Apparently, Joel didn't think so.

"Scotty," he asked mildly, "what exactly is it you want me to do?"

"Make it go away!" And that was when I realized, too late, that I had just given him his opening to say the last thing I wanted to hear.

"Why?"

I knew instantly that, if I had been cagier, I could have steered him in another direction; I never would have given him an opportunity like that. For in one syllable, he stopped the merry-go-round and made me get off—no brass rings and no return ticket. Three days without any sleep, three days of staring at myself in the mirror to see if I had grown horns, and three days of wishing I were anybody else but me—all brought to a dead halt by one word.

Why?

Good question.

"Uh, Joel," I said, not quite sure that he had understood me. "My catcher. Jason. He's a guy."

"No kidding."

"And while we're on the subject, so am I."

He leaned back in his chair, a look of triumph on his face. "Now we're getting somewhere."

We are?

"Don't you see?" I insisted. "Two wrongs don't make a right. Two no's don't make a yes—"

"Whose rules are those?"

I thought about it for a moment, then shrugged. "I don't know. The American League's, maybe."

He nodded as though I had just said something worthwhile. "Right. They also have the designated hitter, don't they?"

Touché.

Maybe it was because he obviously did understand and wasn't fazed, or maybe it was because I can't stand the DH either—but at that moment, I realized I was in good hands. I think what had been paralyzing me up until then was the belief that I was all alone in this thing—you never could have convinced me that anyone else had traveled the same route before. Then again, apparently Joel had been through this song and dance so many times, it had become old hat. And for that, I was grateful.

"So what do we do now?" I asked tentatively.

"Do? We don't do anything. We find out why it happened, and *then* we think about what comes next." He propped up his feet on the edge of his desk and reached for a pack of Benson and Hedges. "You smoke?" he asked, extending it to me.

"No."

He smiled knowingly. "This may be a good time to start."

Once he had lit the cigarette, he got down to business. This is what I have come to hate about therapy. They never let you know when they're just making small talk, and when they've started doing a number on your head.

"Scotty," he began, "what does it feel like when I say 'Jason?'"

He needn't have waited for an answer, because while I was fumbling for words, the smile that has accompanied that name for the last four weeks slipped out of its cage, unchecked by either my conscious or its sub.

"Ah-hah," he declared, noticing it immediately.

"Ah-hah what?"

"Go on."

"What do you mean, 'go on?' I haven't said anything yet." Pause. "Okay, his eyes."

"What *about* his eyes?"

"I like them."

"Tell me about them."

Swell. For this I'm paying fifty dollars an hour.

"They're blue," I began politely, "and there's two of them—"

"Eighty-six the sarcasm," he snapped.

That did it. "What do you expect?" I exploded. "Eyes are eyes. You see them every day." Then the tipoff, before I knew it was coming. "They're Tommy's eyes."

Pain.

"Tommy?" he asked quietly.

"Uh, yeah. He's this guy who—My roommate in the minors, and—*Sports Illustrated* said it was a drug overdose, but—"

I don't know why I'd waited until then to start crying. I'd had forty-eight hours to get used to the news after I'd heard it, and then of course the funeral, and I still hadn't wept once. Now it felt like I was never going to stop. Tommy Higgins. The first person who had ever believed in me. The only person who never stopped pushing me up to the starting gate, even when I would have preferred to hang back at the paddock, scared to death of what I might really be able to do. Tommy Higgins, for whom I'd apparently no longer had time once I'd made the cover of *Newsweek* and he was selling lamb chops in Michigan. And what I could have given him—what I *should* have given him—doesn't count for a goddamned thing anymore, because he's gone to sleep for good, and I'm mourning something I never had to lose.

Joel waited until I had stopped shaking before he said anything. "Scotty, it's not your fault he died," he insisted.

"No," I replied slowly, my cheeks streaked with tears. "But if I'd taken my face out of my navel long enough, maybe I would have heard him in time."

There was a long moment of silence; the unexpected detour had taken a toll I hadn't anticipated paying when I'd first walked in the door. And if that was only an hors d'oeuvre, I began to suspect that I wasn't going to like the main course at all.

"Can I ask you something?" I said finally. "What does this have to do with Jason?"

Joel automatically returned to Response A, Column 1. "You tell me."

Here we go again.

"That's *your* job," I retorted, wiping my eyes. "*You* want to go out and pitch against Cleveland tomorrow?"

"Scotty," he said earnestly, leaning in, "you really loved Tommy, didn't you." Nice observation. I'd only said it three times.

"Weren't you listening to me?"

"Did it bother you?"

"Of course not."

He sank back into the vinyl chair, which was suddenly the ugliest thing I had ever seen on four legs, and smiled smugly. "Well?"

I immediately squinted up at the degree on his wall to make sure that it wasn't stamped "Woolworth's" on the bottom. The dog, sensing what I was doing, frowned.

"It's not the same thing," I retorted. "I wasn't *in* love with him."

"What's the difference?"

I groaned. Loudly. "You're the shrink and you're asking me? Look, Joel, Tommy needed me and I wasn't there. I'm not going to let that happen again. Okay?"

"Okay." He smiled insincerely. "So tell me. Do you think you're apologizing enough by falling in love with Jason?"

What?

When I didn't come up with an immediate reply—as if I had one—he promptly gave me one of his "you-don't-know-what-you-just-said, but-it-was-loaded" looks, which I have since found he wears like neckties.

"Well, that tells me something, anyway," he replied, glancing at his watch.

"What?" I cried. "What did I say?"

"We're going to have to stop for now."

Little shit.

*   *   *

August 16—

Locker Room Tips

1. Drop a lot of hints that you and Joanie are talking marriage.

2. Stop slapping the other guys on the ass. When they do it to you, pretend it didn't happen.

3. *Never* say "Fuck you" to Jason.

4. Get rid of the Aqua Velva. Buy Jock, Stud, Macho, He-Man, and Raunch. Family size.

5. Periodically ask if anyone knows a doctor who specializes in abortion. When they begin kidding you, act sheepish.

6. If Jason walks up to you and he's not wearing anything, stare at the ceiling.

7. Throw out the Jordache jeans. Go back to Levis. *Baggy* Levis.

8. Start subscribing to *Hustler*. Have them send it to the stadium.

9. Always take a shower before or after Cornell. If he should happen to come into the shower room while you're

still there, pretend you have shampoo in your eyes—and if you drop the soap, tough.

10. Point out somebody's tits at least twice an inning.

11. Avoid the press. They can sense *anything*.

* * *

August 17—

Thought: No wonder Jason's underwear ads bothered me. I didn't think they *bothered* me.

* * *

August 18—

Headline of the Week—Joanie got a commercial for something that wasn't a beverage. Yet, while I'd have expected her to be rejoicing, she was busy trying to convince herself that it hadn't been a left-handed compliment.

"I don't get it," I said. "What's the problem?"

She looked up from her script and frowned. "Scotty, it's for Arrid Extra Dry."

"So what?" I shrugged. "They're not going to make you *drink* it, are they?"

"Well, no," she replied hesitantly. "But you don't suppose I got the job because I smelled funny, do you?"

This is why the grass is always greener on the other side.

* * *

Although I feel I am making some real headway in Project Jason, I still haven't come up with any answers. Yet. I have, however, found out why his teeth are so white. He polishes them. Literally.

"Like shoes?" I ask doubtfully. Jason never appreciates it when I compare his cuspids to a pair of loafers.

"Hand me the floss, will you?" he replies, circumventing the question by pretending I haven't asked it. I hand him the floss and watch in amazement. First he brushes, then he flosses, and then he dips a small rag into a bottle of polish and shines each tooth individually. When he can see his reflection, he is satisfied.

"Do you do this often?" I inquire.

"Three times a day."

And he's not even left-handed.

* * *

Joel suggests that I've come to terms with the problem well enough to be able to discuss it with Jason. *I* suggest that Joel take a long walk off of Key Bridge.

"Don't be silly," he retorts. "What's the worst he could do?"

"Knock all of my teeth down my throat and break my face," I reply.

He then wonders out loud how long I think I can keep it a secret, correctly pointing out that Jason knows me a little too well to be fooled for long. I tell him my figures are rough, but I plan to aim for ten years.

"I'd think about it if I were you," he advises.

"We have to stop for now," I tell him.

* * *

STEVE KLUGER

Fantasy Sequence "A"

Scotty tells Jason.

We are sitting in an empty clubhouse after a doubleheader with the Orioles. I have pitched a shutout, Jason has hit three home runs. He has noticed that I've been a little quiet, so he asks me if I'll tell him what's wrong.

"Jase," I sigh, staring at him bravely. "I have a problem. Can I trust you?"

He puts an arm around my shoulder, which, considering the circumstances, is the last thing I need. "We're friends, Scotty," he says quietly. "Doesn't that say it all?"

I nod. "Jason."

"What?"

"I'm in love with you."

Cornell freezes for a moment, then chuckles. "You're what?"

"I'm in love with you."

By now he is roaring. His head is thrown back, peals of laughter shaking his entire body. "Who put you up to this, Scotty?" he gasps. When he sees that I am not smiling, he sobers. Fast. "I don't get it," he says, bewildered. "What's the joke?"

I take a deep breath and face him squarely. "It's no joke, Jason. I mean it." I can tell that it is starting to sink in, because his mouth has begun to curl in a rictus of disgust.

"This is for real?" he snarls.

I nod.

He rises and goes into the men's room, where I can hear him throwing up. When he returns, he strides over to his locker and begins clearing it out.

"Where are you going?" I ask in dismay.

CHANGING PITCHES

"I don't care," he snaps, tossing his sweats into a suitcase. "Seattle, New York, Tokyo. Anywhere to get away from you. You make me sick, MacKay."

"But Jase," I cry. "It doesn't mean anything. I just wanted you to know."

He pauses and turns to me calmly. "Uh-huh." He nods. "And there's something I want *you* to know, Scotty."

Splat!

If Joel really thinks this is going to work, he's more screwed up than I am.

* * *

August 20—

𝕿𝖍𝖊 𝖂𝖆𝖘𝖍𝖎𝖓𝖌𝖙𝖔𝖓 𝕭𝖚𝖑𝖑𝖊𝖙𝖎𝖓

Budlong To Return

August 19—Washington, D.C.—Washington Senators catcher Warren Budlong, who earlier this year was placed on the disabled list for the remainder of the season with an arm injury, will be reactivated next week, Senators manager Doug Hoyt said tonight. Hoyt plans on alternating Budlong between designated hitter and the outfield until he is back to 100 percent. At that time, the catcher will return to his duties behind the plate, splitting responsibilities with Jason Cornell, who was acquired in a trade with Cleveland on June 2.

Abraham Lincoln once made a bases-loaded observation when he said, "He is my friend, and he is me." I have always felt that the simple eloquence behind this particular statement speaks for itself; yet, as is often the case with sentiment

STEVE KLUGER

of a clichéd variety, I wondered if it could ever bear close scrutiny.

Buddy was in his typically nimble frame of mind. His arm had just come out of the cast, and against all medical admonitions, he had gone directly from the doctor's office to the batting cage. I suppose I may have known several more profound moments during the course of my career, but none that has compared to the way I felt standing there on the mound facing him, our conversation interrupted once again by the punctuation Buddy has mastered so well.

"Give me something outside."

Crack!

"Hey, take it easy on your arm, willya?"

Crack!

"Aw, don't be such an old lady."

Crack!

"Okay, you asked for it."

Crack!

His commas were line drives, his semi-colons were home runs, and by the time we had finished a ninety-minute workout, Buddy Budlong had just sewn up his master's in English.

"Jesus Christ, that feels good," he said while we were walking back to the dugout. I noticed that he wouldn't even wipe the sweat off his face, preferring instead to wear it as a badge of honor, a readmission to that working class of athlete called the starting lineup.

"When do you think you'll be ready to play?" I asked, as we plopped ourselves down on the bench.

Buddy flashed me one of his "look-at-me-I'm-a-catcher" smiles and popped his customary piece of bubblegum into his mouth. "Give me twenty minutes to change."

As a matter of fact, that's why Doug Hoyt had already made plans for this particular development, suspecting in advance that Buddy was as likely to remain on the disabled list all year as Doug was likely to take a swan dive off the

National Archives into the Ellipse. And as long as he's back in uniform, Buddy has no ego about sharing the job that was formerly his.

"Ah, fuck Cornell," he grumbled. "Who needs him?"

An unfortunate question. I did not reply. Buddy was acutely aware of the fact as we sat silently in the deserted dugout; and moments later, he turned to me with a worried frown on his face.

"Scotty," he said quietly, "whatever it is that's eating you up alive, you'd better tell me."

He is my friend, and he is me.

Despite the shared years and the thousands of shared moments, from the champagne of victory to the stale malt of defeat, I felt I was finally about to present Buddy with an equation he couldn't handle. Oh, I knew he would factor it and he would cube it, but in the end he'd regard it as insoluble. Even so, from that moment on the mound—facing Brett and Kansas City—when I had first discovered the truth, I knew that Buddy was the only person to whom I would turn. Not Joanie, certainly not Jason, and notwithstanding Joel, who's *paid* to tell me I'm normal. It was Buddy I knew I could trust; yet as I sat silently next to him in the empty dugout, trying not to answer his question, I feared I was about to stretch the parameters of friendship beyond their elasticity. One snap, and I knew that the piece of myself called Buddy Budlong might be banished forever to the sepia-tinted treasure trove called memory. He knew me well, but not well enough to suspect the horrible secret I was hiding that would ultimately turn him away.

"You're hung up on Cornell, right?" he guessed, concentrating on a large Bazooka bubble that was forming in front of his face.

Suspecting that I had just been robbed of a monologue, I made him repeat himself. When he did, it was the same thing I'd *thought* he said.

"How did you know that?" I demanded, a little irritated.

STEVE KLUGER

Buddy began picking the bubblegum off of his glasses and chuckled. "Scotty, I've been catching you for thirteen years. You never looked at *me* like that."

I was hit with a wave of relief, amazed that he seemed to be taking it so well; then immediately began second-guessing myself in the event it was only because he was in an advanced state of shock.

"Does it bother you?" I asked nervously.

Buddy groaned. "Yeah sure, Scotty," he said by rote. "If it'll make you happy, it bothers me. Look, what are you worried about? Sometimes these things happen."

"But what am I supposed to do?" I challenged. "There's a little problem here, you know?"

Buddy frowned. "What? That he's right-handed?"

Big joke. Either he was unwilling to take the whole thing seriously, or he didn't really think it was much cause for concern. In either event, I decided not to press my luck.

We sat in individual solitude for a few minutes—I needed it, Buddy offered it. The questions, and I knew he had many, were left unasked and unanswered, with the silent understanding that when I had the answers, so would he. For the moment, all that mattered to me was that Buddy was still there; still in a perpetual crouch, backing me up, shoring me up, and ready at the drop of a hat to make any suggestions he felt I needed to hear. That I'd even considered the possibility of anything less was cause for more than a little shame. I was reminded of an exchange we had had several years earlier—one of the few times we had ever disagreed on a pitch—when I'd done it my way and given up three runs along with the game. Later on, as embarrassed as I was, I still found a way to blame *him*, and suggested rather sharply that he get himself traded—anywhere. Instead of becoming angry, he had merely smiled.

"Scotty," he'd said, "it's going to take a lot more than a trade to get rid of *me*."

I guess he meant it.

August 20—

Joel says that telling Buddy was one of the healthiest
things I've done in a long time. Of course when I ask him
why, he won't tell me. This implies that either the reason is
too deep for me to understand just yet, or else he's making
it up. I suspect the latter.

"Now if you *really* wanted to break some ground," he
added, knowing I really don't, "you'd think about discussing it with Jason and Joanie too."

I pointed out that I saw no purpose in doing that yet,
seeing as I don't even know if my feelings for Jason are
real.

Actually, that wasn't the whole reason. J.J.'s got
enough on her mind this week. She's playing a flo-thru tea-
bag for Lipton, but I always get embarrassed when I have
to tell Joel things like that.

* * *

August 21—

Joanie thinks we need more culture. She says that we
are living on a programmed diet of celluloid junk, and re-
solves the matter by buying a painting from the gift shop at
the Hirshhorn. It is, beyond a doubt, the ugliest piece of
work that has ever been put on canvas—a large, abstract
madonna that bears a close resemblance to Janis Joplin.

"You've got to be kidding," I tell her.

"You're just not broad-minded, Scotty," she replies.

Obviously, she does not suspect that I am in love with
my catcher.

* * *

If it never rains in Southern California, that's only because it's always pouring in Oakland. This afternoon's doubleheader was finally cancelled, but not until we had sat in the dugout for three hours, wondering whether the drizzle was going to turn into a rainbow or a typhoon.

It was Joey Tobin, of course—he of the telephone numbers acquired from sanitized tile—who came up with the contest. For points, and Joey was the scorer, we each had to think of a word that we felt was clearly the most obscene we had ever heard. The usual four-letter profanities were out; these had to be Webster-approved, and offensive solely by reason of implied suggestiveness.

Joey started the ball rolling with *turgid* and automatically gave himself seven points. *Plunge* was Mickey Fowler's contribution for six, and *nubile* earned the Skipper an even eight. By the time the rest of the lineup had turned in its votes, we had *meaty* (6), *thick* (5), *slippery, firm*, and *taut* for four apiece, and seven for *tongue*—as a verb only. My own donation was *ooze*, a word I have always found somewhat intimidating, and it looked as if I had walked away with it, with a big nine points. Suddenly there was a voice from the other end of the dugout. Opie Wright, the only country not heard from.

"Uh, I know this sounds silly," he said uncertainly, "but the one word *I* can't stand is *moist*."

He won, hands down.

* * *

Acme Durango and the Texas Boots were on Carson's show last night. If there is any substance to hearsay, the Southwest has just threatened to secede from the nation.

I don't know what Carson was thinking—unless it's true that people have been dozing off during the last few minutes of his program. This would make sense, because Buddy's voice has the effect of a stuck alarm clock. They have, however, made some fundamental changes since their early beginnings last month at The Rawhide. Either Hollywood got ahold of them, or they got ahold of Hollywood, but they are presently dressed in sequined vests and matching cowboy pants, which makes Buddy look like a neon sign with a belt. On the plus side, somebody had the foresight to burn all of their music and suggest that they revert to the classics, a move that is obviously not going to earn them plaudits from Glen Campbell, since the two numbers on which they settled are "Wichita Lineman" and "Rhinestone Cowboy."

> *"Fer the Wichita lahnman,*
> *Is still on the laaaaaaahhhhhhhn."*

Every cat in the United States has been looking for a mate since 12:15 this morning.

*   *   *

August 24—

PROPOSITION: It is better to take a risk and steal second than it is to spend the rest of your life safe at first.

PRO: I might ultimately score a run.

CON: I could be tagged out at the bag.

RESOLVED: I'd rather be safe at first.

Joel likes the baseball analogies. He says it gives us a common language when I don't—or won't—understand what he's trying to tell me. Of course, all it really does is start us sparring a lot sooner. Before, it would take him half a session just to get me to talk; now I can walk in and tell him he's dead wrong before he even opens his mouth.

"As I see it," he muses, "unless you get a guarantee in writing that you're not going to get burned, you make everybody else take all the chances."

I nod. "Uh-huh. It's like no-fault life insurance. You can't lose."

Joel leans back in his chair and lights another cigarette. "You're such an asshole," he says. I am reasonably certain that, progressive training or not, this isn't what they taught him to say in college.

We are presently disagreeing, for a change, over what he terms my tragic flaw, and what I term his cop-out, since I don't really believe he has the slightest clue as to what's wrong with me.

"When are you going to start giving up control, Scotty?" he asks.

"When you stop smoking," I tell him agreeably. He hates it when I say that.

"Then let me ask you something," he retorts, putting out the butt. Bad news. He means business. "Was there ever a time in your life when just once you did something you wanted to do without worrying about protecting yourself?"

"Never," I reply emphatically. Judging by the look on his face, he doesn't believe me for a minute.

He's pretty swift, this guy.

His name was Jay Bass. We were in third grade together, and if there was ever anyone I wanted to be in life, it was Jay Bass. He had everything—blond hair, good looks, high marks. He even had Felicia Weiner, who was the pulmonary artery to every pre-adolescent heart at Thomas Jefferson Grammar.

The word *antithesis* was not in my vocabulary at the

time; had it been, I would have used it to describe the chasm separating Jay and myself. I, of course, had only recently come off the disabled list, having thoroughly bewildered modern medicine the summer before by living. In the ensuing months, I had gone on a crash course, learning how to be a kid. The restrictions were off, the bans lifted. Within weeks, there was not a tree in southern Maryland I hadn't climbed, not a stream I hadn't swum in. I had built log cabins, I had shot at Indians, and I had floated down the Mississippi on a raft. And by the end of the summer, an urbanized Huckleberry Finn given a second chance, I had caught up.

When school started in the fall, I wasn't "the sick kid" anymore. I didn't have to play hopscotch with the girls while the guys were playing Greek dodge, and I didn't have to go home directly after the last bell for the unremitting series of late-afternoon naps. But although I had never been disliked, I'd never had many friends either. Everybody knew I was going to die, so there didn't seem to be much point in making me an integral part of *any*thing. This was not meanness—it was a nine year old's logic, and it could not be refuted. Yet, now that my presence had been renewed permanently, I was suddenly regarded as a variable that had just changed binary value, and had to be reassessed, evaluated, and categorized in the proper spot amongst the other xy components loosely known as my peers. It was not always an easy process. Donald Gettinger and Larry Kessler began including me in everything immediately—scaling the Himalayas in Larry's back yard, playing cold war games in Don's basement (they always let me be the G-man). Andrea Fox conceded that I was cute and permitted me to carry her books home after school, while Nan Omansky, my one true crush, asked me if I would help her with fractions, even though it was common knowledge that she always got 100s in arithmetic.

But there was still Jay Bass.

Jay belonged to that singularly unique inner clique that

has been indigenous to every classroom since Aristotle first stood up and addressed the Greeks. They were "the guys"—the rest of us were merely identified individually, without a group affiliation, by our last names. They were in, we were out; and acceptance into this group—a rare excursion for anyone—was the consummate gold star, the ultimate A-plus. I figured I didn't stand a chance, but with my recent luck in bucking the odds, I was game for anything. Not that it presented itself as an easy task—to the best of my recollection, Jay Bass had said perhaps two words to me since first grade, and those, I believe, were "fuck you." But I persisted. "The guys" made up the third grade softball team, and since I'd already discovered that I had a fastball, I'd hang around the playground watching them practice and waiting for them to ask me to join them. Naturally, they didn't, but they would glance over occasionally and see me standing there, a Senators-capped Oliver Twist, silently begging, "Please, sir—I want some more."

And, finally, there was contact.

It was one of those days where you just knew everything was going to go wrong. First, there was the substitute teacher who was a true horse's ass, who rewrote every rule you'd spent a month learning under the real captain, and who was free to mete out punishment with little or no provocation. Then, at lunch, when you went through the cafeteria line, it turned out they were having that awful Salisbury steak that everybody said was really dead cats with ketchup, and to top it off, the only empty seat at your two tables was right next to Jay Bass, and if anybody thought you were in the mood for twenty-five minutes of silence, they were dead wrong.

I sat down quietly, wondering if I really was invisible, or whether I just felt that way. Jay was talking to Richard Eisen, using the secret language of the inner circle I always wished I was brave enough to try.

"Goddamned White Sox. Three–one in ten."

"Screw 'em."

I had already begun counting the raisins in my bread, a practice born more of solitude than interest, when Jay turned to me. No preliminaries, understand, and no warning. He just turned.

"You want my tapioca?" he asked.

I was dumbfounded. Jay Bass wanted *me* to eat his tapioca. Not Richard Eisen, not Philip Gamble. *Me.* The fact that he hated tapioca and probably would have passed it on to a cocker spaniel if I hadn't been there was immaterial. For the rest of the afternoon, I felt as though I had just been handed the Ten Commandments in the guise of a bowl of custard. It was the biggest thing that had ever happened to me.

From there on, it was much easier. After all, Jay and I were friends, and he owed me a favor. When I finally got up enough nerve to ask him if I could pitch an inning, he sighed, but capitulated long enough to permit me one batter (ground out, 6–3). I knew he hadn't wanted to let me pitch, but he had—and in my somewhat inexperienced eyes, this cemented our relationship for life.

For the next few weeks, all I thought about was me and Jay conquering the world together. I saw us shooting the rapids in a canoe, being the first men on the moon, and riding a couple of horses on our way back to the Triple-R Corral. We were Spin and Marty in as many incarnations as I could dream up. Of course, it wasn't easy asking the fantasy to transcend reality. Although I continued to play softball whenever they would let me, I know now that it was merely a question of diminishing my potential nuisance value with a very infrequent yes. Jay was always cool to me, but I figured that was because he didn't want the other guys to know we were friends. Regrettably, self-deception wears a brittle facade, and it never takes much to shatter it. With Jay, it took even less than that.

It was the day before the last game of the season, and

STEVE KLUGER

I'd been oiling my glove since the preceding Tuesday. I knew I'd never get a full inning, but even a fraction thereof would still contribute to what was certain to be a victory. During our final practice, I wasn't allowed on the mound, as I wasn't really a member of the team, so I watched— pretending that Jay was Mickey Mantle, I was Joe DiMaggio, and we were on our way to Cooperstown for our dual induction. When the last pitch had been thrown and the last bat cracked, I approached Jay with a confidence that wasn't really there and asked, "What time should we be here?" He paused as he was picking up his glove, then turned briefly to Richard Eisen as they exchanged a secret look. At the time, it escaped me completely.

"Pinkney Park, eleven o'clock," he said.

I showed up at Pinkney Park at eleven. Nobody else did.

I never understood why they did it to me. I was never quite able to comprehend what it was I had done. Eisen and the others didn't bother me—I was only nine, but I knew a fart-breath when I saw one, and those guys were definitely case studies. But I've never forgiven Jay. I probably lost more at Pinkney Park that morning than I'd ever lost before, and possibly since. That was the last time I trusted anybody on sight, and the last time I failed to look before I jumped.

Not that it really matters, but it was also the last time I ever ate tapioca.

"Kids can be brutal," was Joel's only comment.

As is my wont whenever I am in his presence, I glared at him. "For fifty bucks a pop," I snapped, "you can do better than that, can't you?" Now that he had made me bleed again, he promptly relit his cigarette. Reneging already, I thought.

"Tell me something," he said suddenly, throwing me his

usual curve. "Suppose Jason had been there. What would he have done?"

I didn't even need to think about it. "He'd have tracked down those guys and beaten the shit out of them."

"For whom?"

"For me."

He stared at me cryptically for a prolonged moment, inhaling thoughtfully. "Scotty," he said slowly, "I think you'd better tell me about your father."

I *knew* I was going to hate this.

*   *   *

August 24—

Fantasy Sequence "B"

Scotty tells Jason.

We are sitting by the Jefferson Memorial; the cherry blossoms are in full bloom. Jason has noticed that I've been a little troubled, so he asks me if I will tell him what's wrong.

"Jase," I sigh, staring at the ground. "I have a problem. Can I trust you?"

He puts an arm around my shoulder, which, considering the circumstances, is the last thing I need.

"We're friends, Scotty," he says quietly. "Doesn't that say it all?"

I am somewhat reluctant to believe him. Fool me twice, shame on me.

"Jase."

"What?"

"I'm in love with you."

Jason freezes. Uh-oh. Here we go again.

"You're what?" he says.

"I'm in love with you."

His face melts immediately. "Me too, Scotty," he breathes. "I just didn't know how to tell you."

I, for one, am shocked. "You *are*?" I ask dubiously. "You're not just saying that?"

"Look," he replies, "why don't we find an apartment somewhere, just you and me, and we can move in together, with . . ."

Yeah, right.

* * *

August 25—

Benny Fisk says that we're in an optimum position to renegotiate my contract. This is not because he is especially interested in my well-being, but because his two favorite words are "legal tender."

"We'll take them for a ride," he chortled.

"But Benny," I reminded him, "I'm not that young."

My words did not sink in. Benny Fisk acquires selective hearing when he's got his eye on my credit rating.

* * *

August 26—

One of the smart-ass reporters from the *Metropolitan* took yet another potshot at major leaguers in general, by pointing out that we're nothing more than a bunch of grown men playing a game created for little boys. He claims that when we hold out for free agency or seek salary arbitration, we should be sent to bed without dinner. This is why most of us read the *Bulletin*.

"Hey, Scotty," called Jase from the other side of the clubhouse. "The *Metro* says we're little boys. What do *you* want to be when you grow up?" Since we had just swept a doubleheader and closed in on the Orioles for first place, we were all feeling pretty loose, journalistic criticism or not.

"A soy bean," I retorted. If I'd thought I was being imaginative, the air of athletic rapaciousness proved me the least creative of anyone in the lineup.

SKIP HATTEN	Permanently Stoned
MICKEY FOWLER	A Twelve-Incher
OPIE WRIGHT	A Black Tenor Sax
JOEY TOBIN	A G-String
JASON CORNELL	Sicilian
DON WEINBERG	A Logarithm
RICK JACKSON	Don Knotts
GARY PETRY	Mother Superior
BOB DELANOY	Jason's Capo
DOUG HOYT	Doug Hoyt

Buddy claimed that he wanted to be an arsonist—but only for a day. Just long enough to burn down the *Metropolitan*.

* * *

August 27—

Mound Conference

(At Seattle. Spike Owen at the plate with a 2–2 count. Scotty calls time; Buddy trots out to the mound.)

BUDDY *(raising his mask)*:   Something wrong?

SCOTTY: I'm depressed.

BUDDY: In Seattle? Who isn't? What about Owen?

SCOTTY: Buddy, how come nobody ever gave me a nickname?

BUDDY: What?

SCOTTY: How come you get to be called Boomer and nobody calls me anything?

BUDDY *(brightly)*:   We call you lots of things. Just not to your face.

SCOTTY *(coolly)*:   I don't feel like pitching to you today. Would you go home?

BUDDY *(meekly)*:   Sorry.

SCOTTY: I have an idea—but you've got to help me.

BUDDY *(to himself)*:   Maybe I *will* go home.

SCOTTY *(ignoring him)*:   What do you think of the name Bullet? Bullet MacKay.

BUDDY *(incredulous)*:   *Bullet?*

SCOTTY *(animated)*:   Yeah, me too. So here's what we do. Whenever the press is around, you start calling me that, then they pick it up, and we're in business.

BUDDY *(after a long pause)*:   Scotty, do you do this to torment me? Is that it?

SCOTTY *(archly)*:   *Jason* never complains.

BUDDY: Ah-hah!

SCOTTY *(confused)*:   What?

BUDDY *(feigning jealousy)*:   Is it because my eyes aren't blue, Scotty? You can level with me.

CHANGING PITCHES   189

SCOTTY: Your eyes *are* blue.

BUDDY *(pretending annoyance)*: Then how come you didn't get hung up on *me*? I'm cuter than *he* is.

(There is a long pause.)

SCOTTY *(matter-of-factly)*:   You have ten seconds to go to hell on your own, Buddy.

BUDDY *(shrugging)*:   Just checking to see if you've still got your sense of humor.

SCOTTY: Is that what you call it? *(Indicating the plate.)* Get out of here. Owen looks hungry.

BUDDY *(putting on his mask)*:   Good. Let's starve him to death. Slider?

SCOTTY *(hesitantly)*:   How adventurous do you feel?

BUDDY *(dubiously)*:   The knuckleball?

(Scotty nods.)

BUDDY *(shrugging)*:   It's your ball game, Trigger.

SCOTTY: Bullet.

(Buddy goes back to the plate. Scotty pitches the knuckler, which Owen pops up to the catcher.)

* * *

August 28—

Joanie has been a little curious about what Joel and I discuss. She still doesn't know why I'm seeing him, and I've led her to believe it's the standard "I'm-about-to-turn-forty" crisis. I don't think she believes me.

"Do you talk about me?" she asks, probing.

"Some."

"Do you talk about Buddy?"

"Once in awhile."

"Do you talk about Jason?"

I point to the wall above the television. "You know, I'm really beginning to like that painting after all," I comment. Janis Joplin stares down at me and winks conspiratorially. She knows.

* * *

August 29—

PROPOSITION: An intentional walk with two men on is better than a base hit.

PRO: The next batter may ground into a double play.

CON: The next batter may hit it out.

RESOLVED: Good luck.

"Is that all he ever taught you?" asked Joel, slightly disbelieving.

I gave him a customary shrug. "There wasn't a whole lot more," I admitted. "Nothing important, anyway."

"What, for instance?"

"Well," I replied, "he taught me how to fool a hitter into believing you were getting tired, he taught me that he'd always thought he wanted a son until *I* was born, he taught me what to do with a slider if you—"

"Wait a minute, wait a minute, wait a minute. Back up, Scotty."

I shrank back into the chair and stared down at the floor. "See, he always told me that if you make a hitter think you're getting tired, he might . . ." My voice trailed off meekly under the steady tutelage of Joel's glare.

"The other part, Scotty."

I didn't *think* I was going to get away with it.

One afternoon ten years ago, I was doing my yoga exercises in a small apartment near Georgetown when the telephone rang. It was Benny Fisk, my agent, calling to tell me I had just won the Cy Young Award. To this day, I can still remember the way the plastic felt against my ear when those words came across the receiver, and how I was standing in the middle of my living room in my underwear and a blue T-shirt, looking down at myself and illogically thinking, at that moment, how little I looked like a pitcher.

Once Fisk had hung up, I threw on a pair of jeans, hopped into the Vega, and broke every speed law on the way to my parents' house. I suppose the electricity of the moment had somewhat garbled my speech and impeded my ability to communicate, because it took me a good fifteen minutes to make them understand what had happened. My mother, of course, responded in characteristic fashion.

"That's wonderful, dear." She smiled. "If you get a chance, you must invite Mr. Young over for dinner."

My father, on the other hand, absorbed the implications instantly. He walked across the room and put his arms around me, mumbling under his breath. "I'm proud of you," he said.

It occurred to me then, in that blazing moment of triumph, that he had never said that to me before.

To understand my father is to understand how badly some people want to be parents—and how deep the letdown can be when the realities sometimes don't measure up to the expectations. I was one of those disappointments. I didn't intend to be, and God knows I would have done it differently if I could have, but the truth was simply that I didn't know how to be a son, either.

It was 1945. The Axis had collapsed, FDR was gone—a

STEVE KLUGER

much-mourned symbol of, ironically, a happier time—and the country was attempting to adjust itself to the nuclear era, under the enthusiastic leadership of Harry Truman, the atomic ghoul. In New York, the war clouds had blown away, to be replaced once more and forever by that bright golden haze on the meadow borrowed from a musical about Oklahoma, and Washington, D.C., was the capital of the world. Business was booming, families rediscovered picnics—and each other—and an epidemic of prosperity infected the national consciousness in the form of two cars and 2.3 children.

My father had returned from Europe at the beginning of that year, eager to shed the *Wehrmacht* and anything else that sounded like it was spelled with an umlaut. He had a lucrative partnership in a southern Maryland law firm waiting for him, along with my mother, who had also been doing a little waiting, and who, for three lonely years, had supported him in the same fashion as several thousand other war brides—as a Woman Ordinance Worker ("The Girl He Left Behind Is A WOW!").

With the war over, my father was anxious to become a small percentage of the National Average, and I was the first thing on the agenda. Originally, I had been scheduled to put in my first appearance around Thanksgiving, but either through poor planning or an unexpected change in the lineup, I showed up two months early. I've often thought this was an elective choice on my part, considering that I was born during Game Two of the World Series between the Tigers and the Cubs. But this was the last thing I did right for quite some time.

My mother says that when I was first handed to my father, it was the only time she had ever seen him cry. He was thinking fishing trips and touch football; he was imagining varsity letters and stern lectures on immorality delivered under the aegis of a barely concealed smile. What he *wasn't* visualizing were the incubators and dialysis machines—and for awhile, it looked like that's all he was going to get.

One of the reasons I have always been so cavalier in my approach to what was to have been my early demise was my father. Though I wasn't supposed to know about my expected rendezvous with the dark side, the acquisition of that information was inevitable. I was sick, but I wasn't deaf. Yet, it didn't matter, because there was always my father. It was my father who first told me about the boy called Wart who wasn't afraid to pull a sword from a stone and become King Arthur. It was my father who pointed to the statue of Abraham Lincoln and reminded me that he had been a sick little boy too, but one who had gone from a log cabin in Kentucky to the White House. And it was my father who held me on those nights when I would wake up crying, making me promise I wouldn't be afraid, because he would never let anything hurt me. And I'd stop because I believed him.

By the time I reached my eighth summer, my father was no longer young. His hair had gone gray, his stride had lost its former bounce, and what had started out to be the Great American Dream had turned into a nightmare. Though I didn't realize it until years later, I might as well have been a vampire. While he had put everything he had into keeping me alive, I, in turn, had effectively drained him of his youth. There were no football games, there were no trips to the country. The dreams that had been born on German soil had died there too.

Ironically, it was when I was pronounced officially well that our relationship ended. I was jettisoned to go my own way, with as little paternal involvement as possible. I don't suppose it does any good to understand it now, in retrospect, but I do. Finally. I know he was tired, I know he thought I didn't need him anymore, and I know he wanted to put together some of the pieces of his life that I had effectively broken by being born. When I made Jayvee in high school, it was my mother who attended all the games. When I won my first varsity letter, she was the one who did all the boasting. My father and I no longer knew how to talk to one another, and by the time I turned sixteen, the language barrier was impenetrable.

There is one memory that stands out. Just before my high school graduation he had turned forty-six, and I had come up with a present—*the* present, I thought—that would most clearly show him how I felt. There was a snapshot of the two of us, taken when I was seven—he had his arms around me, and I was wearing my Senators cap—and we were laughing about something. What it was is dimmed by memory. Laughter was too precious a commodity in those days to be questioned. For his birthday, I had the shot enlarged and framed—walnut, I think. If there was anything that was going to remind him of what we had been and what we might still be, that was it.

Just before he came home, I put the wrapped gift on his bed. I visualized him walking into his room and discovering it; then I methodically went through every step from that moment on in my mind. The look of surprise, the look of curiosity, the sound of paper tearing, and then the gasp. My cue to enter with the speech I had been rehearsing for weeks.

Naturally, that's not the way it happened. I peeked out of my door and saw him entering his room; but instead of the sounds I had anticipated, all I heard was a series of sharp cracks. With a sinking feeling in the pit of my stomach, I did a little investigating, and found him staring curiously at the parcel upon which he had just sat. He opened it wordlessly as I watched, and when it had been done, what I saw was a splintered frame and shards of shattered glass piercing our faces. For a long moment, nobody knew what to say.

"I—I—" I stammered, looking up at him.

I have pitched in the major leagues for thirteen years. I

have faced George Brett with the bases loaded, and I have been one strike away from throwing a no-hitter. Yet the hardest thing I have ever done in my life was trying to tell my father I loved him.

*   *   *

August 30—

Buddy Budlong is becoming a real pain in the ass. Yesterday I confessed to him that every time I stare at Jason, feeling the things I feel, I begin to wonder what would happen if the press ever found out. Buddy pretends he doesn't understand.

"What if *The Sporting News* hears about it?" I demand.

"What if they do?" counters Buddy.

"Don't you see?" I retort. "They'd cancel my subscription like that."

He tosses it around as though he's gotten my point, then looks up brightly. "I have an idea," he says.

"What?"

"*Baseball Digest* has this new introductory offer . . ."

Yeah. A real pain in the ass.

*   *   *

The Washington Bulletin

Senators Expand Roster

August 30—Washington, D.C. —With the final month of the season under way and major league rosters permitted an additional 15 players, the Washington Senators have raided their Triple-A franchise in Miami for a wave of younger blood. Notables include Bob Brock, who led the Florida League in batting with a .358 average, and John Walsh, the Gold Glove candidate at first base with the fewest errors of any infielder on the circuit. The bullpen will be also replenished in the form of Mike Gonzalez (13–5) and his screwball, and Rich Bruder (11–2), the rookie phenom whose fastball has puzzled the Panhandle since June.

* * *

September 1—

They say that every circle has a beginning, a middle, and an end; but that unlike any other victim of plane geometry, once it has been completed, it has already been started over again. And so it is with Rich Bruder. The rookie phenom, the kid who has caught lightning in a bell jar ever since he went from Georgetown to Miami, making one brief stop along the way to change his clothes and his numeral. Rich Bruder—the legacy I hope to leave when my own uniform has long since fallen prey to a ceaseless swarm of lepidoptera.

In Florida, they called him Gator, as in "see you later"—which is what his fastball remarked to almost every batter it taunted. The *Miami Herald*, in fact, was pressed to comment, "Rich Bruder has a pitch that does not break and that does not sink. It smirks." Once he arrived in Washington, it became evident immediately, at least to me, that he had shed some of the baby fat he had been pitching in college. In its place and stead, he had acquired the steely edge and the keen eye that separates varsity from the pros. Only his cheerful disposition had remained constant.

"Scotty, this really sucks," he griped.

We were standing on the mound together at Senators Stadium in front of 55,000 people and the California Angels. I had pitched 6⅔ innings with my customary panache, which meant that we'd been in and out of hot water since the second. Now, with a four-run lead, I'd opted for the bullpen, in order to save a little wear and tear on the tendons. Which is the story I handed to the press. What I really wanted to do was give the kid a chance to get his feet wet; partly to finish the cycle we had begun in May, partly because I believed in him, and especially in light of the fact that he still owed me a lunch. Besides, he needed the save a lot more than I needed to go the distance.

Richard, on the other hand, was not especially appreciative of my generous intentions, considering the hulk that was standing in the batter's box. It wore a well-practiced scowl, along with a numeral—44, I believe—and since it was a little early for it to be using its Mr. October alias, it was still going by the name of Reggie Jackson. One thing I'd determined before I'd raised my hand and called time— whatever Bruder was going to do, he was going to do it in style.

"You call that getting your feet wet?" he complained, pointing to the plate. "That's drowning, Scotty."

"Listen, mouth," I reminded him, "*you* were the one who said you'd kill for a uniform." I indicated that batter's box. "There's your mark."

As I turned to leave, Bruder displayed an uncharacteristic uncertainty for the first time since I'd known him. "Scotty," he said quietly, like a six-year-old whose parents

have just left him in a first grade classroom, "say something, okay?"

This was a shorthand I hadn't used in thirteen years, but
I still remembered the translation well. Subtitled it meant,
"I've been waiting for this moment my whole life, so why
do I suddenly wish I was someplace else?" Now if only I
could remember the response.

"What do you hate more than anything in the world?" I
asked finally.

He replied without even thinking. "Wheat germ."

I nodded and pointed to Jackson. "Go for it."

Bruder's first appearance did not resemble baseball as
much as it resembled ballet. It was as though Mikhail Ba-
ryshnikov had picked up a glove and changed careers mid-
stream. The timing and coordination were that of a man
who was born to dance; the natural choreography was that
of a man who was born to pitch. Combined, it only proved
that my suspicions of spring were about to be revealed to
anyone who had ever picked up a sports page and fancied
himself a hero.

"Jesus Christ," breathed Buddy, awed, as Bruder unwound with his last warm-up toss. I was seated next to him
on the dugout bench, a study in hawk-eyed concentration.
Whether Bruder liked it or not, he was getting a post-game
critique—pitch for pitch—on everything he had done
wrong and everything he had done right. And everything
he had done wrong.

"How did he learn to *do* that?" asked an incredulous
Budlong, watching the smoke disappear in the direction of
the reserved seats.

"Alfalfa," I replied noncommittally.

Buddy chuckled. "You wish."

And then number 44 stepped into the box.

Reggie Jackson never knew what hit him. I can say that
categorically, emphatically, and without any presupposition
that I am clairvoyant. It was as if a diesel engine had risen

out of the outfield turf, charged across the basepaths, and cut him down in the prime of his life. I had followed Bruder's progress in the pages of *The Sporting News*, but nothing—*nothing*—had prepared me for what I saw. The fastball—that thing that had kicked up sparks on the college circuit, that spheroid that had single-handedly turned the Floridian peninsula into the personal property of one Rich Bruder—had, somewhere in the course of its metamorphosis, become invisible. You saw him wind up, you saw him go into his stretch, and then you heard the umpire cry, "Steeee-rike!" There was nothing in between. After two of these, Jackson had turned to Jason and asked to see the thing, mildly surprised to discover that there was, indeed, a ball. Well, there was, but not for long. Because Rich Bruder—nervous, frightened, and uncertain—reared up for the third pitch of his very new career, and yawned. Yawned right at Reggie Jackson. Then he threw the fastball that screamed, "Hit me. I dare you."

Jackson was left standing at the plate. He had come to bat expecting to bail the Angels out of a four-run deficit and ended up wondering if he hadn't been the victim of an optical illusion. Yet, as the newly crowned King of the Hill stepped off the mound and headed back toward the dugout, to that rarefied sound of several thousand people adopting him on the spot, it was still my catcher who offered the last word.

"Scotty?" said Budlong, after a reflective moment of silence.

"What?"

"What's a lepidoptera?"

I sank back into the bench and sighed. "It's a moth," I finally told him.

He nodded and turned away, exasperated. "Then why didn't you just say so?"

*　*　*

DO NOT REMOVE

From Doug Hoyt:

𝕿𝖍𝖊 𝖂𝖆𝖘𝖍𝖎𝖓𝖌𝖙𝖔𝖓 𝕭𝖚𝖑𝖑𝖊𝖙𝖎𝖓

THE STANDINGS

American League East

	W	L	Pct.	GB
Baltimore	85	53	.616	—
Washington	82	56	.594	3
New York	79	58	.572	5½
Detroit	75	63	.544	10
Milwaukee	75	64	.544	10½
Toronto	74	65	.536	11½
Cleveland	71	67	.514	14
Boston	70	68	.507	15

At Washington

California	ab	r	h	bl
Downing, lf	4	0	0	0
Carew, 1b	4	1	1	0
Jackson, rf	3	1	1	0
Baylor, dh	4	0	2	0
Lynn, cf	4	0	0	0
DeCinces, 3b	4	1	0	1
Grich, 2b	4	0	1	1
Boone, c	3	0	0	0
Kelleher, ss	3	0	1	0
Totals	33	3	6	2

Washington	ab	r	h	bl
Tobin, 3b	4	1	0	0
Weinberg, lf	3	0	0	0
Budlong, lf	1	1	1	1
Wright, ss	4	2	2	1
Cornell, c	3	1	3	3
Delanoy, dh	4	0	1	0
Jackson, cf	3	0	2	1
Fowler, 2b	4	0	0	0
Petry, rf	4	1	1	0
Hatten, 1b	4	1	2	1
	34	7	12	7

CHANGING PITCHES

```
CALIFORNIA      000    300    000    3
WASHINGTON      060    001    00x    7
```

CALIFORNIA

	IP	H	R	ER	BB	SO
Stallings (L, 12–9)	2	6	5	5	2	1
Richins	5	5	2	1	0	5
Sorenson	1	1	0	0	0	1

WASHINGTON

	IP	H	R	ER	BB	SO
MacKay (W, 18–5)	6⅔	5	3	2	1	5
Bruder	2⅓	1	0	0	0	2

E—Fowler DP—California, 1 LOB—California, 5, Washington, 6 2B—Petry, Hatten, Budlong, Wright, Cornell SF—Rk Jackson, DeCinces Time—2:24 Attendance—55,112

*　*　*

September 4—

Mound Conference

(Versus Oakland, third inning. Two on, two out, and Rickey Henderson at the plate.)

JASON *(raising his mask)*:   Scotty, what's a cask?

SCOTTY: It's that thing they put wine in. You can buy one over at Archive Liquors—twenty bucks a pop.

(There is a long pause.)

SCOTTY: Why?

JASON: I had this idea. What if we cut off Henderson's fingers, then stuff him into a cask and bury him?

STEVE KLUGER

SCOTTY: Jason, don't you think that's a little extreme? The worst he can do is hit one out.

(Jason shakes his head slyly.)

JASON *(with evil import)*: Nevermore. *(Pause.)* Nevermore.

I knew I shouldn't have given him Poe.

* * *

September 5—

Buddy is crushed. Acme Durango and the Texas Boots are officially dead. Oddly enough, it didn't have anything to do with lack of talent—as a matter of fact, they'd been booked into the Roxy in L.A. for Hallowe'en. What happened was that the Phillie was traded to Tokyo and the Red Sock was released unconditionally; and since the one union card you needed to get into the group was an active numeral, the guitars have fallen silent.

"You know what they say," sighs my downcast catcher. "For every light on Broadway, there's a broken heart." I have tried to be sympathetic, but listening to them sing is one of the greatest personal sacrifices I have ever made in the name of friendship. Plus the fact that if Buddy had called me "pardner" one more time, chances are he'd have been back on the disabled list.

"You know what *your* problem is?" he snaps. "You don't know art when you see it."

Buddy Budlong wouldn't recognize art unless it was printed on the side of a beer can.

* * *

I'm beginning to wish I'd never decided to try a knuckleball. It's not a question of the pitch itself—that could pass muster as the curveball's fraternal twin—it's the grip on the damned thing. As the name implies, the ball must be released off of the knuckles. This gives it an unusual spin that causes it to break just about anywhere you're not expecting it to. Well, the only problem is, it doesn't break so hot yet.

Yesterday's game was a good illustration. I was cooking with gas on a mixture of pitches—mostly curveball, fastball, and slider—and by the time we had gone into the sixth, I was feeling so smug with a 7–zip lead, I figured I'd give my embryonic knuckler a chance to grow up a little. Yeah, sure. Seventeen pitches later, I had yet to throw a strike. As a matter of fact, throughout the remaining four innings, it worked exactly once—and even that was not especially reason to celebrate. I had a 2–2 count on the batter and a runner at first, whose eyes were fixed on second base, felony clearly on his mind. The first three pick-off moves worked fine.

"Get back there, sucker," threatened my arm.

It was the fourth time around that caused the problem. I was so intent on making the knuckler work, that when I pivoted left for one more routine throw to first, I forgot that I was still gripping the ball in my pitching mode— knuckles and all. Well, the thing finally broke. Three feet in front of first base, to be exact. It was about to fall into Skip Hatten's glove, when the bottom dropped out, it took a sharp turn, and landed in right field.

Oh, I got the win, all right. Barely. Six outs later, we had managed to hang on, 7–6.

Why is it that no matter how good you are, every game makes you feel like an amateur?

* * *

Scotty tells Jason.
Take one

Joel says my prior speculations on Jason's reactions are, to put it clinically, bullshit. He further adds that if I don't tell him now, it's only going to get more difficult. I am beginning to think he's right—so I'm standing in front of my locker after a doubleheader, staring at myself in the mirror and comparing my face to the guy in the Marlboro ads. I am wondering if a mustache will make me look macho, when I hear a voice behind me. Jason.

"What are you doing?"

I promptly drop a bottle of cologne on the floor and whirl.

"Mustache!" I shout, startled. "I was thinking of growing a mustache! How do you think I'd look with a mustache?"

"Like a badly mowed lawn." He chuckles. Jason is wearing a towel, which, considering the circumstances, is the last thing I need. "Are you okay?" he asks.

"I'm fine," I reply, shaking. Yeah, he bought that. There is a long silence as he stares at me thoughtfully.

"Sit down," he commands after a moment. I sit; so does he.

"Scotty," he says quietly. "This afternoon you almost took my head off with three wild pitches. Then when I signaled for the curve, you said okay and threw the slider." His voice begins to rise. "Now I'm standing here in my bare feet on broken glass. You got something against short people?"

The moment of truth.

"Jase," I tell him, trembling. "I have a problem. Can I trust you?"

He smiles benevolently and leans back. "We're friends,

Scotty. Doesn't that say it all?" Yeah, you little fucker. The last time you said that, I wound up on my ass.

"Jase," I begin. This is zero hour and I know it. As long as it has taken me to get here, as slowly as I have permitted my feet to move, it has all come down to this moment. The next words, you hear, Jason . . .

"What is it, Scotty?" he asks, genuinely concerned.

"Jase—" Pause. No way. "Uh—you ever hear of a guy named, uh—Ron Miller?"

"No. Who's he?"

Beats the hell out of me. My mind is racing. "Uh— shortstop. Miami Senators."

"What about him?" he asks blankly.

I try to make my mouth move, wondering if this has the slightest chance of working. "I watched him grow up, Jase," I say sadly. "I watched him go from high school all-star to the minor leagues. Now he's got the state of Florida in his back pocket."

"That's a problem?" asks my catcher.

It will be in a minute. I take a deep breath and add the postscript. "He's also in love with his second baseman," I say.

Like a hawk, I watch Jason's face for any and every sign. The slightest hint of sympathy and I have my opening. On the other hand, if I see him recoil—or even pretend not to—I will write off the whole venture as a closed book. As always happens with the best laid plans, however . . .

"Now, *that's* a problem," says Cornell. Early returns: inconclusive.

"What am I going to tell him?" I sigh, probing for more tangible evidence. "The rule books don't say anything about that." Pause. "Poor Steve."

Jason stares at me quizzically, thoroughly in the dark. "I thought you said his name was Ron."

"Uh—it is," I stammer hastily. "Steve's his nickname."

Why am I such an asshole?

September 7—

Benny Fisk got me the new contract. He'd gone in asking for five years, $700,000 per, and a signing bonus. When he came out, we had three years, no bonus, and a salary that guarantees that if my car breaks down on Independence Avenue I might be able to afford a bus.

"I thought we were going to take them for a ride," I protested. Benny shrugged and shook his head.

"Scotty," he advised, "you're not that young."

I've *got* to get a new agent.

* * *

September 7—

Joel is not pleased. Not pleased at all.

"Ron's nickname is *Steve*?" he shouted incredulously.

I squirmed in the chair, wondering if I could steer him back to my parents. He loves talking about them.

"What do you want from me?" I shrugged. "I'm lucky I remembered what *team* I had him playing for." Joel groaned. "You know," I added hastily, "it reminds me of something my father said, when—"

"Forget it, Scotty. It's not going to work." I seriously doubted it would. And after a moment, I finally leveled with him.

"I was afraid," I told him quietly. "Okay?"

"Scotty, you're too far along for this," he said, leaning in toward me. "What are you running from, will you tell me that? *What*?"

Yeah, well . . .

He wants me to say I'm running from myself. That's what he's getting at, isn't it? I probably am—but at least

I'm not blind to it anymore. There is one question, though, that keeps presenting itself. What *am* I afraid of? Until this moment, I had myself believing it was the obvious—that my confession to Jason would successfully terminate everything good we have between us. Uh—wrong. Because I'm beginning to suspect that the real fear is what would happen if it *didn't* bother him. What if he smiled and said, "I understand"? Even worse, what if he put an arm around me and suggested, "Let's work it out"? What would I have to do? What would he *want* me to do? It gives me this terrible feeling of weakness, as though loving him makes me less strong. And in telling him, aren't I taking some sort of inflexible step that can't be retracted? Not only that, when the words do leave my mouth, they're not mine anymore. I've lost all control, and he's involved as much—

Control.

That's what the shrink means by control. Maybe what he's trying to tell me is that if I stop worrying about remaining at the helm, I'll find out that was the whole problem. Let go, Scotty. But you'd have to be crazy to take a risk like that. Look what could happen. Sure, I think I can trust Jason, but I could be wrong. Maybe he *wouldn't* understand. And if he didn't, who knows what he'd do? Tell the other guys, tell the press, make me feel like an errant child who ought to be ostracized just for saying, "I love you." Does the punishment really fit the crime?

RESOLVED: Take the risk, and Jason gets all the power.

There's my argument. But will Joel buy it? Do *I*? And if I'm wrong, what other combinations are there?

Too many questions. Back to something I know.

If I use my fingertips to grasp the ball, but I still let my knuckles do all the work, maybe . . .

* * *

DO NOT REMOVE

To All Players, From Doug Hoyt:

1. A reminder that the American League Playoffs begin on October 6th in the Eastern Division city, and the Series starts on the 12th in the National League. I would strongly recommend that you leave those dates open and not make any other plans.

2. Public Relations asked me to remind you again *that, winning record or not, sportsmanship is* still *the name of the game. They are talking suspension if they ever find out who it was that hired the skywriter to spell out "Yankees Suck" over the South Bronx.*

3. I am advised that with the September roster expansion and the influx of new rookies, several of you would like a few games off. Tough shit.

4. Fan Appreciation Day is coming up shortly. Let's not have a repetition of last year. When they ask for pictures or autographs, we say, "Thank you." "Nice tits" is not what they mean by fan appreciation.
Any questions, see me.

DH

●

PR ought to be grateful. It's better than squeezing them.

Skip

●

It is?

Mick the Man

●

Fowler:

I'd suggest that you do something about your predicates. They're supposed to rhyme *with the name. "Stan the Man," for instance, would be acceptable. "Dan the Man" would also work. "Mick the Man" destroys the whole concept. Do you see what I'm getting at?*

Don Weinberg

●

How about "Mick the Prick"?

Buddy

●

Anybody hear what Kansas City says? They say that facing us in the playoffs would be like going on vacation.

Scotty

●

Yeah? Kansas City can sit on it. Say, Tobin, why don't you hire somebody to spell that *out over the stadium?*

Opie

●

I wish you'd watch it. Nobody's supposed to know it was me.

Joey

●

Then next time, don't tell them to put your initials at the end, moron.

Bob Delanoy

●

STEVE KLUGER

Listen, when we get to K.C., does anybody want to switch roommates? I'm getting sick of Opie. He snores with an accent.

Mick

●

Look who's talking. You *never take showers. Now I know what it's like living in a skunkhole.*

Ope

●

You always did. You were born in Louisiana, weren't you?

Buddy

●

Smell? You want to talk about smell? *My* roomie *hasn't done his laundry since basketball season.*

Skip

●

Three weeks, Hatten. It's been three weeks.

Don W.

●

Oh, yeah? The last night in Cleveland, I stubbed my toe on a pair of jeans.

S.H.

●

Did somebody really *say "nice tits" to a fan?*

Jason

●

Yeah. Wanna guess?

Rookie Ricky

•

Tobin, don't you have any *class?*

Jase

•

Nope. Sold it to pay for my car. Anybody know when we get fitted for Series rings?

Little Joe

•

Come on, Joey. Don't you think we'd better wait until we win it first?

Scotty

•

Tell you what. If any one *of you guys doesn't feel the same way, put down your names, and I'll keep my mouth shut, okay?*

Joe

_____

_____

_____

_____

_____

_____

_____

_____

_____

"Kismet"—an inevitable outcome.

The Washington Senators

* * *

September 9—

Joanie finally got rid of the Janis Joplin painting. Unconditional surrender, they call it.

"Where is it now?" she'd ask, coming into the bedroom and noticing the vacant spot on the wall.

"Guess," I would reply. Sometimes I'd hide it under the bed, other times in the closet, and once she even wound up behind the refrigerator. Joanie finally took the hint and returned it to the Hirshhorn. At a loss. As a matter of fact, she nearly had to pay *them* to get it off her hands.

"What I don't understand," she said, "is why you just didn't tell me you didn't like it." I did—about eleven hundred times—but Joanie doesn't like dealing with contradiction.

"You know what we do need?" she mused, looking around the room. "We need a little sculpture."

I hope she gets one small enough to fit in the linen closet.

* * *

September 10—

PROPOSITION: It is better to take a chance and give up a grand slam than it is to fan the side without even trying.

PRO: *You* know you weren't afraid to be the challenger.

CON: Your ERA rises like a helium balloon.

RESOLVED: I'll take the higher ERA.

"That's the first intelligent thing you've said all month," commented Joel.

"But what good does it do?" I insisted. "You know what? This isn't getting easier—only worse."

Joel's face lit up like 100 watts. "I never promised you a rose garden." I pretended I hadn't heard him, deciding that the remark did not deserve the courtesy of an intelligent reply. Joel apparently felt the same way, as he began blushing for the first time since I've known him. "Sorry," he mumbled. "I've been waiting six years for an opening like that."

"Can I ask you something?" I countered. "And you don't have to answer if you don't want to."

"Don't worry—I won't."

"I'm not getting any better, am I?"

"You don't think so?" He chuckled. "You just said you weren't afraid of giving up a grand slam anymore." As if he didn't know what I was talking about.

"What I mean," I retorted, "is that when I first came in here, Jason was this little problem—"

"That's *your* opinion."

"Shut up. Jason was this little problem that I could work around if I had to. Not anymore. Last night, I pitched a two-hitter against Texas. Know why? For nine innings, I was so busy watching the way his eyes crinkle whenever he smiles, I forgot to worry about my arm."

"Would you have preferred being shelled in the third?" he asked studiously.

"You don't understand. Right now I'm leading the American League in shutouts and wins. If they knew the reason, they'd revoke my resin bag."

"I don't see why." He shrugged. "It's not as if you're sleeping with him."

Fear. Abject fear. In the microcosm of a second following this most unwelcome statement, I held my breath, praying that the other shoe would not drop.

"Yet."

It dropped.

Joel insists on knowing why the prospect of loving another man is so terrifying to me. *That*, he says, is the problem, not Jason. He thinks that the implications I attach to my feelings are ridiculous; I tell him he's not a ballplayer. In defense, I also add that I wasn't afraid to love Tommy, and I wasn't afraid to love Buddy. Joel has a ready answer for that—big surprise. He says that they each loved me first, so I was safe in reciprocating—no risk involved. Jason, on the other hand, has made no such indication; it is *my* turn to take the lead off the bag, because if I don't, nobody else will.

This brings me to his last remark—and I have no clues. I am now so successfully confused, I can no longer make the distinctions that were once so simple. Why, for instance, I have been able to share a bed with Buddy, to whom I am welded for life, without once considering doing anything there beyond sleeping; while I have also shared a bed with Joanie, to whom I am equally as tied, yet very rarely get much sleeping done there at all. I am beginning to suspect that if I were to multiply Joanie by Buddy and divide by two, Jason would undoubtedly come out on the other side of the equal sign. This implies that either I am coming to terms with myself as a human being, or I am extremely fucked up. I mean, when Jase first showed up in the clubhouse, it's not as if I thought, "Boy, does he have a cute ass." Nor did I notice anything *else* about him that is usually reserved for discussion behind closed doors. What I saw was, having spent my whole life thinking I was the soli-

tary piece in a different jigsaw puzzle, I had found someone
who was the interlocking part—the piece with the sky on it.
And if I have to take that one extra step to make sure I
don't lose it . . .

"Would you do it?" asked Joel.
"Do what?"
"Sleep with him."
I glanced over at the cloud of cigarette smoke and tried
to get around answering. "Couldn't I just buy him a beer
and call it a night?" The usual frown. "I don't know." I
hesitated. "If it came to that, I might ask myself—" Suddenly I sat up, noticing for the first time the direction in
which we were going. "Joel, you're not going to talk me
out of this, are you?" I demanded, slightly panicked.
"Do you want me to?"
Suddenly it was a highly loaded question. "I don't
know."
He put out the cigarette and addressed me with sincere
concern, a tactic he actually uses once in a while. "Scotty,"
he said quietly, "I'm not trying to talk you into or out of
anything. What happens is immaterial. It's what *feels* right
that counts."
"Look, I'm a pitcher and I'm left-handed. You want to
tell me what that means in English?"
"We have to stop for now."

That's what *everything* means in English.

*　　*　　*

September 11—

Mound Conference

*(Versus Milwaukee. Mitchell Brokaw at bat. Scotty calls
time and signals Jason, who jogs out to the mound.)*

216   STEVE KLUGER

JASON *(raising his mask)*:   Problem?

SCOTTY: Question. Who's Mitchell Brokaw?

JASON *(reciting)*:   Just up from Triple-A. .327 average, .628 slugging percentage, 22 home runs, 18 walks.

SCOTTY *(amazed)*:   How do you know all that?

JASON: They flashed it on the scoreboard. You know, you *miss* a lot when you're facing the backstop.

SCOTTY: You do?

JASON: Uh-huh. But you know what else? You never complain. That's a very princely thing to do, Scotty. I'd be mad as hell.

SCOTTY *(in the dark)*:   About what?

JASON *(insistent)*:   About not being able to see what's on the scoreboard. *You* know—the scores and the beer ads and T-Shirt Night.

SCOTTY: Yeah, well I'll let you be my rearview mirror, okay? If you see anything up there that's important, you let me know.

JASON *(putting on his mask)*:   If they wanted to be fair, they'd turn some of these parks around, so that when you were on the mound, you'd really be facing the outfield.

SCOTTY *(somberly)*:   That's a very wise idea. Why don't you send it to the Commissioner?

JASON: Yeah. Yeah, maybe I will. Throw the curve, Scotty.

(He starts to leave; Scotty calls out after him.)

SCOTTY: Hey, Jase?

(Jason turns around.)

JASON: What?

CHANGING PITCHES   217

SCOTTY *(after a pause)*:　Nice eyes.

(There is a beat.)

JASON:　Thanks.

(He leaves.)

SCOTTY *(to himself)*:　I don't believe I said that. I don't *believe* I said that.

(Jason reaches the plate, crouches, squints up at the scoreboard, then stands and trots back to the mound.)

SCOTTY *(seeing him)*:　Uh-oh.

JASON *(reaching the mound)*:　Scotty?

SCOTTY *(nervously)*:　What?

JASON *(pointing to the scoreboard)*:　Next Friday. Jacket Night.

SCOTTY *(nodding)*:　Thanks.

(Jason returns to the plate, and they nail Brokaw on the curve.)

＊　＊　＊

September 12—

Periodically I find myself wondering whether or not Joel is truly legitimate. It just seems that his occasional lapses into self-contradiction and digression belie the piece of paper on his wall, and lead one to suspect that a year ago, he was really something else. A mailman, perhaps.

I have told him repeatedly that I believe it is a bad idea to discuss Jason with Joanie. His response?

"Have you ever noticed that the most important people in your life have names that begin with a *J?* What do you think that means?"

I think that means he's waiting for me to remember that his name is Joel.

On the surface, he tends to agree with me that there's no point in dragging Joanie into this when it clearly does not—yet—concern her. At the same time, however, he always seems to be pushing me in that direction, forcing me to weigh the possibility. Either he can't remember his lines, or he sees a golden opportunity to clean up on me, should he ever go into marriage counselling.

"Let me ask you something, Scotty," he says, lighting a match. "What's the first thing you feel when you think about Joanie?"

"Fear."

"Uh-huh. And what's the first thing you feel when you think about Jason?"

"Fear."

He frowns and puts out the match. "Something stinks," he observes.

In the event I didn't say it before, he also has a great deal of difficulty with his syntax.

* * *

September 13—

Buddy's issue of *Playgirl* finally hit the stands. According to a reliable poll—Joanie—his body has become the most popular piece of anatomical art since Mona Lisa first decided to smile.

Normally when something like this happens, you can pretty much expect not to be able to live it down, clubhouse-wise, for at least three seasons. Buddy is no different.

"Hey, Budlong," shouted Mickey Fowler, looking up from the centerfold. "Is this your ass? I thought it was your face."

"I heard they paid you ten dollars an inch," called out Joey Tobin.

"Big deal," retorted Skip Hatten. "How far can you get on twenty bucks?"

This lasted until after the game—when Buddy was mobbed by every woman in Washington, D.C. Assuming that he actually calls each one of the numbers that was left on his windshield, Chesapeake and Potomac Telephone will be able to cancel all the rest of their clients.

Yeah, we're still laughing.

Ha-ha.

* * *

September 14—

I finally told Joanie that all Joel and I do is argue for an hour. I tell him I'm right, and he tells me I'm full of shit.

"I don't get it," she frowns. "I do that all the time. How come you don't pay *me*?"

I should have seen *that* coming.

* * *

September 15—

The world came to an end for a change. But this time, it was for different reasons. I found out this evening that Jason's already in love with somebody else, and they're about three boxes of Minute Rice away from the altar. This means that if I had even a ghost of a chance before, I'm out of the running for good now.

I don't know much about her except that her name is Kristin, she lives in New York, and she's either very rich or she loves him a lot—because the phone call ran three hours, and New York to Milwaukee's a lot of message units.

I didn't intend to eavesdrop. I'd merely stopped by Jason's room to see if he wanted to hunt down some zucchini with me. The fact that the door was ajar was unfortunate; the one-sided dialogue from within even more so. I can only speculate on the other end of the conversation, but then you didn't exactly have to be Harry Houdini to figure it out anyway.

JASON: Milwaukee's Milwaukee. I just wish *you* were here, that's all.

KRIS: You think we're doing the right thing by getting married?

JASON: Of course we are. Tell you what. You go looking for an apartment, and when I get back, we'll put down a deposit, okay? Something near Central Park.

KRIS: How many bedrooms?

JASON *(chuckling)*: At least one.

KRIS: You know, some of those places don't allow children.

JASON: Then we'll have to find one that does. We *want* one, don't we?

KRIS: Uh-huh. What have you got in mind for a name?

JASON *(laughing)*: Kris, isn't it a little early for that?

KRIS: Come on, Jase.

JASON *(joking)*: *I* don't know. How about something classical? Either Sebastian or Juliet.

KRIS: That's awful. But I still love you.

JASON: I love you too.

CHANGING PITCHES   221

I found a zucchini place by myself—something which was ultimately immaterial, since I couldn't taste my food anyway. On the one hand, I'm miserable, and on the other, I'm relieved. If I was worried that I might have to do some soul-searching with Jason, that's out of the question now. At least I'm off the hook—no matter *what* Joel says. Then why do I feel so terrible?

Maybe it's because I hate the name Sebastian.

* * *

September 16—

I told Buddy that Jason was planning on marrying Kris, so he could forget about the whole problem.

"Why?" he said blankly. "What's changed?" Once in a while, Buddy likes to be obtuse.

"Don't be a schmuck," I told him. "It was bad enough before. You think I want to get involved in a triangle?" All he did was frown. "What's the matter?"

"Well, there's her, Jason, you, and J.J."

"So what?"

"Scotty, that's a square."

Sometimes I really appreciate having someone to talk to.

* * *

September 17—

One of the benefits of therapy, I thought, was that my nightmares would need no longer go unexplained. This is what I thought.

I recently dreamed that I had gotten on the Metro at the DuPont Circle station, and once the doors had closed,

STEVE KLUGER

discovered that I had become a prisoner. All I noticed was that I was the only passenger in the car, and that most of the advertisements on the walls were for retirement homes. As the train sped through the tunnel, refusing to slow down, I saw through the windows various scenes flashing in front of me on platforms along the route. Jason was making love to Joanie on one, while on another, Buddy was white-washing a billboard with my face on it, and pasting over it a much larger poster of Richard Nixon who, according to the print at the bottom, had just married Goldie Hawn. Further on, I saw myself in full uniform, locked in mortal combat with Darth Vader, who had just sawed me in two with his laser, and as my torso fell to the ground, Doug Hoyt leaned over me and shouted, "Yer out!"

I had begun to believe I was doomed for good, when it suddenly hit me. Of course! The steering wheel! I located it just where I'd expected it to be—right below the windshield—and after I'd made a left turn into the stadium parking lot, Jason came over to me and stuck his head in the window.

"Tokens are thirty cents," he snapped. "Hurry up."

"What do you think?" asked Joel.

I told him I took the whole thing as a good sign. I am obviously a layman at these things, but it was clear, even to me, that I'd had the strength to extract myself from danger without having to be rescued.

"What do *you* think?" I asked.

"I think you still haven't forgiven your father for tuning you out."

Sometimes I get the feeling that either I'm on the wrong channel, or he's reading last week's *TV Guide*.

* * *

I've been trying to get Jason to talk about Kris, but so far it's been like barking up a dead tree. My only recourse has been in the form of hinting, seeing as I would be hard-pressed to explain what I was doing with my ear pressed up to his keyhole in Milwaukee. For my opening, I choose the usual dialogue in which we presently engage, thanks to the *Metropolitan*'s article, whenever I've just given up a two-run homer.

"I *hate* this stupid game," I grumble, lying on top of a Minneapolis hotel bed in my gym shorts. Jason calls out from the bathroom, where he is brushing his teeth. Again.

"Say, Scotty, forget it," he calls out, attempting to wrest me from the mood of the moment. "What do you *really* want to be when you grow up?"

I fight off the impulse to reply, "Yours," when I suddenly see the chance of a lifetime. "Hell, I don't know." I shrug, pretending indifference. "All I really want's to have an apartment by the park." There is a pregnant pause. I can hear Jason spitting into the sink. "*Central* Park," I add darkly. The gargle. "One bedroom." That doesn't get anything out of him either, except the Lavoris, which is now en route to joining the toothpaste. "I thought maybe I'd have a couple of kids," I shout, a little exasperated. "A boy and a girl." Jason comes out of the bathroom, a towel around his neck.

"Hey, Scotty, you mind if I use your Old Spice? Mine's in the clubhouse."

It should come as no surprise that I flunked out of Innuendo 101 at Maryland.

* * *

Rich Bruder has officially made it to the big leagues. Statistically, of course, this happened the day he faced Reggie Jackson—but initiation by box score is not the same as initiation by clubhouse.

This afternoon he threw four innings of brilliant shutout relief and was convinced, as we all were, of his invincibility. The only one who seemed to express any doubt at all was Bob Delanoy.

"Aah, big deal," he shrugged, after the game. "Anybody with a strong arm could do that."

"Oh, yeah?" demanded Rich. "Could you?" As a matter of fact, Bob had set him up for just that opening. The rest of us, knowing what was coming, gathered around gleefully.

"Sure I could," retorted Delanoy. "If I can pick up three guys with one arm, I could shut out the Twins."

Rich, naturally, refused to believe he could pick up three men with one arm, which is what Bob was counting on. He called for two volunteers—me and Joey—to lie down on the floor with Bruder. Rich was in the middle, Tobin on one side, me on the other.

"Okay," said Bob, standing over us. "Scotty, you and Tobin lock arms around the kid. Bruder, you grab onto MacKay, then I'll lift all three of you."

Once this had been accomplished, Rich was effectively trapped between the two of us—and just as he was about to dare Delanoy again, realization flooded his face. "Oh, no," he groaned, squirming and unable to move.

Bob stepped back and addressed the rest of the team. "Gentlemen," he said politely, "he's all yours."

The guys were on him in seconds. His clothes were pulled off and his shoes tied together, while shaving cream, cologne, and other wet cosmetics within reach were poured—liberally—all over him. By the time we were

CHANGING PITCHES

through, Rich Bruder resembled The Thing That Wouldn't Die—and he *hated* it.

Welcome to the major leagues, Gator.

*　　*　　*

September 20—

The choice had been narrowed down to *Raiders of the Lost Ark, E. T.,* and *Star Wars.* Joanie and I have always been of the opinion that if Steven Spielberg and George Lucas had been put in charge of creating the heavens and the earth, they not only would have written a much tighter script, but the special effects would have been a lot better. As it happened, however, *Raiders* was playing clear out in Silver Spring, and the lines for *E. T.* were longer than my adolescence. This left us with the perennial standby.

I am ashamed to admit that, for once, I did not especially give a damn about Han Solo and the Millenium Falcon. Even the jump to hyperspace left me totally cold. I suppose I could have chalked it off to inevitable tedium— even with Luke Skywalker—but the fact of the matter was simply that, while my eyes were fixed, unseeing, on the screen, my thoughts were centered on my right arm, which was momentarily wrapped around J.J.

I don't know why I've been feeling so vulnerable lately—except it hurts. Joel would say that's a good sign— that I'm getting in touch with something. This is an easy observation for him to make, considering I'm the one who's depressed. I only know that every time I stare at Joanie, I have this insane urge to touch her, or to hold her, or to tell her I love her—as though I expected her to be taken from me at any minute and put into carbon freeze. It isn't too farfetched, either, because as open-minded as she is, there are certain limitations beyond which she might indeed feel well entitled to suggest I remove my name from our door-

　　　　　　STEVE KLUGER

bell. Sharing me with somebody else would undoubtedly be one of those eventualities. Sharing me with a catcher? Well, just add an exclamation point.

In the protective darkness of the movie theatre, I felt my arm grip her tightly—as though I were trying to shield her from the pain I was feeling. Love is the funniest damned thing. The closer you get, the more alienated you become. How simple it would be if only we could hang on to those earlier days, when commitment is a kite whose string has been broken, sending it free-floating into the lower atmosphere, visible, but still hovering above the horizon line, out of reach.

It's *always* easier when you're just starting out.

J.J. says she let me pick her up. I insist that she found me irresistibly overwhelming, so she had no choice.

"When do you want me to gag?" she says in response.

Actually, if you decided to be fair, it was pretty mutual—although at first, it didn't seem as if we were going to connect at all. After we'd met underneath Channel 5's weather map, she had said good-bye in a somewhat offhand manner and left the television studio before I could even offer to show her my barometer. When I followed her to the parking lot, she was indeed gone, leaving me to wonder if it was my breath or my personality that had offended her. It was neither, I found out; because just as I reached my car, I saw the piece of paper stuck underneath the windshield. It read: *Don't panic—you're being followed. Suggest we meet in neutral territory to discuss further game plan.* Sure enough, as soon as I had turned on my ignition, a pair of headlights filled my rearview mirror.

"You're so easy," I mumbled to myself, throwing the car into first.

We wound our way through the avenues of downtown Washington, heading for K Street, a silver Porsche and a red Firebird nosing south, trying to pretend they were merely close friends. I am convinced that the pilot of the police helicopter on patrol above us took one look and said to his partner, "*Some*body's not going home alone tonight." Somebody knew what he was talking about.

"How did you know which one was *my* car?" I asked, seated across from her in a booth at Mr. Natural's. Why I'd expected to be able to seduce her over a pair of celery milkshakes was beyond my comprehension. Joanie's too, for that matter.

"Your license plates," she replied, making a horrible face as she took a tentative sip. "Who else is going to have plates that say 'PITCHER'?"

Wise observation, I thought, grateful for no unexpected twists of Fate. One missed cue and she might have followed Ron Guidry all the way to New York.

"Can I ask you something?" I said, looking her right in the eye. "Why?"

"Because." The logic was inescapable.

"That's it?" I asked, simultaneously bewildered and amused.

"That's it."

Which is how we wound up in front of my fireplace. Which is how we wound up going to bed on Friday night and not getting up until Tuesday morning. And which is how, coincidentally, we wound up falling in love along the way. Because that *was* it. For both of us.

In the beginning, commitment was something to be discussed—like death—when one was feeling masochistic. There were no strings at all for that first year. When we were together, we were together, and when we weren't, we weren't. When I learned that J.J. had gone out with a buyer for Lord and Taylor, it didn't bother me one bit. I even commended her on their line of men's shirts. When she found out that I'd had dinner with a Delta Airlines stewardess, she was overjoyed. And when we were together, lying in one another's arms, we even learned not to wonder whether or not we'd had an understudy the night

STEVE KLUGER

before. Isn't it wonderful to be so civilized?

"Scotty, I hate this," she finally exploded. "Know what I did last night? I'll tell you what I did last night. I fell asleep listening to your telephone ringing."

"Oh, yeah?" I retorted, putting aside my sushi. "How about Thursday?"

"What about it?"

"You said you had a Coke rehearsal."

"I did," she insisted.

"For eight hours?" I was livid. "Who wrote it, Eugene O'Neill? Where were you?"

"Where were *you?*" she snapped.

The following morning, we went looking for an apartment—two days later, we signed the lease. Lord and Taylor is now buying elsewhere, and as for Delta Airlines—well, they're still ready when I am, only these days I prefer to fly American.

If there is one thing in my life I have done right, it is J.J. If there is one decision I have never regretted making, it is loving her freely, without reservation, and with everything that isn't nailed to the very walls of my heart. Perhaps this is why Jason has become such an overwhelming threat. He has borrowed—no, he has stolen—what once belonged to her alone. And that makes it wrong. Doesn't it? Were it not for Joanie, Jason would not be an issue. Because of her, he is.

There is a clue in here someplace. I wish I knew what it was.

"Scotty, what's bothering you?"

The film had ended, the Imperial Death Star had once again been detonated, and we were walking by the reflecting pool beneath the Washington Monument. I knew I wasn't going to give her a direct answer; I debated whether or not to give her an answer at all.

"Nothing," I finally lied. Her rebuke came in silence, and she was right. I owed her more than that.

"Joanie," I said quietly, kicking a pebble into the water. "Did you ever notice how apples make better sliders than limes? Did you ever wonder why Melville didn't make Moby Dick a shark?" She was very much in the dark. I don't blame her.

"It never occurred to me."

"Me either," I sighed. "That's what's bothering me."

We took a few more steps before she turned. Apprehension—clearly. "Scotty," she began bravely, "is it another woman?"

"No," I said emphatically. "Joanie, I swear to you it's not another woman."

Her face broke into a relieved smile. "Things are looking up." She sighed, taking my hand. "You know, if it was, I'd understand."

For the first time all evening, I grinned. "No, you wouldn't," I told her, putting an arm around her shoulder.

After a moment, she grudgingly conceded. "No, I wouldn't," she mumbled.

Against my better judgment, I laughed.

"You want to go for dessert?" she asked, changing the subject.

I was, by then, feeling malicious. "Celery shakes?"

The immediate frown. "Dessert, Scotty. *You* know—banana chip, rocky road."

"That *is* dessert," I protested.

"Scotty," retorted she, "that's a salad."

Arms around one another, we walked back toward the car, en route to Mr. N's. Halfway to the curb, J.J. stopped and turned to me.

"Scotty," she said quietly, "when you feel like talking, I wish you would." She briefly put a hand up to my face and smiled. "You can tell me anything, you know?"

If only I could believe her.

*   *   *

From Doug Hoyt:

𝕿𝖍𝖊 𝖂𝖆𝖘𝖍𝖎𝖓𝖌𝖙𝖔𝖓 𝕭𝖚𝖑𝖑𝖊𝖙𝖎𝖓

THE STANDINGS

American League East

	W	L	Pct.	GB
Baltimore	94	60	.610	—
Washington	92	61	.601	1½
New York	88	65	.575	5½
Detroit	87	67	.565	7
Milwaukee	85	70	.548	9½
Toronto	83	71	.539	11
Cleveland	81	72	.529	12½
Boston	79	75	.513	15

●

This gives us a week to overtake the Orioles and achieve the impossible. First place. Considering that this isn't the Twilight Zone, it's difficult to believe that we're that close to doing it. Of course, I keep my pessimistic speculations to myself and let the banter around the clubhouse say it instead. "Fuck the Orioles" and "Baltimore Bites It" are standards, along with the general consensus that the Washington Senators have it all sewn up.

If only I could believe them.

* * *

Jason thinks Oliver Twist was a schmuck.

"They had schmucks in those days, didn't they?" he asks. I nod. It is his contention that being an orphan wàs the kid's first mistake; doing it in England was the second.

"If he'd been born in New York," he insists, "none of that stuff would have happened. They have Little Leagues. They have libraries."

"They also have orphanages," I remind him.

"Yeah, but they call them private schools."

He has been attempting to cross-pollinate the Dickens book with *Wuthering Heights*, holding that, if Twist had to ally himself with an unorthodox mentor, Fagin was definitely the wrong choice.

"Now if he had wound up with Heathcoate," says Jason, "he might have turned out all right. He'd have been a *spooky* little kid, but he'd have turned out all right."

Jason is making me tick. I don't know why—but I can now keep time better than a quartz crystal. This comes from learning how to look at the world through the wrong end of his kaleidoscope and finding my balance while I'm doing it. Maybe because I'm suddenly asking questions I've never asked before. Maybe because, instead of waking up to find I've gone over the hill in my sleep, I'm beginning to feel like the new kid on the block. Is it confidence? Is it karma? After all of this, is there really a reason? Sure there is. Because the kid *should* have wound up with Heathcliffe and because they *do* have Little Leagues in New York, and even if he *wasn't* born in England, it wouldn't matter because Oliver Twist was a schmuck anyway.

I think I'm losing my mind.

* * *

STEVE KLUGER

It's funny how the most meaningless combination of words can move mountains—how a casual remark can turn into the cure-all that sets everything right. Like a car horn that has been stuck for three hours while countless excursions under the hood have proven fruitless—only to have matters settled by a hair pin.

I was beginning to feel like a first-class Judas because of Joanie. Despite Joel's suggestions and Buddy's proddings, I had not been able to tell her about Jason, only because there didn't seem to be much point in upsetting two of us, when *one* couldn't seem to do the job right. And so it was pain I felt rather than joy when she told me last night that she loved me more than Luke Skywalker.

"Is that good?" asks Joel.

I glare at him. "Are you kidding? It's like you telling somebody you love her more than Jung."

It was at that moment that Joel Humphries set me up for the biggest hit of my life, and I was the prize clay pigeon.

"Then why don't you level with her?" he demanded.

As soon as he asked the question, I was on my feet, enraged. All I saw was Joanie—the sweatshirts, the commercials, the apricots, and me—and all I knew was that some unnamed force was gathering deadly speed and finally compelling me to tell her something that would not only destroy her, but us as well. And that was when I made my fatal mistake.

"Don't you understand?" I screamed. "Don't you get it? I want to marry her!" I heard the words at the same time he did, yet our reactions were entirely different. He was smiling cryptically; *my* mouth, on the other hand, was hanging open in slack-jawed shock.

I didn't know that.

I suppose I wasn't too surprised. For all of my various reasons for *not* getting married, I had just been brutally shoved face to face with the only reason that counts: I want to—and that automatically renders caution a lie. I want to more than I've ever wanted anything in my life. More than winning the Cy Youngs, more than pitching a no-hitter, more than eating Jay Bass's goddamned tapioca. Perhaps if Jason hadn't come along, I'd still be living in my vast network of deception—but thanks to Buddy's broken arm and Cleveland's overabundance of catchers, I have just been spared another thirty-six years of single tax exemptions. Because Joel was right.

The problem isn't Jason. The problem never *was* Jason. The problem is me.

Is there any reason I have gone through my whole life without committing myself to anyone? Is there any reason that the only thing I've permitted myself to feel close to is a fastball? No. And yes.

So whom do I blame for nearly having my life taken away from me when I was eight? My parents? God? Fine. I'll have all three of them open a vein. You'd think I'd have had ample opportunity to get over it by now, wouldn't you? And while we're on the subject, there's my father—okay, so he tuned out. He was still there, wasn't he? Did he beat me? Or did he buy me the cleats and the bats and the gloves while Tommy Higgins had to wrestle with bicycle chains? Is he supposed to be condemned forever because I wore him out too soon?

And what *about* Tommy Higgins? Isn't it conceivable that with so little effort, I could have talked him into a coaching spot? Talked to him, period? Naaah, forget it. Who wants to get that close? Besides, he was a lot happier weighing in chopped sirloin at $1.89 a pound, wasn't he? Or Buddy. When was the last time I lifted the world off of *his* shoulders? But, hey—that's Buddy. He's self-sufficient. Everybody knows that. Come on Buddy, catch—*Oomph!* No, it's not a medicine ball—just my latest neuroses. Could you wash them, dry them, air them out, and have them back to me by noon? And if I'm out to lunch again, just leave them with the doorman, okay?

So what does it all mean? It means that I'm thirty-six years old, and I'm still waiting for the whole world to strand me at Pinkney Park.

Get over it, Scotty.

It also means that I was so frightened of being a complete person, I let Tommy Higgins die. It means that I love Buddy so deeply and so unwillingly, that when he was knocked out of commission, I had to hate Jason to keep from feeling the depth of my loss. And it means that when I came that close to asking Joanie if she would share my life, I had to fall in *love* with Jason to make sure I'd be running in the opposite direction.

No, it isn't Jason. It's the wooden puppet who wears the number 37. And like it or not, somebody with a wand has just turned him into a real little boy. Nerve endings, pain sensors and all.

It isn't Jason. It's me.

"Is that all there is?" I asked, shaking like a leaf.

"Well, you get the general idea, anyway," cracked the smug shrink.

"Then the only reason I fell in love with Cornell was because I was afraid of marrying Joanie?"

He shrugged into his cloud of smoke. "Give or take a few hang-ups. It's called transference."

"Why didn't you tell me this before?" I wailed.

"Because you wouldn't have believed me." After a pause, he added, "You've always had the power to return to Kansas."

I stared down at the floor and nodded slowly. "Fuck you," I replied.

That, I think, is what they call solving a problem. Oh, there are still a number of issues to be settled. First priority is Joanie. We're going to have to do something about her monograms. Soon. Then, of course, there's Jason. I can't undo the fact that I love him, and I don't really know if I *want* it undone—because now that it doesn't mean what I thought it did, maybe it won't stand in our way anymore. Joel has always thought I should tell him, and I'm beginning to see his point. Right after I pitch my next no-hitter. I'm not *that* well yet.

The shrink also says that, emotional bloodshed or not, I've come out of this thing way ahead of everybody else. While being in love with another guy is no longer something with which I am concerned, I now possess that capability should the need ever arise. He says it's a rare faculty for a person to have.

With all due respect to the sweethearts of Sigmund Freud, I hope he'll forgive me if I leave that off of my roster of specialties the next time I'm interviewed by *Sports Illustrated*.

*   *   *

September 26—

Vegas odds say the Senators are going to fall just short of beating out the Orioles for first place in the division. Jason, on the other hand, believes the Vegas people should stick to keno.

"Don't you think we're asking a little bit much?" I point out. "I mean, going from the bottom to the top in one season."

Jason shrugs. "Why not? *You* did it, Scotty. You think *we* can't?" He pauses before making the challenge. "I'll tell you what. Ten bucks says we pull it off."

"You're on," I reply.

We shake hands somberly; and as Jason turns away, he leaves me with a parting shot. "You're going to lose, Scotty."

I like the sound of that.

* * *

October 1—

DO NOT REMOVE

From Doug Hoyt:

𝔗𝔥𝔢 𝔚𝔞𝔰𝔥𝔦𝔫𝔤𝔱𝔬𝔫 𝔅𝔲𝔩𝔩𝔢𝔱𝔦𝔫

THE STANDINGS

American League East

	W	L	Pct.	GB
Baltimore	98	64	.605	—
Washington	98	64	.605	—
New York	90	72	.556	8
Detroit	90	72	.556	8
Milwaukee	88	74	.543	10
Toronto	87	75	.537	11
Cleveland	84	78	.519	14
Boston	82	80	.506	16

* * *

The Washington Bulletin

SENATORS FACE ORIOLES IN
DIVISION PLAYOFF

October 1—Washington, D.C.
—With the Senators' victory today over the Toronto Blue Jays,
along with the Orioles' loss to
Cleveland, Washington and Baltimore have pulled into a tie for
first place in the American
League East. The division-decid-
ing one-game playoff will be held
tomorrow at Senators Stadium at
1:00 p.m. EDT. League Playoffs
begin Tuesday at Dodger Stadium between the Los Angeles
Dodgers and the Philadelphia
Phillies in the National League,
and on Wednesday in the home
park of the American League
Eastern Division champions versus the Kansas City Royals.

* * *

October 2—

I knew in advance that last night I was going to ask
Joanie to marry me. I didn't know *how* I was going to do it,
but I knew that the time had come. Actually, I had several
alternatives, all bad—flowers were trite, candy worse, and
hiring an airplane to spell it out over the Tidal Basin was
too expensive. I even contemplated taking her to Yuet
Sun's and bringing along a fortune cookie whose message I
had pulled out with a safety pin, substituting one of my
own. I opted for multiple choice—(e) none of the above—
only because Joel would say I was trying to remain in control by being cute. When the words come, they come.
Period.

We had dinner on the floor; we both disdain dining

room convention. The menu was sushi and alfalfa muffins, something that touched me to no end because she was the one who made the muffins, entrusting me with the sushi despite my track record. Neither of us said much while we were eating. *I* knew what was going to happen, and I'm fairly certain she had a pretty good idea too, as it was one of those rare occasions when I didn't make any jokes about our food swimming up the Potomac. The last time that happened was the night I'd suggested that we live together.

When we had finished with the dishes, she was the one who took *my* hand and led me into the bedroom. That was obviously where we'd been heading all night, so nobody actually had to make the overture. I lost track of how many times we made love to each other—not that it was important, as I was unconscious of anything else in my life except Joanie. All I did know was that I permitted myself, for the first time, to give and take in equal measure, so that when we finally fell back on one another, spent, I felt—with more than a little wonder—that there was the distinct possibility I had just become a man.

"Joanie?" I whispered. Her head was buried in my neck, her arms wrapped around my chest.

"What?"

"You want to marry me?" There was a long silence, which I took for indecision, until I realized that my shoulder was wet.

"Yes."

That was all.

We began dozing, lightly at first, and then slipped into the darker blanket of slumber. Just before I succumbed, I heard her voice once more, softly, as though she were talking to herself.

"I love you, Scotty."

"I love *you*."

MORAL: If this is what taking a risk is all about, I have spent my whole life living in a tree.

October 2—

Dear Mr. MacKay,

A couple of months ago, I met my fiancée, Judy. It was love from the start, so it didn't take long before I'd popped the question. We planned on getting married around Thanksgiving, so I thought I had it all sewn up. Then last week we saw you signing autographs on the Mall. All she talked about for the rest of the night was your designer jeans, your blue sweater, and the gold chain. The next day, she called off the whole thing.

Thanks a lot, pal.

Tom Hastings

Dear Mr. MacKay:

Every year, our school selects a member of the national community, whom we believe we would feel comfortable having our children emulate, to speak at our annual Father-Son Banquet. Our guests have ranged from politicians to industrialists to an occasional movie actor. This year, our choice was fairly simple, although quite frankly we have never selected an athlete before. However, when we took into account leadership, dedication, and a sense of fair play, the vote was unanimous.

Do you know how we could get in touch with Joe Montana?

Very truly yours,
Kenneth MacArthur
St. Michael's Academy

Dear Mr. MacKay,

Last Saturday during the Sabbath service, we interrupted our reading from the Torah in order to listen to the last inning of the Senators game. *This is not as blasphemous as it sounds—Cantor Rosenfeld and I are both fans, as is half our congregation—and by Genesis 6, there were so many transistor radios plugged into so many ears, we didn't have much of an audience anyway.*

Mr. MacKay, even at our various weddings and bar mitzvahs, I have never seen as much joy under one roof as there was during the final out. The cantor and I discussed it at length afterwards, and decided that, even though you are already spoken for, we would like to make you an honorary Jew. Services will be the second Saturday in November. Please come.

> *Best wishes,*
> *Rabbi Harold Goldman*

Dear Mr. MacKay,
Thank you for your recent application for an American Express Gold Card. We are sorry to inform you that, based on the information you have provided, you do not qualify.
Please do not take this personally. We are very selective.

> *Sincerely,*
> *Mrs. M. Satara*
> *New Accounts*

Dear Scotty,
You don't know me, but I've been a Senators fan my whole life. I am nine. I'm sending you the red rabbit's foot because the green one turned yellow in the washing machine, and maybe it doesn't work anymore. Anyway, I am the only one in my class who wants you to win, because everybody else is for the Orioles. If you do win, I'll probably get beat up, but I don't care.

> *Signed,*
> *Brian Denny*

Dear Mr. MacKay,

I read in Marilyn Beck's column that you live with a tele-vision actress. Is this true? If it is, are you serious or is it just temporary? I know it is none of my business, but I always thought if we ever met, it would be like fireworks. I'm only 16, but I am very mature for my age. Think about it.

> *Love always,*
> *Linda Leck*

Dear Mr. MacKay,

The only reason I'm writing this is because sometimes I have a lot of trouble saying things, and anyway if I get em-barrassed, you can't see it this way.

When they first traded me, I thought I was going to hate it. I know this makes me sound like a schmuck (your word), but I figured I knew it all, and being on a last-place team would probably drag me down. I also thought I was going to hate you, on account of all the awards, and also because I never knew anybody famous who wasn't a pain in the ass (my word). And this was even before you were being pissy to me at the beginning, when I really thought I was going to hate you. But when we started playing together and I'd go out to the mound and make you throw the curve even if you didn't want to, you listened to me. You really did—not just pretended to, like some of these other guys who say okay, but you know they're really thinking fuck you (both of our words). It was like, hey, I'm just a couple of batting titles and this guy's Hall of Fame, but he's letting me do my job and not just block the plate, which is what a lot of people think is all I'm supposed to do. It made me feel like I was a part of something—and not just the team either. Like you really needed me, you know?

Also the other thing is—and this is the part I probably couldn't say to your face—I'm proud of you, Scotty. And not just the way everybody always says the word without thinking about what it means. Know how many guys would have had the guts and a couple of other things to go for a comeback at 36? And with a new pitch? I'll give you a hint— exactly none. But you did it. And the reason you did it wasn't just because you're good anyway, but because you believed in yourself. And when that sometimes wasn't enough, you believed in me. So Scotty, when they ask you how you made it back to the top and you tell them what you always do, that is was half you and half me, I'll make out like I believe it. But just between us, you were there first.

Anyway, I figured you ought to know that when I grow up, I want to be just like you. Hey, that's only a joke, okay?

> *Very truly yours,*
> *Jason Cornell*

*   *   *

October 2—

He *does* love me. Know what? It isn't scary anymore. Know what else? I'm going to tell him.

October 3—

		R	H	E		
					BALL	1
BALTIMORE	000 000 00	0	0	0	STRIKE	2
WASHINGTON	000 001 00	1	6	0	OUT	2

My timing, as usual, left a great deal to be desired. However, there are certain eventualities that can only be postponed for so long, and as far as Jason went, my statute of limitations had just expired. The fact that we were one strike away from sewing up both the game and the division was immaterial. The fact that the same out also represented the last hurdle standing between me and that evasive no-hitter was equally unimportant. What mattered most was the guy behind the plate, whose compassion, whose unyielding optimism, and yeah, whose heart, had put me back on magazine covers. And all because I was able to love him.

The preceding eight innings had been a fantasy trip through Space Mountain, The Haunted Mansion, and Pirates of the Caribbean combined. Jason smelled a no-hitter in the fourth when I challenged Kenny Singleton with a 3–2 fastball; Singleton, apparently, was betting his life on a 3–2 curve. After he had gone down looking, Jason trotted out to the mound and removed his mask thoughtfully.

"That's the ball game, Scotty," he'd said—and from that moment on, it was in the bag. Not because I was supremely confident, but because Jason was.

Which brings me to the ninth inning, two out, a 1–0 lead, and Rich Dauer at the plate with a two-strike count—Dauer, whose clutch home runs have kept the Orioles on top since April. For the first time all afternoon, I hesitated. This is where they always get me. Remember Boston? I had a no-hitter going there too. One more out was all I needed. Then *Pow!* But even there, we were merely fighting for last place. This was something else entirely.

I stared down the pipe into Jason's eyes, looking not for a sign, but for the assurances I always find there. Those eyes had gotten me through twenty-six batters; yet now, with so much on the line, I needed more. More than just a smile, more than just an encouraging word. Because as Dauer took a few practice swings, I realized the time had come for me to gamble—and I knew if I didn't, I'd come to the end of the line. No more second chances.

Jason, Dauer. It was all the same thing.

PROPOSITION: It is better to take a risk and steal second than it is to spend the rest of your life safe at first.

I raised a hand and called time.

Mound Conference

(Versus Baltimore, 1–0 in the ninth. Rich Dauer is at bat; Scotty is pitching a no-hitter.)

JASON *(raising his mask, worried)*:   Are you all right?

SCOTTY *(with no false moves)*:   Jason, I've got to talk to you. *(Pause.)* Do you have a minute?

JASON *(incredulously)*:   Do I *what*?

SCOTTY: Jase, do you remember Ron Miller—that guy I told you about? The shortstop who was hung up on his second baseman?

JASON *(groaning)*:   Scotty, you picked a hell of a time to play Rona Barrett.

SCOTTY *(slowly)*:   Jason, it was *me*. *(Pause.)* And you're him.

(There is a long moment of silence, as Jason stares at Scotty.)

JASON *(shrugging)*:   *I* know that.

(Scotty is astounded.)

SCOTTY *(irritably)*:   What do you mean, you *know* that?

JASON: What do I look, stupid or something? There *is* no shortstop named Ron Miller. *(Pause.)* Tell you what. Fan this guy and I'll *marry* you, okay?

SCOTTY *(disappointedly)*:   Aren't you even upset?

JASON *(agitated)*:   Scotty, if I faint, will you strike out Dauer?

(They stare at each other for a long moment.)

SCOTTY *(pensively)*:   Curve?

JASON *(shrugging)*:   Naah, we got more class than that. Nail him on the knuckler, Scotty.

(He puts on his mask and starts back toward the plate. Scotty calls out after him.)

SCOTTY: Jase?

(Jason turns.)

JASON: What?

SCOTTY *(troubled)*:   You know, this is awfully anticlimactic.

JASON *(nodding)*:   I'll make a deal with you. After the game, I'll belt you in the mouth, okay? Will that make you feel any better?

(He returns to the plate.)

I wasn't so much dazed as I was relieved. I'd actually told him and lived. What's more, judging from the slight smile on his face as he crouched behind Dauer, it really *hadn't* been a surprise. Only to me. Oh sure, we've got a lot to talk about—later. But for now, at least, the earth is once again rotating on its axis. Business, they say, as usual.

I dug into the rubber and took my stance. Dauer was a genuine threat, all right, but then I had Jason on my side, along with a lot more. On the other hand, there *was* the matter of the knuckleball. That elusive pitch—the ultimate risk. One slipped digit, and it's Boston all over again.

Dauer leaned over the plate, bat raised.

Jason crossed his fingers.

Ready on the left, ready on the right. No time to be afraid, Scotty. What did Joel say about fear itself? No, that was Roosevelt.

The windup.

The stretch . . .

*   *   *

𝕿𝖍𝖊 𝖂𝖆𝖘𝖍𝖎𝖓𝖌𝖙𝖔𝖓 𝕭𝖚𝖑𝖑𝖊𝖙𝖎𝖓

MacKay
No-Hits Birds

THEY
DO IT!

* * *

DO NOT REMOVE

From Doug Hoyt:

𝕿𝖍𝖊 𝖂𝖆𝖘𝖍𝖎𝖓𝖌𝖙𝖔𝖓 𝕭𝖚𝖑𝖑𝖊𝖙𝖎𝖓

FINAL BASEBALL STANDINGS

American League East

	W	L	Pct.	GB
Washington	99	64	.607	—
Baltimore	98	65	.601	1
New York	90	72	.556	8½
Detroit	90	72	.556	8½
Milwaukee	88	74	.543	10½
Toronto	87	75	.537	11½
Cleveland	84	78	.519	14½
Boston	82	80	.506	16½

At Washington

Baltimore	ab	r	h	bi		Washington	ab	r	h	bi
Singleton, rf	3	0	0	0		Cornell, c	4	1	2	0
Sakata, ss	3	0	0	0		Budlong, lf	4	0	2	0
Dwyer, lf	3	0	0	0		Wright, ss	4	0	0	0
Murray, 1b	3	0	0	0		Tobin, 3b	3	0	1	1
Ayala, dh	3	0	0	0		Delanoy, dh	3	0	0	0
Dempsey, c	3	0	0	0		Jackson, cf	4	0	1	0
Bumbry, cf	3	0	0	0		Fowler, 2b	3	0	0	0
Ripken, 3b	3	0	0	0		Petry, rf	3	0	0	0
Dauer, 2b	3	0	0	0		Hatten, 1b	3	0	0	0
Totals	27	0	0	0			31	1	6	1

CHANGING PITCHES

BALTIMORE	000	000	000	0
WASHINGTON	000	001	00x	1

BALTIMORE

	IP	H	R	ER	BB	SO
Parker (L, 14–8)	8	6	1	1	2	4

WASHINGTON

	IP	H	R	ER	BB	SO
MacKay (W, 21-6)	9	0	0	0	0	7

DP—Baltimore, 2 LOB—Washington, 5   2B—Cornell SF—Tobin Time
—2:56 Attendance—57,012

* * *

October 3—

The Washington Bulletin

To the Editor:
They say that sometimes you have to take the bad with the good. Maybe that's so, but if you're a Senators fan, you've always had to take the bad with the bad. I guess we used to complain a lot that we never had a winner, and now that we do, there's a lot of us who owe them an apology. Well, the line forms here.
Sorry, guys. I didn't mean any of it.

DAVID JALOWSKY
Rockville Center, MD

To the Editor:
Do you suppose if Doug Hoyt were elected President, he could do something about the economy too?

MARY LOU WESTERFIELD
Broomes Island, MD

To the Editor:
What is all this talk about pennants? Everybody *knows* they'll fold in the clutch. Look at the '78 Red Sox. Look at the '80 Royals. Oh, and '79—good show, Baltimore. Nice way to rise to the occasion, Baltimore.

Bring on the Redskins, I say.

ERNIE GREEN
Upper Marlboro, MD

To the Editor:
About that woman from Pittsburgh who called us savages. Okay, maybe we do get a little carried away—like cheering until we're hoarse. Maybe we do shout a couple of things that we shouldn't. But I don't know. If manners are so important, what are the Pirates doing in last place when we're in first?

ANDY BURSTEIN
Lanham, MD

To the Editor:
In 1955, a lot of people said the Giants were going to do it because Brooklyn was a bunch of bums. Then *everybody* started laughing at the Dodgers—until they won the World Series. It doesn't mean anything, but I thought you'd like to know.

STEVIE SOLOMON
Georgetown, Washington, DC

To the Editor:
My daddy almost moved us away from here because he said the baseball team was a crying shame. Guess what? He just bought a new house and we're not going anywhere.

BEVERLY SMALLEY
Anne Arundel, MD

To the Editor:

If George Washington were still around, he'd say the Senators were "first in war, first in peace, first to holler, 'We win!'"

JOAN DANTO
Hagerstown, MD

To the Editor:

Somebody ought to buy those guys a drink. I don't know how they did it, when everybody *knew* that they couldn't but if you ask me, they're living proof that it pays to dream. Boy, do we need them now.

ALLEN GREENE
Baltimore, MD

* * *

STEVE KLUGER

𝔗𝔥𝔢 𝔚𝔞𝔰𝔥𝔦𝔫𝔤𝔱𝔬𝔫 𝔅𝔲𝔩𝔩𝔢𝔱𝔦𝔫

HAIL TO THE CHAMPIONS!

How The Good Guys Finally Won

BY MARK LITVIN
Washington Bulletin Staff Writer

It has happened. To a very grateful city and to a ball club that wouldn't die, it has happened. And when we wake up tomorrow morning, convinced that our immortality was a brief excursion from reality, we need only take a second look at the bunting draped all across Washington, D.C., to know that we have arrived. Finally.

To those with keen memories, it was only six weeks ago that Senators fans first began permitting themselves to think the unthinkable. True, the June swoon had, for once, passed over the city, unnoticed and unheeded, like a truant cloud on its way to the storm. And perhaps the dog days of August *had* slipped away, more a whimper than a bark. But first place? Suddenly one could empathize with Moses, who had stood on the banks of the Red Sea, staff raised and thinking to himself, "Is this really going to work?" Yet, such is the stuff of miracles; and as one cynic was moved to admit, "Today the Senators, tomorrow the Cubs."

There has not been a time in
See Senators Page Three

CHANGING PITCHES

recent history when an entire city has been quite so unified by singlemindedness. Petty grievances have been put aside, enmities temporarily shelved. Along Constitution Avenue, strangers discuss standings on street corners, while across town, dinners are going uncooked, meetings unattended, and vacant storefronts are explaining their absence of occupancies in signs which read CLOSED. GONE TO BALL GAME. It seems that "home" is no longer a dwelling defined by deeds and mortgages—for until further notice, it has been relocated to a handful of acreage at Florida and Georgia Avenues.

And behind those walls . . .

Scotty Does It

Perhaps it is only fitting that the man who put the candles on the cake is the same one who couldn't get himself arrested six months ago. So much has been written recently on the comeback of Scotty MacKay, his first career no-hitter was almost superfluous; less a surprise and more a celebration. A triumph, really. A triumph of will that guaranteed there *would* be a tomorrow. For him. For us.

MacKay is no longer the stuff of wonder or awe. He has proven that he is a man who is not afraid to take a chance—and 86 pitches against Baltimore proved it. There are those who still claim that Scotty MacKay is a fluke, and perhaps some of us once felt the same way. It is strongly suggested that we hop into our Edsels and go for a long drive.

Orioles Flutter

Of course, it was MacKay who stole the whole show. The lanky 6-foot-2 lefthander took the mound in the first inning with a poised yet cocky calm that clearly seemed to say, "Goodbye Birds, Hello Playoffs." Baltimore, in fact, didn't have a chance. MacKay was simply overpowering. Five strikeouts after he had fanned the first batter, he seemed to be gathering strength, rather than losing it, from each successive pitch that left his glove. And when Rich Dauer stepped up to the plate representing the 27th out, it was all over. The cheering began on ball one. It crescendoed on the next two strikes, and when Dauer's bat missed the 1–2 knuckler by more than a foot, it wasn't shouting you heard—it was nuclear fission. Grown men wept, strangers embraced one another, and Washington, D.C., the city that was previously

See Senators Page Five

STEVE KLUGER

known for its senators and not its Senators, found itself in the winner's circle, courtesy of 25 men who refused to give up.

It's All In The Team

And what a supporting cast. The somewhat nerve-rending 1–0 score was helped along by key singles courtesy of catcher Jason Cornell and left fielder Buddy Budlong, the former scoring the game's only run on a sacrifice fly by third baseman Joey Tobin. This was the same Joey Tobin whose diving catch of a Ken Singleton bunt in the seventh saved MacKay from the afternoon's only serious threat. But that's what they call teamwork, and that's why October has finally come to the Capitol city for something other than Hallowe'en.

It should also be noted that the Royals, the Western Division champions, had expected to face Baltimore in the American League Playoffs. If reports are true, when they learned that the opener would be played on the banks of the Potomac and not the Patapsco, champagne was poured. They claim we cannot field. They swear we cannot hit, and they really believe that our pitching won't stand up under the light of day. As an addendum, they also remind us smugly that everything's up-to-date in Kansas City.

Not quite.

The Handwriting On The Wall

Because it has finally happened. For the millions of tears that have been shed, for the millions of cheers that have reverberated through a city whose name, until now, has been angst, for a population that has never stopped believing, and for the boys of summer who have never known the autumn crocus, it has happened. The Day of Reckoning has arrived—and the meek have inherited the earth.

* * *

October 4—

Except it's never over when you think it's over. . . .

Jason and I were seated alone on the dugout bench in our street clothes. The champagne had been poured, the flashbulbs had snapped; and while the rest of the team had

CHANGING PITCHES

taken leave of the premises in favor of a victory celebration at Giorgio's, my catcher and I had hung back, preferring instead to watch dusk settle over Washington, D.C., from the sanctity of a stadium we called home.

We didn't say anything for the longest time—but the silence was not uncomfortable. It was a quiet moment between two people who share a lot more than a division title. Yet, knowing there were still a few matters to resolve, I was the one who spoke first.

"So what do we do now?" I asked quietly.

Jason shrugged. "How about a third Cy Young?"

In spite of myself, I couldn't help chuckling. "That's not what I meant," I reminded him.

Jason turned to me slowly, a look of serious concern on his face. "Scotty," he said quietly, "why didn't you tell me? I would have understood."

That was when it all came out. That awful day on the mound against Kansas City, the nightmares, trying to tell him, trying not to tell him, Joel. And as I sat there for an hour, flexing the muscles I'd discovered in the freedom of the spoken word, I realized at last that what it had all boiled down to was the simple fear of losing him. Nothing more. Jason responded with an exasperated sigh.

"Scotty, you should be ashamed of yourself," he said flatly. "You know me better than that."

I shrugged in self-defense. "What good would it have done?" I replied reasonably. "I have Joanie, you have Kris. So why bring it up at all? It'd only mean trouble, right?"

Jason seemed to freeze for a long moment, as though I had just poured ice water down his back. His features wore a look of confusion mixed with apprehension. "You know about Kris?" he said in a small voice.

"Yeah," I told him. "I heard you on the phone in Milwaukee. How do you think *she'd* feel?"

There was a brief double-take on Cornell's part before

STEVE KLUGER

he began to smile. And in seconds, the smile had turned into a resonating laugh.

"You don't know about Kris."

By now, I was thoroughly bewildered. "I know you're in love with her, aren't you?"

He leaned in toward me and put a gentle hand on my shoulder, all traces of mirth gone. "Scotty," he began earnestly, "think hard. Did you see *Inside Sports* last month?" My mind raced. August, September, Boswell's piece—oh, yeah. Pigskin.

"The football preview," I replied. "Why?"

"Remember who was on the cover?"

Helmets. Blue and white. "That quarterback for the Giants," I said automatically. "Chris Brody."

Whoa.

The words reached my ears a fraction of a second after I had said them. Even so, there was only so much I could absorb in a given afternoon. The no-hitter, the division title, telling Jason, and now this. Of course, it all began assembling itself immediately, like a jigsaw puzzle whose pieces have whirled into place courtesy of a summer zephyr. Chris—the neutergenderous name I'd heard over a hotel transom in Wisconsin. And naturally *I'd* thought—

Jason. *That's* what he'd been trying to tell me on the flight back from Philadelphia. That's what he'd meant when he'd said his best friend was a football player, and that's why he'd never told anybody he was in love. That's also why he'd taken my news so well. I thought he'd regard it as alien corn, when apparently he'd been reaping it all along. And yet maybe, after all, I didn't understand him correctly.

"You mean—?" I asked, pointing to him.

He nodded.

I understood him correctly.

Perhaps it doesn't make sense, but in comprehension, the first thing I felt was rage. Violent, unwelcome rage. As sure as I was sitting in a dugout on Georgia Avenue and not in India or Brooklyn, was as sure as I was that he'd known all along. After the pure hell I had lived for six weeks, I irrationally saw him crouching behind the plate and chuckling to himself. "Let's have some fun," he thinks. "Call a mound conference and watch Scotty shake." And in the meantime, *I'm* scared to death of saying, "Hi, Jase," because I might give myself away. Nice guy.

"You knew, didn't you?" I snapped. "What was it, Jason, some kind of a joke?"

He pulled back, burned, and returned my glare—dagger for dagger. "Now, wait just a second, Scotty," he retorted.

"No, *you* wait just a second. You could have told me."

"Oh, yeah? You could have told me too, you know."

We squared off, yielding to the distinct possibility that the afternoon's victory might be capped off by a couple of black eyes. Then, suddenly, as quickly as it had appeared, the anger evaporated, leaving in its place a pronounced terror that was growing by the minute. I sank back onto the bench and stared at the dugout floor.

"Well, this changes everything," I grumbled, trying to hide the fear as well as I could.

"Why?" Jason was wary—distrustful of the sudden change in temperature, and still ready to resort to pugilism if necessary.

"Because," I shouted, "I didn't expect you to feel anything back." Jason looked me straight in the eye and let me have it.

"The hell you didn't."

And instantly, I knew he was right.

There had to be some reason *why* I'd picked Jason. I even forgot to ask Joel that. If I was going to fall in love with another guy just to run away from myself, I could have picked *any*body—Buddy, Joey, Skip, even Marty, the guy who runs the deli across the street from my apartment.

STEVE KLUGER

Then why Jason? Simple. Because there are no accidents. That 90 percent of our brain that we never use knows a couple of things the other 10 percent would rather not face. In simpler terms? Jason is my catcher. I can read his signs.

Oh, brother.

This means that everything Joel and I have just solved is once again open for discussion. Or is it? Are things the same as they were, or does it really make a difference?

"I don't see why it should," said Jase. "Nothing's changed." The one thing I wanted to hear him say.

"You're right," I added quickly, hastening to agree with him. "We wouldn't want to take it any further even if we could, *would* we?" Instead of replying, Jason stared down at his left hand and began worrying his thumbnail.

"*I* would," he said finally, looking up.

Under the circumstances, I did the only thing I could in the face of his response. I ignored it. I was sweating a lot, but I ignored it. Then something occurred to me.

"Who were you going to name Juliet or Sebastian?"

Jason punched my right shoulder lightly. "Boy, Scotty, what *don't* you know?" He chuckled. "We just got a golden retriever." I felt like the biggest schmuck that ever lived.

We looked at each other for a moment and then, as if on cue, we lost it completely. Come to think of it, I haven't roared that loudly since the time Joey Tobin left a rabbit in Mickey Fowler's jockstrap. And Jason? Well, somehow, the mood of the moment had infected both of us, making us realize at the same time how stupid it all really was. Baseball may be a kid's game, but it can't hold a candle to real life when it comes to the unexpected base hit.

"I'll tell you what," I finally said, eager to lay the whole thing to rest. "How about if we call it even? You know about me, I know about Chris, and we've got a pennant to win. Okay?"

Jason Cornell put an arm around my shoulder—a gesture I could now appreciate and accept—and nodded.

"You've got a deal," he said.

I stared out toward center field at a deep blue October sky darkening over the city that now belongs to the Washington Senators, and took my first deep breath since August 5. There were a lot of tomorrows to be faced, and a lot of questions to be answered, but suddenly it was possible to anticipate each one of them. I didn't even mind that in about twenty minutes I was going to be thirty-seven—the same configuration of digits as my numeral. What did it matter? I now had it all.

It was then, I realized, however, that once again I was lying to myself. Because it wasn't quite everything I'd wanted. Yet. Of course there were the playoffs, and of course there was Joanie; but as I glanced over at the catcher to my left who was staring at me thoughtfully, I knew there was one more thing I needed to make it all complete.

If only I could get a grip on the knuckleball . . .

STEVE KLUGER

Other books of interest from
ALYSON PUBLICATIONS

☐ **BOYS' TOWN,** by Art Bosch, $8.00. Scout DeYoung's four basic food groups are frozen, bottled, canned, and boxed — but this warm-hearted story of two roommates who build an extended gay family is a gourmet's delight.

☐ **EIGHT DAYS A WEEK,** by Larry Duplechan, $7.00. Can Johnnie Ray Rousseau, a 22-year-old black singer, find happiness with Keith Keller, a six-foot-two blond bisexual jock who works in a bank? Will Johnnie Ray's manager ever get him on the Merv Griffin show? Who was the lead singer of the Shangri-las? And what about Snookie? Somewhere among the answers to these and other silly questions is a love story as funny, and sexy, and memorable, as any you'll ever read.

☐ **THE GAY BOOK OF LISTS,** by Leigh Rutledge, $7.00. Leigh Rutledge has compiled a fascinating, informative and highly entertaining collection of lists that range from the historical (6 gay or bisexual popes) to the political (17 outspoken anti-gay politicians) and the outrageous (16 famous men, all reputedly very well-hung).

☐ **DEAD HEAT,** by Willyce Kim, $7.00. Dancer and the crew meet up for a new adventure involving Vinny 'The Skull', horse racing, and a kidnapped gypsy, but the result is one fast-paced, entertaining story you'll read again and again.

☐ **A HISTORY OF SHADOWS,** by Robert C. Reinhart, $7.00. A fascinating look at gay life during the Depression, the war years, the McCarthy witchhunts, and the sixties — through the eyes of four men who were friends during those forty years.

☐ **HOT LIVING: Erotic stories about safer sex,** edited by John Preston, $8.00. The AIDS crisis has encouraged gay men to look for new and safer forms of sexual activity; here, over a dozen of today's most popular gay writers erotically portray those new possibilities.

☐ **WORLDS APART,** edited by Camilla Decarnin, Eric Garber and Lyn Paleo, $8.00. Today's generation of science fiction writers has created a wide array of futuristic gay characters. The s-f stories collected here present adventure, romance, and excitement; and maybe some genuine alternatives for our future.

☐ **THE LITTLE DEATH,** by Michael Nava, $7.00. As a public defender, Henry Rios finds himself losing the idealism he had as a young lawyer. Then a man he has befriended — and loved — dies under mysterious circumstances. As he investigates the murder, Rios finds that the solution is as subtle as the law itself can be.

☐ **GOLDENBOY,** by Michael Nava, $15.00 (cloth). Gay lawyer-sleuth Henry Rios returns, in this sequel to Nava's highly-praised *The Little Death*.

Did Jim Pears kill the co-worker who threatened to expose his homosexuality? The evidence says so, but too many people *want* Pears to be guilty. Distracted by grisly murders and the glitz of Hollywood, can Rios prove his client's innocence?

☐ **IN THE LIFE: A Black Gay Anthology,** edited by Joseph Beam, $8.00. When Joseph Beam became frustrated that so little gay male literature spoke to him as a black man, he decided to do something about it. The result is this anthology, in which 29 contributors, through stories, essays, verse and artwork, have made heard the voice of a too-often silent minority.

☐ **ONE TEENAGER IN TEN: Writings by gay and lesbian youth,** edited by Ann Heron, $4.00. One teenager in ten is gay; here, twenty-six young people tell their stories: of coming to terms with being different, of the decision how — and whether — to tell friends and parents, and what the consequences were.

☐ **REFLECTIONS OF A ROCK LOBSTER: A story about growing up gay,** by Aaron Fricke, $6.00. When Aaron Fricke took a male date to the senior prom, no one was surprised: he'd gone to court to be able to do so, and the case had made national news. Here Aaron tells his story, and shows what gay pride can mean in a small New England town.

☐ **BETTER ANGEL,** by Richard Meeker, $6.00. For readers fifty years ago, *Better Angel* was one of the few positive images available of gay life. Today, it remains a touching, well-written story of a young man's gay awakening in the years between the World Wars.

☐ **ALL-AMERICAN BOYS,** by Frank Mosca, $6.00. "I've known that I was gay since I was thirteen. Does that surprise you? It didn't me..." So begins *All-American Boys,* the story of a teenage love affair that should have been simple — but wasn't.

☐ **SOCRATES, PLATO AND GUYS LIKE ME: Confessions of a gay schoolteacher,** by Eric Rofes, $7.00. When Eric Rofes began teaching sixth grade at a conservative private school, he soon felt the strain of a split identity. Here he describes his two years of teaching from within the closet, and his difficult decision to finally come out.

☐ **SECOND CHANCES,** by Florine De Veer, $7.00. Is it always harder to accept what is offered freely? Jeremy, who is just coming out, could easily have the love of his devoted friend Roy, yet he chooses to pursue the handsome and unpredictable Mark instead.

These titles are available at many bookstores, or by mail.

— — — — — — — — — — — — — — — — —

Enclosed is $_____ for the following books. (Add $1.00 postage when ordering just one book; if you order two or more, we'll pay the postage.)

1. _____   2. _____

3. _____   4. _____

5. _____   6. _____

name:_____ address:_____

city: _____ state: _____ zip: _____

ALYSON PUBLICATIONS
Dept. H-55, 40 Plympton St., Boston, Mass. 02118

After Dec. 31, 1991, please write for current catalog.